I0588169

JOHNNY APOCALYPSE

BOOK 1:
Johnny Apocalypse
and the Nuclear Wasteland

BOOK 2:
Johnny Apocalypse
and the Fight for a New World

BOOK 3:
Johnny Apocalypse
and the Battle for Freedom

BOOK 4:
Johnny Apocalypse
and the King of New York

Join the Johnny Apocalypse Discord:

ymBcADDZFR

JOHNNY APOCALYPSE
AND THE BATTLE FOR FREEDOM

MARK ROBIJN

BLUE FORGE PRESS
Port Orchard, Washington

Johnny Apocalypse and the Battle for Freedom
Copyright 2019
By Mark Robijn

First eBook Edition March 2019
Second eBook Edition March 2022
First Print EditionMarch 2019
Second Print Edition March 2022

ISBN 978-1-59092-864-6

Blue Forge Press is the print division of the volunteer-run, federal 501(c)3 nonprofit company, Blue Legacy, founded in 1989 and dedicated to bringing light to the shadows and voice to the silence. We strive to empower storytellers across all walks of life with our four divisions: Blue Forge Press, Blue Forge Films, Blue Forge Gaming, and Blue Forge Records. Find out more at www.MyBlueLegacy.org

Blue Forge Press
7419 Ebbert Drive Southeast
Port Orchard, Washington 98367
blueforgepress@gmail.com
360-550-2071 ph.txt

DEDICATION

To my wife, Laura, who has given me twenty-five years of fun and adventure.

ACKNOWLEDGEMENTS

I'd like to thank all the great writers and friends who gave me feedback and encouragement over the years, especially my good friends Carl Palmer and Rob Miller, who sadly is no longer with us. I'd like to thank Blue Forge Press for believing in me and my stories enough to take a chance on my novels. I'd also like to thank all the great authors who fueled my imagination through the years, including Jack London, Isaac Asimov, Ray Bradbury and Sir Arthur Conan Doyle. Without their great examples and inspiration, this series of books would probably not exist.

JOHNNY APOCALYPSE
AND THE BATTLE FOR FREEDOM

MARK ROBIJN

PROLOGUE

The days of the Great War with its Mushroom Monsters, death and destruction are over. After 100 years, life has slowly begun to return to the desolate wasteland.

Johnny Apocalypse and his people, who call themselves the Tribe lived in an abandoned mall they called Sanctuary in the city that used to be called Philadelphia. They are forced to leave when they are attacked by a roaming group of evil mercenaries called Gangers led by a man named Ripper. They travel to a new city that used to be called Washington D. C. Here with the help of Misterwizard, a short, bald old man who is very smart and possesses the knowledge of the magic from before the Great War, they hope to rebuild a new society built on the ancient principles of democracy and freedom.

They settle into a new place they call New Sanctuary,

an old museum known in the past as the Museum of American History. But Ripper and the Gangers follow them, and Johnny and his Tribe also find a new enemy waiting in their new city. He is a mad man who calls himself Lord Algon. Lord Algon has organized the people who wander the wasteland, known as Wildies into a fighting force and declared himself their king.

Johnny and the Tribe battle Lord Algon and his army, and Ripper and the Gangers make the mistake of thinking the Tribe is allying itself with Lord Algon, so they attack Lord Algon as well, allowing Johnny and the Tribe to win the day. At the end of the battle, Johnny and Ripper finally meet face to face and fight. Johnny wins when a tiger-beastie attacks Ripper. Ripper dies, or at least that is what Johnny thinks.

Johnny finds a new friend, a dog-beastie he names Deecee. Johnny's girlfriend Deb and her friend Super fall into a hole above an old subway tunnel and discover a race of people living there who called themselves the Undergrounders. Deb and Super find out there is another, monstrous race of creatures living in the subway who prey on the Undergrounders, a people called the Rat People. When the Rat People attack, Deb and Super help the Undergrounders fight them, and they almost lose until Johnny and his friend Starbucks show up to help fight the Rat People off.

Johnny and his friends convince the Undergrounders that they no longer have to live in the subway tunnel, for the world is safe now.

Meanwhile, Lord Algon has mounted an even more deadly attack on the Tribe, and this time, it seems he is winning. And Ripper is still alive, and he's watching the battle, aiming a rifle at Misterwizard.

CHAPTER 1

Johnny, Deb, Starbucks and Super walked out the door of the subway tunnel and onto the street, which was bathed in yellow light from the half-closed Yellow Eye.

Deb moved up against Johnny and collapsed in his arms. He quickly grabbed her and looked at her face, concerned. What he saw made him less afraid, for she looked simply exhausted from the long ordeal. Her eyes were closed, and she seemed to have fallen asleep on her feet.

Super had the opposite reaction. She screamed with joy and raised her fists in the air. "Yee-haw, we're free!" She ran, and Starbucks laughed and hurried to catch up to her.

Behind them, the Undergrounders slowly walked outside, eyes wide with wonder and fear, but also with excitement and joy. Their pale white bodies shone in the faint light of the Yellow Eye, making them look like ghosts. They held onto each other and looked around at their first sight of a street, of a night sky, and of the world. Loki walked up to stand next to Johnny and Deb. He was so excited he shook. He tried to look everywhere at once, a big grin on his face. Loki's parents, Bot and Pak walked beside him gripping each other's hands nervously. Pak's long white hair shook as she trembled, her face shaking with fear and amazement.

Deb woke up and smiled at Johnny.

"What happened?"

Johnny smiled. "You conked out. You must be really tired."

Deb looked around and realized where they were. She smiled again. "I never thought I'd be so happy to see this dark, empty street again."

Slon gazed around in wonder, turning around in a full circle. He looked this way and that, taking in what to him were sights beyond belief. Then he looked at Johnny and Deb. He started sobbing, and soon big tears fell on his cheeks. He shook, crying loudly. Johnny and Deb walked over and put their hands on his shoulders. He looked up at them. "How can we ever thank you? You don't know what our life has been like. If you hadn't shown up…"

He wrung his hands and looked tortured. "We had given up hope. We were out of food, and the Rat People attacked almost every night. We had nothing left. We were about to…" He stopped, not able to even say what he was thinking. "But you have saved our lives. We can never thank you enough.

Johnny looked at Deb, who smiled back at him, tears in her own eyes. Johnny looked back at Slon. "When we lost Deb and Super, we were afraid. But now I'm glad they fell in that hole, for it gave us a chance to save you."

The Undergrounders stood on the street laughing and giggling, trying to look in every direction at once. The danced in the pale light of the Yellow Eye, strange white creatures with long arms and black eyes in a world that seemed even stranger, to them.

Loki walked up to an old car. He peered inside it, fascinated. Slon looked up at the Yellow Eye, transfixed by its beauty. Bot and Pak held each other's hands, looked around and grinned.

Harp walked up to Loki. Loki didn't see at first, because he was busy looking in the car, but then he noticed her. He stood up and smiled at her and she smile back. "This is all because of you, Loki," she said.

Loki smiled humbly. "Anyone would have done the same thing."

Harp took his hand. "Let's explore the new world together."

Loki grinned, happy. "Yes, let's, if you want to."

Suddenly in the distance they heard an explosion. Johnny, Deb, Starbucks and Super all turned and looked. Then they looked back at each other. They all knew what it meant.

"The Wildies are attacking the Tribe!" Starbucks said.

"We have to go fight," Johnny said. He turned to Slon. "Slon, you know our people that we told you about?"

"Yes," Slon said.

"They are in a battle right now with some very bad people. We have to leave and go help them fight. You and your people stay here. We'll be back as soon as we can."

"NO!" Slon said, frowning with determination. "We will fight for you, as you fought for us. We owe you our lives, how could we stand by while you fight your enemies?"

Slon turned to the Undergrounders and spoke to some of the men. "Bot, Loki, Farg, Lop. Go collect our weapons. Tonight, we will try to pay our friends back for the kindness they have shown us!"

The Undergrounders all agreed, nodding and talking. All the Undergrounder men ran back into the subway tunnel to do what Slon asked. Slon turned to Johnny.

"Just tell us what to do, Johnny. We are at your command."

Lord Algon's Wildies swarmed over the grounds like ants. The men from the Tribe stood on the top of the car wall and shot and shot, but most couldn't hit anything. Soon the wall was crawling with attackers. Misterwizard threw bombs as fast as he could, and they had the desired effect, killing the enemy Wildies and causing others to run and hide, but there was just too many of them.

Foodcourt's aim grew better and better with practice. When he fired now, he almost always hit a target, and Wildies learned quickly to avoid the area in front of him.

Misterwizard bent down to pick up a grenade launcher, and it was just at the right moment. Suddenly a loud "ping" sound came from the top of the car he stood on, and a bright shiny mark appeared right next to Misterwizard's feet. Both he and Foodcourt looked behind them.

"Someone's shooting at us from behind!" Foodcourt said, straining to see who it was. "I didn't think the Wildies had guns."

Misterwizard looked in the direction of the rifle shot as well. Far in the distance, next to the side of the Museum of American History, he saw a lone man. The man wore an ugly, evil grin, and Misterwizard's heart skipped a beat. He couldn't believe his eyes. He wondered if the strain of battle was becoming too much for him, for he swore the man was none other than Ripper. That couldn't be, he told himself. Johnny killed Ripper. Was he seeing a ghost? Msiterwizard squinted harder and looked again, and this time he was almost positive. It seemed impossible, but Ripper somehow survived the tiger-beastie attack. Ripper was still alive. Ripper raised his gun. He was getting ready to shoot again!

"Quickly, Foodcourt, aim at that man on the side of New Sanctuary, right there! Do you see him?" Misterwizard pointed, and Foodcourt nodded. Quickly he raised his rifle, aimed and fired. The figure darted back behind the building. Foodcourt frowned, disappointed. "I missed him."

Suddenly Foodcourt pointed out at the field. "Misterwizard, look what's coming!"

Misterwizard looked and was dismayed at what he saw. A large bear-beastie bounded across the ground, whipping its head around, snarling.

"We have to sound retreat, Misterwizard. There's no way we can fight that!"

Then they looked to the left and saw two huge dogs coming as well.

"And look there!   Look at that fearsome creature!" Foodcourt pointed in another direction. They both looked. The gorilla-beastie howled and bounded towards them on its huge strong legs, pounding its chest.

"What are we going to do, Misterwizard?"

Misterwizard thought about it, and decided his only choice was to sound retreat, but then they saw something that made them both laugh out loud.

"Look!" Foodcourt said, pointing again. "His beasties are attacking his own men!"

Just as Foodcourt said, the beasties leapt on the Wildies running towards the wall and killed them. The Wildies screamed in terror as they were mauled by the dog-beasties and the bear-beastie. The gorilla-beastie grabbed a man and flung him in the air. He sailed back away from the car wall as if he was flying.

Misterwizard grinned darkly. "It seems Lord Algon didn't sufficiently train his pets before sending them into battle. They have become our unwitting allies."

"That'll teach him!" Foodcourt said.

The Wildies near the beasties screamed in abject terror and scattered, and the beasties chased them. But many more of the Wildies took the men's places.

But then Misterwizard looked at the wall. Wildies swarmed at the bottom of it. In the distance he saw Lord Algon on his king carrier being carried by four large guards. Next to him was someone else on a king carrier, also being carried. A man with a sword stood in front of the two, barking orders. Misterwizard suspected this was the captain of Lord Algon's army.

"Lord Algon has added some new weapons to his arsenal which are quite formidable," Misterwizard said to Foodcourt, yelling so he could be heard over the din of men yelling, gunfire and explosions.

"He's got some new tricks up his sleeve, that's for sure!" Foodcourt replied as he aimed at another Wildie.

Two huge men leapt onto the top of the wall. Misterwizard and Foodcourt turned and looked at them. They wore short chains around their waists and metal bands around their necks. Their faces were scarred with cuts and burned with primitive tattoos. Their eyes were red, wild and crazy. They both let out bloodcurdling war cries that sent shivers up Foodcourt's spine. Then they looked around and found the nearest Tribe member to attack. They leapt on their victims, biting and clawing. The men near screamed in fear and ran away.

Foodcourt took aim at one of the crazy creatures, but it and the man it fought tumbled and rolled, the man screaming in fear and pain.

Misterwizard saw with dismay that the wall was lost. "Foodcourt, despite the help of the beasties, I'm reluctantly certain it is time to sound the retreat!" He yelled. "We will have to regroup in New Sanctuary!"

Foodcourt nodded and cupped a hand over his mouth. "Retreat! Tribe! Back to New Sanctuaray!" He yelled, and quickly men all along the wall turned and jumped off the wall to follow his orders. Some couldn't, for they were already fighting Wildies or the Crazies in desperate life and death struggles. Badluck the Ganger climbed up on the wall. He yelled and started shooting his gun at the retreating Tribe members. Misterwizard saw him and picked up a grenade.

"You over there!" Misterwizard said. Badluck looked. "Catch!"

Misterwizard threw the grenade and Badluck caught it. He looked down at it with a blank expression, just before he blew into a thousand pieces.

Foodcourt looked at Misterwizard. "Let's go, Misterwizard!"

"Yes, I'm afraid discretion is now the better part of valor. We are hard pressed indeed." Misterwizard gathered up the rest of his bombs and weapons and was just about to leave, when he looked out over the wall.

"Foodcourt, come take a gander at over yon wall. Am is experiencing hallucinations, or do you see what I see?"

Foodcourt turned and looked. His eyes went wide with disbelief. "I am having hallooginations too I think. What are those?"

Misterwizard smiled. "I have no knowledge, but whatever they are, they seem to be our allies. Look!

Misterwizard and Foodcourt watched as strange white creatures poured in from the right side of the street and attacked the Wildies. They carried spears and knives. The Wildies took one look at their ghostly forms, screamed terror ran away.

Misterwizard and Foodcourt smiled at each other.

"This is a most unexpected and bizarre turn of events that nonetheless is very fortuitous," Misterwizard said.

"I agree!" Foodcourt said, not even bothering to wonder what Misterwizard had just said.

Ripper steadied the rifle and stared at Misterwizard's head in the scope. With a heart as cold as steel, he squeezed the trigger. Suddenly Misterwizard's head was gone from view. He lowered the gun and looked. Then he cursed. The old man had moved at the last minute. A new shiny spot gleamed in the light of the Yellow Eye on the top of the old car next to Misterwizard's feet. He had missed!

He cocked the rifle again to get ready for another shot. Misterwizard and that old fool Foodcourt turned and looked at the spot. *They heard the shot,* Ripper thought. He'd have to shoot again fast, before the old man had time to hide. He raised the gun again and stared through the scope again. But this time he saw Foodcourt raising a gun of his own and pointing it at him! Ripper quickly lowered the gun and stepped back behind the building. A bullet hit the ground right where he'd been standing. He moved just in time.

"You can't be alive."

A soft female voice spoke in amazement and disbelief. Ripper spun around in a panic. He'd been spotted!

Standing behind him was Carny, Johnny's sister. She was no longer heavy with a wriggler, and she looked thin and strong. Her wriggler was nowhere to be seen. In her hands she held a sword, pointed at him.

Ripper knew he had to act fast. He rushed her using his rifle like a club. But things seemed to be very different this time. She was not slow and awkward, but strong and fast. As Ripper reached her, she deftly stepped aside and slashed at him with the sword. He yelled as it cut his hand, making him drop the rifle.

"That's for Buildabear!" Carny snarled, her eyes full of fury.

Ripper backed up and grabbed his now bleeding hand. Carny followed him, her eyes narrowed with hatred. "I don't know how you're still alive, but I'm going to make sure to fix that right now!"

Ripper grit his teeth and made fists with his hands. Carny's courage and brave words didn't scare him a bit. Now that the surprise of her attack was over, he smiled. Ripper had been fighting since he was a scrabbler, and rifle or no rifle, no mere girl recently heavy with a wriggler was going to beat him in a fight.

"Buildabear hated you," Ripper said, sneering. "He couldn't wait to turn you over to me, because you were a fat, lazy cow-beastie. And ugly too."

Ripper's words didn't hurt Carny, but she had already made her peace with Buildabear's treachery, and now she merely frowned and remained unfazed. She advanced on Ripper. He circled her like a wolf-beastie, looking for its chance to strike.

"Thegap! Come here!" Carny called over her shoulder. "Bring your gun!"

Ripper could tell that despite his ability to beat Carny, events were quickly turning against him. He rushed at Carny. She yelled and stabbed at him, but he dodged the sword and slapped her face. She screamed in anger and fury and stabbed at him again. Ripper grabbed her sword arm and held it high in the air. She bit at him and kicked at him like a tiger-beastie. He grinned, laughing, enjoying the struggle.

Thegap ran around the corner, a rifle in his hand. It was time for Ripper to leave. He threw Carny to the ground and took off running towards the broken white stick building.

Carny called from the ground. "Shoot him, Thegap! It's Ripper!"

Thegap just stared, amazed by what she was saying into immobility. "Ripper? Ripper?"

Carny struggled up and grabbed the gun from

Thegap's hands. She turned and aimed. But by the time she did, all she was darkness. Ripper had made his escape. She lowered the gun, angry and disappointed. Her cheek was red where Ripper had hit her, but what really hurt was the feeling she'd had a chance to get revenge on him and missed.

"Was that really Ripper?" Thegap said, staring into the darkness after him.

"I'm afraid so," Carny said. "He's as hard to kill as a roach-beastie. We have to tell Johnny."

CHAPTER 2

Lord Algon watched with dismay as his beasties attacked his own men. He had made a serious miscalculation with the beasties, forgetting that they would attack whatever was nearby.

Still, he chuckled, barely able to contain his glee. His Wildies were wining easily despite the beasties attacking them. It seemed the old man and the Newcomers were not as prepared as Lord Algon had feared. They created a simple wall, and that was the extent of their defenses. His men, nearly outnumbering the Newcomers by two to one, covered the wall and would soon over-run it. He barely had time to use his cannon or his catapults. It looked like it was going to be over so fast he wouldn't even get to use his beasties.

Pity, he thought, *the battle was over so quickly.* He thought of how only a few hours before he had thought about running away. Now it seemed like dumbest idea he'd ever had. He looked over, smiled and waved at Facegash. Facegash grinned, looking mildly impressed, and waved back.

Lord Algon looked towards the battle again, his heart merry. *Soon, stupid Ganger,* he thought, the battle with the Newcomers will be over, and I will have the pleasure of killing you and all your annoying Gangers slowly, painfully. He couldn't wait, it was going to be so much fun.

"Release the crazies!" Lord Algon yelled with dark glee. The Wildies holding the chains of the Crazies let them go and the Crazies took off, laughing insanely. Lord Algon couldn't wait to see the terror and mayhem the insane Wildies would cause. He looked down at his guards.

"Move me closer!" He yelled impatiently, waving his arms. "I want to see the ending!"

The guards fell into a trot, carrying Lord Algon towards the battle.

Suddenly a strange scream filled the air, followed by another and another. They were screams of fright, of even terror. And they seemed to be coming from Lord Algon's own Wildies on his left. "Stop!" He yelled, and his guards halted. He looked to his to see Facegash looking that direction too.

In the distance, a scene out of a nightmare unfurled before them. From between the buildings and the street beyond his troops, strange creatures of the night ran towards his men. They were pale and bloodless in the light of the Yellow Eye, with huge black eyes and large hands with long fingers. As Lord Algon watched with horror, they swarmed towards his Wildies with spears and sharp sticks.

Lord Algon felt all the blood drain from his face and a new, cold, clammy fear gripped his heart. "What new deviltry be this?"

Just when he thought he was finally winning against the Newcomers, they came up with a new and terrifying magic. They had called up people from the grave!

As Lord Algon watched, the tide of battle instantly turned. His men, out of their minds with fear, turned and ran for their very lives. Like a wave of the ocean receding, his men melted away in the wake of the new creepy onslaught of strange dead men.

Even the Crazies had enough sense to be terrified, for Lord Algon saw them run past him, hooting with fear. The men on the wall also turned and looked. They saw the rest of the army running away. They panicked and jumped off the wall to run after the rest of the retreating army. In an instant, Lord Algon's victory was shattered.

His guards set him down. *No, not again!* he thought. He stood up, terrified of the new strange creatures heading his way. He watched with dismay as once again, his guards took off, deserting him! "I'll kill ye, like I did the swine before ye, ye scurvy cowards!" Lord Algon hurried to stand up and run away before the horrid white monsters reached him.

Hardhitter ran up, his face a white sheet. "Lord Algon! Monsters!"

"Sound retreat, ye fool, before we lose everything! Collect the beasties and pull our catapults back 'fore we lose 'em to our enemy!"

Hardhitter hurried to comply. "Retreat! Turn around! Back to the castle!" He yelled but it was too late. The men pushing the catapults had already deserted them.

The men with cannons had already abandoned them too. The beastie cages lay open and unoccupied. Hardhitter grabbed some new men and forced them to start rolling the catapults back but they only lasted a few minutes until the strange white creatures grew near, then they too turned tail and ran.

The Wildies carrying Facegash's throne dropped him and ran away too. Facegash stood up in front of his chair, just staring at the strange creatures. And then he and Lord Algon saw Johnny.

Johnny Apocalypse came into view. He wore a big smile of victory and courage. Next to him holding his hand walked a beautiful girl with blond hair. Johnny looked like a hero. Next to him stood a black man and a white girl with long black hair. Johnny and his black friend both held magic weapons in their hands, the exploding kind. Next to them were two of the grave creatures. *So, Johnny and his Tribe did have control of the monsters,* Lord Algon thought.

Lord Algon stepped off his carrier. He thought to himself, maybe these weird white creatures are too powerful. Maybe there was no way they could beat them. The thought depressed him and made his spirit sag.

He looked once more at Johnny Apocalypse. A fire of hatred ignited in Lord Algon's heart. It was identical as the one that burned constantly in Ripper, and it came from the same source. Lord Algon realized he now hated this Johnny more than he even hated Crooked Walk, the piratt who had betrayed him.

He looked at Facegash, and he could tell by the look on the Ganger's face he felt the same way. It made Lord Algon feel a kindred spirit with the Ganger, though not enough to make him decide not to kill him some day.

"There be your Johnny," Lord Algon declared. "Knew ye about these monsters?"

"No," Facegash said, looking thoughtful. "This is something new."

"Let's be getting gone, afore they scuttle us!" Lord Algon said, as he turned to run. But Facegash wasn't running, he just stood there. Lord Algon grew anxious. He didn't want to appear more terrified than the Ganger, but terrified was exactly what he was. He hopped up and down, first on one foot then the other with impatience.

"Come along! Ye think ye can fight these monsters?"

"No," Facegash said. "But they're not monsters I'll bet."

Lord Algon groaned. "They're heading this way!"

Finally, Lord Algon decided he didn't care what happened to the Ganger. He took off running back towards the river.

Facegash stood still for a few more minutes, until the white creatures had almost reached him. Then slowly he turned and ran away. He vowed to himself that he would be back, with or without Lord Algon. Johnny and his Tribe had been a thorn in the Gangers side for too long. He would continue to harass them and kill as many as he could, until finally they were all dead.

Misterwizard, Foodcourt and the men on the wall watched with joy as Lord Algon and the Widlies turned and ran. All along the wall men jumped up and down and cheered. From inside New Sanctuary, the rest of the

Tribe walked out onto the porch, hearing the cheering. Curious, they walked out onto the Mall to see what was happening.

The only people who didn't seem happy were Microsoft and Abercrombie. They stayed inside, still searching for their daughter. The rest walked over to the wall and climbed up, for it appeared as if the battle was over.

Cinnabon stood at the base of the wall with Wheaties. "What happened?" She yelled up, but no one answered. They were too busy staring at the strange sight on the other side of the wall.

Johnny, Starbucks and the girls walked up to the wall. Behind them, the men and women of the Undergrounders followed, looking like white ghosts in the light of the Yellow Eye. When everyone saw the heroes they cheered and jumped up and down even more, waving their guns and swords in the air.

"Johnny saved us again!"

"Johnny's our hero!"

"Yahoo for Johnny!"

Starbucks frowned, annoyed. He muttered, "What about us? He didn't do it alone, you know!" But then he smiled, just happy to be back with the Tribe in one piece.

Misterwizard looked down at Johnny, a smile beaming from his face. "Well met, dear colleague. Once again you have proved your inestimable worth. And how you manage to do it in such superlative and evocative ways continues to amaze and entertain. I see you found the fair maidens."

"Hi Misterwizard!" Deb said, waving.

"Hello, Dear!" Foodcourt said, grinning down.

"Who is this you've brought with you, Johnny?"

Misterwizard said with interest.

Johnny looked at Slon and waved to him to join him.

Slon walked up and so did Loki.

Johnny grinned up at Misterwizard. "Misterwizard, this is Slon. And this is Loki. They are called Undergrounders. They lived in a hole in the ground."

"A hole, you say?" Misterwizard said, stroking his beard. "How fascinating."

"It's a long story, Misterwizard," Starbucks said. "A really long one."

"Well," Misterwizard replied. "Thanks to your timely routing of Lord Algon, we seem to have the leisure to hear it. What say we have an old-fashioned picnic by the light of the moon to celebrate and get to know your new-found friends?"

Everybody cheered. Johnny looked at Slon, who smiled and nodded. Johnny grabbed Deb around the waist and kissed her. Then they all walked around the wall to join the Tribe.

"Yee-haw!" Super said, as she held onto Starbuck's waist and walked. "I can't believe how good things turned out. Maybe we're going to make a go of it here in this new place after all."

"You bet we are," Johnny said. "There's nothing that's going to stop us now!"

CHAPTER 3

Ripper walked down the street leading to the bridge over the river that led to Lord Algon's castle at the cemetery. He had managed to bandage his hand where Carny had slashed it, but it throbbed with pain. He knew he would have another bad scar. Someday, he vowed he would pay her back. He'd pay them all back. He moved his fingers on the hand that was cut. They were stiff and sore. He hoped he didn't lose some movement in that hand. How he hated Johnny and his whole family!

Ahead of him, the last of Lord Algon's troops ran across the bridge, hurrying back to join Lord Algon and his army in cowering back at his fortress.

Ripper had seen the whole thing. He watched as the Wildies swarmed over the makeshift wall, and his heart soared with the feeling of victory. It looked like the Tribe was finally going to get what they deserved.

And then he saw Johnny appear, just like he always did, and somehow find a way to win. It was infuriating, frustrating, and totally maddening. What did Johnny have that made him so hard to kill? Was he truly magic? Had Misterwizard somehow put a spell on Johnny that gave him super power? Ripper didn't understand how Johnny always managed to steal victory from the jaws of defeat. It wasn't fair. He tried and tried, but Johnny always came out on top, and always with that disgusting smile on his face, like he was some big hero. And always with his girl by his side, the beautiful Deb. Ripper hated Johnny so much he couldn't barely stand it. It didn't matter if Johnny was magical, Ripper vowed. He was going to kill him anyway. And then he'd have Deb for his own, or maybe feed her to a wild beastie.

During the battle he watched the strange, white creatures follow Johnny and his friends and fight for them. What were they? Were they some kind of strange new creature? They appeared human, and yet they were so weird, with pale, white skin, dark eyes and long fingers.

Ripper wasn't stupid enough to think they were ghosts. He wasn't a simpleton like Lord Algon or his Wildies, who were nothing more than mindless rabble. It didn't matter what they were, the addition of their numbers to the Tribe made Johnny and his people even harder to fight. Now the Tribe not only had the Wildies who joined them, but these weird white creatures too. If Ripper didn't act soon, Johnny's Tribe would grow so big in numbers it would be almost impossible to defeat them.

The thought of that depressed Ripper. He walked across the bridge, turning his mind to Lord Algon. Lord

Algon was a fool. He was so steeped in superstition, he even believed guns were some kind of magic. What an idiot! And the way he talked, like a crazy person. What Ripper needed to do was kill Lord Algon and take over his army. With Facegash's help, he could do it. Then he would have a force to use to deal with Johnny. *That would be his next move,* Ripper thought. I will kill that fool, and then fight Johnny and his Tribe, and nothing will stop me until I win. *But what if he just beats you again?* he thought. The idea depressed him some more.

He reached the other side of the bridge. The half-closed Yellow Eye shone bright directly overhead. In its light, he saw a huge building far ahead away from Lord Algon's cemetery and castle. It was different than most of the others. It was only one story high with square walls, but the front wall connected to one on either side, and they connected to others behind them. The square walls on one side ended up connecting to the others on the other side until the building formed a star shape. Ripper decided to go inside it and investigate.

He stopped at the front of the building. The words on the wall above the door said, "Pentagon." Ripper shrugged, not knowing what it meant, and walked in the front door.

The front door was huge and made of heavy wood, and he had to push it hard, for the hinges on it were rusty. The hinges made a loud groaning sound but finally Ripper was able to get the door to move. He walked inside and peered around at the dark, gloomy interior.

He saw nothing of interest, just a hallway with old suits of armor and some rotted flags on sticks, just like a lot of other buildings he'd been in. The room seemed boring, with nothing interesting inside. He entered the hallway first that seemed to run along the wall in both directions. In front of him, two more doors led into a large open area.

He decided to walk down the hallway. As he did he peered in open doors, finding nothing different in any of them, just rotting junk. He saw a set of marble stairs going down. With nothing else to do, he walked down them. He entered another large room, more rotted desks and chairs. The walls had colored paper on them with lines all over them and push pins stuck in them. Nothing of interest.

Ripper heard a loud clicking sound. It echoed off the empty walls ominously. Scared, he tensed and hid behind a rotted desk. He pulled out his knife, for he'd lost his rifle when he ran from Carny at New Sanctuary. He scowled and bolstered his courage by telling himself he could still defend himself if he had to.

Something was definitely in the room with him, for now he heard a loud clank sound on the other side of the room. He peered slowly over the desk. What he saw standing on the other side of the room was even stranger and more bizarre than the white people.

A huge, dark shadow stood near the back wall, at least ten feet tall and square, but it had arms and legs like man. It had a square body and a square head on top of its shoulders. In the darkness, Ripper couldn't see its face, but two round eyes glowed red.

Ripper made sure to keep very still, for he the strange creature terrified him more than anything he'd seen before. This thing was new and frightening, beyond just a man to fight. It was something else, something terrifying.

Suddenly the strange creature lifted its big thick leg, which bent at the knee. It took a step forward and brought its food down, making a loud banging on the floor. Dust rose from where it stepped, creating a small cloud that floated off to the side. The creature picked up its other food and stepped again. It was coming towards Ripper! Ripper tried to shrink down as small as he could and lay perfectly still, his heart pounding in his ears. No knife would stop this creature, Ripper could easily see. If it saw him, he was dead, there was no question about it.

Ripper lay in a ball, not looking up, but with fear he heard the footsteps growing closer. He decided if it drew too close he'd have no choice but to jump up and run for it, hoping the creature didn't have some sort of weapon to kill him with. The clanking grew closer. It was almost on top of him! Ripper got ready to run. And then the creature spoke!

Its voice was funny, as if it was being spoken a mile away, and there was no inflection in the speech, like it was dead or asleep. There was something terrible and menacing about the dark, deep voice, however, and as it spoke Ripper felt like a cold wind whistled through him.

"State your name and nationality. Stand and be recognized."

Ripper didn't stand. He lay where he was, so frightened he peed his pants. He didn't move, he couldn't. He was sure he was seconds from death.

The creature tramped around to where Ripper could see him. Ripper looked up at it, his eyes wide with fear. He saw it now plainly. It looked like a man, but it was made of metal! The metal was a dull gold color, the color of rings Ripper had seen. The head was square, but had the eyes, nose and mouth of a man. The lips didn't move when it spoke, but the sound seemed to come out of a little hole in the middle of the lips with a mesh covering it. And its eyes had two red orbs that shone out from its face like little bits of the Red Eye.

Ripper saw nothing he could do but stand up and face it. The creature tilted its head down, for it was ten feet tall, and looked at Ripper. In the darkness, the two red orbs of its eyes made little red dots on Ripper's face.

"State your name and nationality. Be recognized."

Ripper didn't know what to say. He thought. What did he hear Johnny say once?

"This is Ripper of the Unided Sates," Ripper said, swallowing hard, his knees shaking.

"Ripper of the United States. Awaiting orders. What is your command?"

Ripper smiled. Suddenly he realized this wasn't a creature at all, but some kind of machine. And it was waiting for him to give it orders. Ripper knew somehow that the fortunes of battle had just shifted in his favor.

CHAPTER 4

Johnny, Deb, Starbuck and Super led the Undergrounders around the wall to stand in the grass of the Mall. The people of the Tribe stood a little distance away from them. Everyone in the Tribe stared at the strange, white-skinned Undergrounders with curiosity and a little fright. Their pale skin and black eyes made them look totally foreign to the Tribe, as if they came from another world. The Undergrounders in turn stared back at all the pink and brown skinned people who looked totally alien to them as well. They continued to gaze about at the world they had never seen before with amazement and awe, now that the light of the Red Eye began to brighten the landscape. The Red Eye had just begun to rise over the distant horizon, bringing with it light that already hurt the Undergrounders' eyes. Some began to shield their eyes and look distressed, frowns on their faces.

Foodcourt and Teavana, Johnny's parents, didn't care about the Undergrounders. They were too overjoyed with seeing Johnny again. They ran up to him, big smiles of happiness on their faces, and threw their arms around him. Deb's parents came and hugged her. Starbucks and Super's parents ran up to them with joy as well and hugged their children.

"Johnny, my boy! I can't tell you how glad I am to see you!" Foordcourt said, putting an arm around Johnny and squeezing his shoulder joyfully.

Starbucks's father named Apple, a big black man with strong arms and a happy smile, put an arm around his son's shoulders and said, "Johnny, thanks for bringing my boy back safe."

"He brought me back safe, if you want to know the truth," Johnny said, laughing.

"Johnny, we're so glad you're safe!" Teavana said. She gave him a big hug.

Johnny turned to the Tribe and with a smile and the flourish of his hand said, "Everybody, meet Slon, Loki and the Undergrounders. They are our new friends. Thanks to them, we beat Lord Algon and the Wildies."

The people of the Tribe smiled nervously and waved at the Undergrounders, frightened of them but still trying to be friendly. None of them moved, as if waiting for someone else to be bold enough to step forward first.

The Undergrounders stood still too, looking uncomfortable, studying the Tribe with wide eyes. Foodcourt finally broke the stalemate. He strode over and with a big grin on his face stuck out a hand to Slon.

"I for one am very glad you and your friends came

along. You scared the pants off that old nutty leader of theirs. Welcome to our Tribe!"

Slon smiled back, nervous and shy himself, though Foodcourt's bright smile made him feel more at ease. He looked at Foodcourt's hand extended to him with puzzlement, as if he'd never had someone ask to shake his hand before.

Foodcourt grabbed Slon's hand with his other hand and put it in his. Then he shook Slon's hand vigorously.

"Glad to meet you." Foodcourt glanced back at the other Tribe members and then back at Slon. "Don't worry, they're friendly, they've just never seen white people with black eyes before."

The Tribe members laughed and slowly made their way towards the Undergrounders. But before they reached them, Misterwizard burst through the crowd. The rest of the Tribe stood back to see what Misterwizard would do.

At first Misterwizard didn't even notice the Undergrounders. He just looked overjoyed to see Johnny and his friends again. He walked over and gave Johnny a big bear hug as the others watched and laughed. Then Misterwizard stood back and shook Johnny's hand vigorously.

"Johnny, I am exponentially ecstatic to see you! Your disappearance had me discomfited, concerned and discombobulated. I mentally berated myself for not accompanying you on your quest. But now I'm happy to see my apprehensions were unfounded, as always, for you are a resourceful and intelligent young man. You have returned," Misterwizard finally looked at the Undergrounders, "and by the appearance of your new acquaintances, with quite a tale to tell!"

"I sure do have, I mean, I think so," Johnny said, not really understanding half of what Misterwizard said. "Misterwizard, as I said before, this is Slon. His people are called the Undergrounders."

"And this is Loki," Deb said, leading Loki forward. "He's the one who helped Super and I first. He's our good friend."

Loki grinned, for Deb's words him happy. He looked to see if Harp had heard but was disappointed when he couldn't spot her anywhere.

Misterwizard walked over to Slon and smiled at him warmly.

"Welcome and solicitations, my dear Slon. You and your people are most appreciated, for your arrival was very fortuitous, most fortuitous indeed."

Slon frowned, not understanding, but then he smiled again weakly. Misterwizard put out his hand, and this time Slon knew what to do. He took Misterwizard's hand and they shook.

Miserwizard looked Slon and his people over with eager interest. "You and your people are simply remarkable. Perfect examples of the change in skin pigment from the lack of sunlight and the detrimental effects of a lack of Vitamin D."

Slon just nodded, not sure if Misterwizard was complimenting him or insulting him.

"I really hope that you will be willing to relay to me a detailed description of your people's history, when we have a moment of leisure. I am endeavoring to document all of the events not only relating to Johnny and his Tribe, but to everyone else who has survived since the Great War."

"I am Slon," Slon said, starting the conversation over.

"And I am called Misterwizard," Misterwizard said. "But let's not stand out here talking like strangers on the doorstep. Why don't you and your people join us at our place of residence where we can all get to know each other and celebrate our victory together?"

Slon nodded, but then he looked at the horizon. The Red Eye rose into the sky, and the land was growing light. The rest of the Undergrounders noticed as well, and they started to react. They covered their eyes and looked as if they were in pain.

"Please understand," Slon said, "we want to get to know you, but the brightness, it is very painful."

The Undergrounders turned and ran back around the car wall towards the entrance back into the subway tunnel. Johnny, Misterwizard and the rest of the Tribe watched with dismay.

"We understand, Slon," Johnny said. "But now that you're free, hopefully your eyes will begin to adjust. Soon you'll be able to come out whenever you want."

"I hope you are right. I'm sorry to cut this short, but..." Slon turned and soon he, Loki and the other Undergrounders were running to get back too, their eyes closed and their hands out to keep from running into something.

Johnny walked over to Misterwizard. "They've lived underground all their lives."

"Yes," Misterwizard said, nodding. "It will take some time for their eyes to be able to tolerate the light of the Red Eye. But I think once they do, the Undergrounders are going to be very happy to have a whole new world to explore."

As the last of the Undergrounders ran back down the tunnel, Johnny and the rest slowly walked back to New

Sanctuary, laughing and talking to each other, happy to be together again and at peace, at least for a little while.

After the first night's rest that Johnny could remember in a long time, Johnny Apocalypse woke up the next morning in a real bed in a bedroom all his own. Since the new battle, the Tribe all agreed Johnny should have a room all his own. Johnny agreed, but only if his parents, Carny and Miracle could share it with him. So now, Johnny and his family were christened the "First Family" by Misterwizard and given a much better place to live.

Johnny sat up, yawned and looked around. It was going to be a good day. The fight with Lord Algon and the Wildies was over, at least for the moment, Deb was back safe and sound, and work had progressed well the day before on the wall of the makeshift fortress.

But best of all, today he was going to get to see his new barker again! Misterwizard said it was healed enough to get up and walk around. Johnny couldn't wait. He wondered if it was going to be friendly still or mean like other barkers. Something inside him told him it wasn't going to be mean, that this barker was different, a real good barker. Johnny only knew he already loved it. There was something amazing, wonderful about the way the barker smiled at him and licked his face. It made Johnny almost as happy as being with Deb.

Johnny and his family's new bedroom was in the upper floor of the Museum of Natural History, where he'd fought Ripper. It had dark walls, high ceilings and a cold stone floor. It was on the outer wall of the Museum, and one wall had a huge round glass window that let the light from the Red Eye in. It was nice to have the light again like back in the old Sanctuary, but the glass was broken, and half gone, and so the window also let in the cold. Johnny didn't want to complain, though, because the Tribe had made up the room just for him and his family.

His room and the other rooms next to it where his family slept weren't bedrooms when they found them, but the members of the Tribe all got together, found some nice beds and some furniture and decorated the rooms so they turned out as nice as Misterwizard's bedroom in the Buknker. Now Johnny's room had a big fourposter bed just like Misterwizard's, tables and chairs flowers in a metal vase and even a big white tub in the corner. Johnny didn't know what you used the tub for, maybe to hold food. It was empty now. He thought maybe he'd let the barker sleep in it.

Paintings hung from walls. Most were so faded they had little color left, but you could still see what was in them. Most were men or women just looking at you, or carrying jugs, or playing with dogs. Johnny found them all a little boring, but they were still better than blank walls. A thin red rug ran down the middle of the room. It also was faded, and bug-beasties had chewed on it, so it was full of holes. Pieces of cloth hung from the walls too in long thin strips. Those didn't look like they'd been chewed on, though they were dusty and faded.

Johnny hopped out of bed and right into his black leather boots. He was already in his clothes. Why take them off? He scratched his straw- colored hair that stood up in all directions. He was surprised there were no bug-beasties in his hair. This new city seemed cleaner than

Pilladelpia, where old Sanctuary had been, at least inside the Museums.

Johnny picked up his sword and sheath and buckled them on. He didn't sleep with his sword on, for obvious reasons. He didn't want to risk breaking it. He walked over to the table where a jug of water sat. Picking it up, he opened his mouth, tipped the jug up and let it pour in. He drank too much, coughed, and smiled.

He thought about Sanctuary for moment, and how when he would sneak out, Sephie would catch him. Then he would give her treats from his private collection. That collection of rare and precious things was still back there in Pilladelpia, in old Sanctuary. Some day he would have to go back and get the things there, for there were pieces of gold and little figures of men and strange long sticks that made blue marks on things when you ran them across them. He'd spent a lot of time collecting all those treasures.

He wondered where Sephie was. He hadn't seen her since he came back to New Sanctuary. It was strange that she hadn't come to visit him. Johnny decided he'd have to go find her, but only after he found a special treat to give her. He wanted to see that special smile she always wore when he gave her a present.

A rat-beastie ran into the center of the room. Johnny looked at it and smiled. "Morning, rat-beastie. How are you?"

The rat-beastie just looked at him, rubbed its paws over its snout and then ran off again. Johnny chuckled and headed towards the door to the upstairs hallway.

As Johnny opened the door to his room and walked outside, he saw the dark shape at the end of the hallway. He couldn't see the person's face because light from the

Red Eye streamed in a window behind them, casting them into shadow. Johnny saw the soft, slender shape of the face and the shadow of long hair falling over the dark shoulders, and he knew right away who it was. His heart skipped a beat as pleasure coursed through him like a fire spreading up from his toes to the top of his head. It was Deb.

Johnny walked towards her and she did the same. They met at the top of the stairs. Johnny could see her now, her long, blond hair and her warm blue eyes. Her beautiful, soft lips were turned upwards in a smile. Johnny put his arms around her and she did the same. They kissed deeply, passionately, just happy to be together, sharing that moment, without fear or danger, for the moment getting to simply enjoy each other without some problem interrupting them.

Johnny stopped kissing her and she put her head on his shoulder. He held her and closed his eyes, happier than he remembered being for a long time.

"I love you, Johnny," Deb said. "I love you so much."

"And I love you, Deb, more than anything in the world."

They looked at each other and smiled. "Are you ready to go see my barker with me?" Johnny asked, his face lit up with excitement.

Deb frowned, but in a playful way. "I was almost eaten by a wolf-beastie, not a few cycles ago. And now you want me to go near a barker?"

Johnny took her hand and pulled her down the stairs. "This one is different. You'll see!"

Deb didn't look convinced, but she followed along, deep in thought.

"He saved my life, Deb! I was about to be attacked by

a mean barker, and it fought it off until I could get free. You'll see, he's a good barker."

"Okay, Johnny," Deb said, laughing, as they both trotted down the stone stairs one at a time. "I've never seen you this excited about anything before!"

"Except you," Johnny said. Deb smiled at him, enjoying the compliment.

They came out of the Museum and Johnny pulled Deb along, making her start running!

"Hey!" She yelled as if annoyed, but really amused at seeing Johnny so anxious.

"Hurry, we have to make sure it's all right!"

"Well, you don't have to pull my arm off!"

Johnny came to his senses and slowed down. He put an arm around her and walked slower, looking embarrassed. She grabbed his hand and hurried her pace.

"I can't wait to see this barker. It must be something pretty special!"

Johnny stopped, looked at her and smiled. "You're the most special thing in my life." Johnny kissed her again, and they would have stood there kissing for a long time if Starbucks and Super didn't show up.

"Hey Johnny!" Starbucks said. He walked up holding Super's hand. "Guess what?"

Johnny stopped kissing Deb and looked at Starbucks with pretend annoyance. "What, Starbucks?"

"Nobody's trying to kill us today!"

They all laughed and gathered together in a group.

"What do you say we go on another adventure today?" Starbucks continued. "We haven't gone exploring since way back at Sanctuary. Who knows what cool stuff we could find here?"

"Like another hold in the ground?" Super said,

making them all smile.

"That didn't turn out all that bad, in the end," Starbucks said, looking at Super.

Johnny thought about what Starbucks said. It had been a long time since he and Starbucks explored. He remembered how much fun it had been, searching through old buildings, examining the old relics from before the Great War, wondering what the things they found were for. Even facing danger from Wildies, Beasties or the Gangers was exciting. He realized suddenly how much he missed their adventures.

"All right. I'm game," Super said, squeezing Starbuck's arm. "Now that you both have your Harleys back, let's go a long way away from here, somewhere new and exciting. But this time, we all fall in the hole together."

"That's a deal!" Starbucks said, laughing.

"We can't," Deb said. "Johnny's taking me to see his barker."

Starbucks' eyes opened wide with disbelief. "His, did you say, his Barker?"

Deb nodded, and Johnny smiled. "Yep. He found it when he was looking for Super and me."

Starbucks looked at Johnny as if Johnny had just gone crazy. "Did one of those Wildies hit your head too hard, Johnny? You brought a barker here, into New Sanctuary?"

"It's different, Starbucks," Johnny said, and suddenly he felt anxious again to go down and see it. "It a good barker."

"Well, this I got to see." Starbucks walked Super over behind Johnny and Deb. "Lead the way, Johnny Apocalypse. If you don't get eaten by this Barker, I'll say you really are the king of the world."

Laughing and joking, the four hurried down the stairs to meet Johnny's new friend.

CHAPTER 5

Misterwizard combed his short, white beard in the mirror next to the wall in his bedroom. The morning light from the Red Eye poured in the window, giving the room a cheery feeling. Being only five feet six inches tall, he had to stand on a stool to see his whole reflection. He stopped combing and gazed at himself with a critical eye. He looked at his bald head and round face, with the twinkle in his eyes.

"Just right," he said with a satisfied smile. "Adam," he said, for that was Misterwizard's real name, "you are still a handsome devil."

The night before while the Tribe slept, Misterwizard had paid a visit to Slon and the Undergrounders in their dark subway lair. He talked with them and they gave him a tour of their small village. Misterwizard learned about the lack of food and water they suffered from. Most of all, he learned all about the Rat People and their threat to Slon and his people. Misterwizard knew he had to find a way to help the Undergrounders escape their sorry existence in the old subway tunnels and join the Tribe. It would take time, however, for their eyes to adjust. Meanwhile, Misterwizard had to find a way to keep the Rat People from being able to harm them. He knew it had to be a top priority, or the Undergrounders were in great danger.

Now Misterwizard stepped off the stool and walked over to the large walk in closet in his new quarters. Once the President's bedroom, his room sported all the fanciest gadgets and perks, including a walk-in closet filled with fancy suits in blacks, browns and blues. The closet also had twenty white shirts, fifty fancy pairs of black leather shoes, a whole wall of colorful ties, a drawer full of socks and a jewelry box filled with cuff links of every description.

Misterwizard stood in the middle of the closet with nothing on but his polka dotted boxer shorts and a pair of black socks with little yellow diamonds on them. He gazed at the clothes, turning around in a circle, scratching his head.

"Where are all the fun clothes?" he muttered. He walked to the back of the closet to a chest of drawers in the corner. Opening a drawer, he looked at the contents with a smile of delight.

"Ah, now this is more like it!'

Misterwizard pulled out a pair tan shorts and held them up to see if they looked like they might fit. Nodding, he lifted his bony legs one at a time and slipped them on.

"Now all I need is a nice, fancy shirt to go along with

it!" He said. He looked around, but all he saw was the black suits and white shirts. "Surely he didn't wear these all the time. Mr. President, you're holding out on me!"

Then he saw what looked like a handle to a door at the far end of the room. He walked over and pulled on it, and to his delight, a whole new section of closet emerged! Here the shirts were colorful and covered with Hawaiian designs. Slippers as far as he could see lay on the floor and thick, fluffy robes in rich reds and royal blues hung from the hangars.

"Heaven! Misterwizard said. "Eureka! I am in Heaven!"

He walked in and checked out the shirts, finally settling on an orange shirt with white birds flying on it. Putting it on, he slipped his feet in a pair of brown leather slippers.

"Wonderful!" He exclaimed. He looked at himself in the mirror. "Stupendous!"

He spied something else and hurried over to look at it. It was a box sitting on a chest of drawers. Misterwizard opened the box. Inside where two rows of long, thick cigars. Misterwizard put his nose over them and took a big sniff. He closed his eyes with pleasure.

"Aaah! Better than the ones I found in the Capitol. And I suspect there is a light somewhere here as well."

He took out a cigar and put it in his mouth. "Mr. President," he said as well as he could with the cigar in his mouth, "I am beginning to like you, even though you turned out to be a scoundrel!"

He walked back into his bedroom, looking forward to finding a lighter and enjoying his new-found treasure. Then he saw Abercrombie and Microsoft standing in his doorway. Their expression of sorrow made him totally forget his cigar, in fact his mouth opened in surprise and the cigar fell unnoticed on the carpet.

Their faces showed such sadness and loss that Misterwizard hurried over to them. He took Abercrombie's hands and looked into her face. "My dear Abercrombie, whatever has you two so distressed? Has Sephie still not been found? "

Abercrombie shook her head, and Microsoft looked down, his eyes haunted.

"No Misterwizard. We've looked everywhere. My little girl is gone. I don't know if I can live, if I can't find my little angel."

She started weeping, and Misterwizard put an arm around her. Soon Microsoft joined her, and finally tears came to Misterwizard's eyes. He wiped his runny nose on the side of his Hawaiian shirt. Then he turned Abercrombie show she faced him and looked into her eyes.

"Abercrombie and Microsoft. I hope you will forgive me for not making Sephie's safety my first priority from the moment you told me about her disappearance. I give you my solemn promise and affidavit that I will endeavor to find your missing progeny, regardless of the perils or obstacles that I encounter on the way. I will neither relent nor relinquish my quest until I have successfully returned your sweet little maiden back safely to your familial domicile. Sephie will return to you, or you shall not see me again on this mortal plain!"

Abercrombie nodded and said, "That's all fine, Misterwizard, but can you just get Sephie back?"

"I will!" Misterwizard said, pointing a finger towards the sky. "I shall gather some supplies and set out on an exploratory mission at once. But you must do something for me."

Abercrombie and Microsoft leaned in, listening closely. "Yes, Misterwizard?" Microsoft said, his eyes wide with curiosity.

"You must guarantee to me Johnny will not discover Sephie's disappearance. Knowing Johnny, he would be stricken to the heart, and I would spare him this sorrow until absolutely necessary and at the last possible moment. Also, he too would immediately begin a search for her, and one of us is needed here to protect the Tribe against another attack. It is difficult enough to keep Johnny in one location for more than a brief moment. We do not need to give him more reason to once again leave on a new adventure."

Abercrombie and Microsoft both nodded. "You're right, of course," Abercrombie said. "Johnny is such a good boy, and he loves Sephie so much. I just hope you find her, for Johnny's sake as well as ours."

Misterwizard turned to head back to his bedroom. "I must prepare for a long and arduous journey into who knows what unknown dangers and adventures. Ha ha!" He laughed. "Today, I am Johnny, on a quest of my own!"

As he disappeared back into his room, Abercrombie and Microsoft looked at each other and smiled through their tear stained faces. But this time, a light of hope shone in their eyes.

Hidden around the corner of a tall building, Lady Stabs watched the strange man and his prisoner as he cooked breakfast over a fire. The man stopped in an open space between the crumbled remains of two tall buildings where rocks and trees kept him hidden from view of the street. The Red Eye just peeked over the distant, and the world still lay in darkness. The man's firelight made shadows puppets of the man and his prisoner on the rocks and the walls of the old broken buildings. The firelight also lit up the man's face, illuminating the cruel scowl he wore and his dark black eyes. Sitting next to him with arms tied behind her back was the man's prisoner. Lady Stabs saw to her horror and dismay that it was the little girl with the frog puppet, Sephie. Sephie looked frightened and cold, and Lady Stabs' heart went out to her. She was only a little girl, and what she'd been through must have been terrifying for her.

The man glanced at Sephie occasionally, then ignored her. He chewed on the leg of a Barker he'd shot and cooked. Sephie stared at the food with famished eyes.

He glanced at her and then smiled. He stood up and brought over a hunk of meat and a tin of water. "Listen. If I untie you, you promise not to try and run away? Because if you do, I'll break your legs. Got it?"

Sephie nodded, looking frightened. "I want to go home."

"You will," the man said as he untied her hands, looking bored. "Maybe, if you prove useful. Nobody's gonna hurt you, scrabbler, as long as your Misterwizard cares about you as much as Lord Algon thinks he does."

Once her hands were free, Sephie rubbed her wrists where the ropes had rubbed against them and then hugged herself. The man handed her a piece of meat and the tin of water. She took them and then said, "Where's Kermit? I want my frog-beastie."

The man sat down again. He picked up his meat and

got ready to eat again. "Well, you can't have it. I dropped it. Some dog-beastie's probably chewing it to pieces right now."

Tears came to Sephie's eyes, but she fought them back. She sniffed. She shivered some more. The man noticed. He grunted, stood up, took his cloak and put it around her.

"See? I'm not so bad. You just behave, and everything will be all right."

Sephie screwed up her eyes with anger and courage. "Johnny's gonna find you. Then he's going to kill you."

The man sat back down, picked up his meat, looked at her and chuckled. "Johnny, eh? Everybody seems to think this Johnny is some kind of magical being who can do anything."

"He's a hero, and he takes care of creeps like you," Sephie said stubbornly.

"Well, I hate to break it to you little missy, but your Johnny is probably dead right now. Lord Algon didn't like the way your Johnny come and tried to take over his land get it? And Lord Algon rules this place."

"Lord Algon is a bad man!" Sephie said. "And so are you!"

The man scowled. "Watch your mouth, little scrabbler, or I'll come over and slap you. I can only be pushed so far. Now eat your meat. It's all your gonna get for a while, so you better enjoy it."

Lady Stabs whole being filled with a supreme, dark hatred for the evil, cruel man. He was another rotten piece of scum, the type that needed to be weeded out of the world like a roach-beastie or a mean Barker. And she'd be glad to be the one to do it.

She held her knife in her hand and got ready to strike.

She'd fought men before, and she was a good, tough fighter. He looked like the type of scoundrel who would fight dirty, but Lady Stabs had fought his type. She could fight dirty too, even though she didn't like to. Whatever happened, she was going to make sure Sephie got away, no matter what.

But just as she was about to leap into the fire light and attack the man, two Wildies walked up out of the shadows. They were both men. One had dark hair and word an old ratty robe. The other was thin with red hair and one eye missing. He wore an old pair of jeans that were so full of holes there were more holes than jean. He had no shirt, and his body was covered with scars.

Lady Stabs moved back into hiding, disappointed. One man she could beat, but three, that would be hard. She couldn't take the chance of losing.

The man looked up at them with curiosity. They approached the man cautiously, almost reverently, and it was plain they were terrified of him.

The one with black hair in the dirty robe spoke. "Master Wolf Fang. Please forgive us for disturbing ye. We thought ye might like to know the news of the battle."

He didn't look up, as if they weren't worth the effort to acknowledge. He just kept eating his meat. "Keep your voices down, fools. Speak quick, and then be gone. Ye stink."

he men looked at each other, as if this was a new idea to them. Then they looked back at Wolf Fang."

"I'm afraid the news not be good. Lord Algon be in full retreat."

Wolf Fang's head jerked up in surprise. Sephie smiled, victorious."See? I told you Johnny would kick your ass," she said.

Wolf Fang glared at her and then turned back to the men. "How did the fool of a king manage to lose again?"

"Everything be going well," the dark-haired man said.

"And then, spirits from the Underworld came to aid the Newcomers," the red-haired man in jeans continued. "We all ran, barely escaping with our lives!"

Wolf Fang spat on the ground in disgust. "Spirits from the Underworld? What kind of stupid fools be ye? And the king believed such nonsense?"

"He be the first to turn and run, of a truth!" The red-haired man said. "He called it deviltry."

Lady Stabs, hiding around the corner, smiled, happy to hear the news. Hope grew in her that maybe the man would just release Sephie now.

"He's a bigger fool than all else," Wolf Fang said. "And a coward to boot. At the slightest sign of danger, he tucks his tail between his legs like a scrabbler and runs away. Bah!"

The men looked at each other with barely perceptible smiles, both thinking the same thing. Wolf Fang's insults of the king might come in handy some time for them, if they told them to the king at just the right moment.

Wolf Fang looked at Sephie. "I took too long getting ye to Lord Algon. I should have thrown ye over my back and ran to his castle. But then, maybe with his cowardice, it wouldn't have made much difference."

"What will ye do now?" the black-haired Wildie asked.

Wolf Fang's lip curled in disgust. "None of thy business, fool. Help me gather me things and tie this scrabbler's hands again. Maybe with her the tide can once again be turned in our favor, though I lose confidence that Lord Algon can win a battle against a scrabbler cat-beastie."

Lady Stabs watched with disappointment as the men tied Sephie's hands again and helped Wolf Fang gather his cloak and supplies. Were they going to follow him the rest of the way? If so, her chance to grab Sephie away would be slim.

When they were done tying Sephie's hands, Wolf Fang, Sephie and the two Wildies marched off again, leaving the fire to burn merrily. As soon as they were far enough away that they couldn't see her, Lady Stabs followed again. She had to find a chance to steal Sephie away before they reached Lord Algon's castle, or it would be even harder to rescue her.

CHAPTER 6

Ripper stood in front of the strange, tall, metal man of gold. It stood ten feet tall, seeming to rise to touch the ceiling. Its face was fashioned to look like a man's face with a slight smile frozen in place, with a small metal hole in the middle of the lips with mesh covering it.

Its body looked human but was boxy and big, with a huge gold chest with buttons on it. Its arms and legs were boxy looking too, with joints at the elbows and knees. Its hands looked like little squares and ended in three fingers and a thumb, with joints so the fingers and thumb could bend. The fact that its face looked human gave Ripper the creeps, for it reminded him of a golden corpse come to life.

It stood in front of Ripper, with the red orbs in its eyes pointed in his direction. Ripper didn't know whether to be terrified or thrilled at finding the strange creature. He didn't know if it was going to kill him or do be his slave.

"What are you?" Ripper asked, tense and ready to run if it showed the least sign of hostility.

"I am G-49682, the Goliath Initiative," it said in a tinny, monotone voice that came out of the small round mesh in its mouth. The voice sounded weird, as if it was speaking from far away.

"What does all that nonsense mean?" Ripper asked. "Speak so I can understand you."

The strange metal man didn't respond, just stood perfectly still.

"Will you obey my orders?" Ripper asked.

"My parameters require I take direction from only two entities. One is the Executive Officer, commonly referred to as the President, and the other is the General in Charge of the Armed Forces of America."

Ripper scratched his temple with his finger and thought. Then he said, "What if I tell you I am the Executive Officer?"

"You are President Winkle Watson?" the strange metal man intoned, turning its head and looking at him.

"Yes, I am!" Ripper said.

"Then I am at your command."

Ripper smiled with dark glee. "Great."

"If you can prove what you say is the truth. What is the password of the day?"

Ripper's smile disappeared, and he frowned instead. "Password? What does that mean? What is a password?"

"A password is a collection of letters and or numerical data chosen randomly to allow access to sensitive data or to assure authenticity of the person wishing to use restricted military equipment, such as myself. If you are the President, relay the password and I will be at your command."

Ripper cursed, suddenly afraid again. Of course, he had no clue what the password was, and he worried that if the metal monster found out he was lying, it might kill him. He had to think fast.

Ripper moved a little closer to the door, just in case the metal man made any move to hurt him. "I can't give you the password because, the President is dead, and I'm his helper. See?"

"The only two individuals who can access my functionality are the President and the General in Charge of the Armed Forces of America. President Winkle Watson or Five Star General Murphy Halftrack. If the President is dead, only Five Star General Murphy Halftrack can access my functionality."

"That don't make any sense," Ripper said. "What if this General is dead too?"

The metal man didn't move, just turned its round head to look forward again. "In the event that both the President and the General in Charge of the Armed Forces of America are dead, then Executive Order 1422 is placed in effect."

Ripper rolled his eyes, getting annoyed. "Okay, give. What is Executive Order 1422, you annoying pile of junk?"

"Executive Order 1422 states that in the absence of the two persons capable of accessing my functionality due to death or impairment, a senior officer may open the secret vault in the Pentagon and use the key code inside to countermand normal security procedures."

"Now we're getting somewhere!" Ripper said. "So, where's the secret vault?"

"Are you a senior officer?"

"Yeah, yeah. Where's the vault?"

The metal man looked at him again. "That is a secret." Then it turned its head and looked forward again. Ripper got so mad he picked up a chair and threw it across the room. The metal man didn't respond, just stood perfectly still.

It was no use. Somewhere in the building was a secret vault, and he had to find it.

Lord Algon sat on his throne in his castle gripping the arms of the chair, tense as a cat-beastie about to spring. Fear gripped his insides, twisting his stomach until he felt like he might get sick, but he fought it down, just like he had been doing since his humiliating defeat at the hands of the Newcomers.

Outside in the cemetery, the Wildies milled about. Some cooked over open fires, others slept or nursed their wounds. But Lord Algon knew they were all talking about him and wondering what was going to happen next. Some had even expressed fear that the Newcomers and their ghosts would come after them and suggested they all run away. Lord Algon wasn't sure they weren't right. He had to think of something, for he felt his kingdom falling apart around him. He'd worked too hard and killed too many people to lose it all now. He loved the power of being king, it was like a drug and he was addicted to it. He would do anything to keep it, kill anyone or sacrifice whatever he had to, just to stay Lord Algon.

But what? What was there to do? These new ghosts, they were not of this world. They probably couldn't even be killed. If you attacked them, they'd pull your heart out and eat it in front of you, and then you would become one of them, the undead. The thought sent chills up his spine. How do you fight what's already dead?

The door to his Throne Room burst open. The Ganger Facegash burst in. Lord Algon scowled, and a new fear gripped him. It was time to get rid of these Gangers, once and for all. He would at least be able to do that as long as they didn't use their magic on him, that was. Why did everyone around him have some sort of special power except him? It wasn't fair.

"How dare ye burst into my Throne Room like this, ye dirty dog?" Lord Algon said, standing up and looking outraged. "I'll have ye thrown in the Arena and torn to pieces, by thunder."

Facegash didn't look at all scared, in fact he smiled, increasing Lord Algon's fear. Was he losing all his power? He had to destroy the Gangers fast, before somehow this scum stole his kingdom away from him.

"You might as well stop all that king nonsense right now and tell me why you and your cowardly Wildies turned tail and ran."

Lord Algon didn't know what to say at first, for no matter what he said, it would seem as if he was justifying himself to Facegash. So instead he just gathered his robe around himself and strode over to a table with bottles of wine on it. He pretended to be relaxed and at ease, and hoped he pulled it off.

"I need not explain meself to the like of ye, thou lowlife Ganger scum. Ye are just lucky I don't have the lot of ye thrown in a pit to rot."

Facegash strode up to Lord Algon, his face a mask of anger. He shook a fist in Lord Algon's face.

"We were beating them. They were almost ready to surrender, and then you and your stupid rabble turned and ran away!"

Lord Algon's fear turned to anger. Who was king, after all? Leisurely, so Facegash wouldn't notice, he picked up a dagger laying on the table. Then with one fast slash, he cut Facegash's cheek. The Ganger staggered back in shock. He put a hand to his bleeding cheek and then looked at the blood on his hand, as if he didn't believe what he was seeing.

"Ye worthless, mangy c7r! How dare ye sally into my Throne Room and talk in such a pompous manner to me. Now ye can even more fit your name, ye filthy mongrel!"

Facegash sat on the floor, holding his cheek as it bled. It was a good, long cut, at least three inches. He didn't know how he was going to stop the bleeding. Suddenly all the bravado Facegash had disappeared, for he really wasn't as confident or cocky as Ripper. He realized he'd overplayed his hand and was in danger of getting himself and all the Gangers killed.

"You'll pay for that," Facegash said, knowing both he and Lord Algon knew it was an empty threat.

Lord Algon was back in control now. He smiled and sat down on his throne again. "We did not wager on the ghosts of these Newcomers. But ghosts or non, we shall fight and destroy them all, whether they be flesh or spirit."

"They're not ghosts, you idiot!" Facegash said, frowning with anger and hurt, blood oozing from his cheek. "They're just some kind of new freak made by this weird world we're living in. They can be killed, just like anyone else."

Lord Algon thought about what Facegash said, rubbing his chin idly. It hadn't occurred to him that the ghosts might be just flesh and blood. If that was the case, then Facegash was right. If they attacked right away before the Newcomers had time to recover, they could still win.

"Think ye I did not know that?" he said. "We just seemed outnumbered. But now I see we will still have the victory, if we attack swiftly."

"It about time you talked sense!" Facegash said, encouraged, despite the blood pouring from his face. "But don't try to make me believe you knew it all along."

"Bah!" Lord Algon jumping up out of his throne and walking to a window in irritation. He looked out at the grass and the strange rounded stones dotting the landscape. For some reason the stones made him uncomfortable. He'd always meant to have them all removed, but never got around to it.

His mind whirled at a thousand miles an hour. Even though the ghosts might not truly be ghosts, they still meant more people to fight. But thinking back, they seemed weak and frail. If they were truly just people, then they wouldn't be very hard to kill. He smiled. He had to get his Wildies ready to fight again fast.

Then he saw something strange. A Wildie ran towards the castle across the grass, his eyes wild and his hands waving in the air. Now what? Couldn't Lord Algon get a chance to deal with one problem before another came along?

The Wildie screamed something. Lord Algon strained his ears to hear. And when he finally did, a cold hand of dread gripped his heart.

"Piratts be attacking! Piratts!"

Lord Algon couldn't believe his bad luck. Just when he need it least, his old enemy Crooked Walk the piratt had returned, come to pillage and destroy! Lord Algon wondered why everything seemed to be turning against him. Could the great god Nucleer really be a god, and angry because Lord Algon mocked him? Could he simply have overstayed his time in the city, letting himself get too settled and relaxed when he should have been ready to leave when the winds of fortune changed? Whatever the reason, he now had a much bigger battle on his hands, one with an enemy he knew was dangerous and fierce. This battle he wasn't sure he could survive, let alone win. He began to wonder if he was simply destined to die.

Like metal sea creatures, swimming towards the shore, the rusted old ships floated slowly towards the wooden docks in the bay. The rotted docks leaned, like old men unsteady on their feet. Most of the pillars holding the docks in place had long ago fallen into the water, leaving the wooden slats tilted. Some of the docks lay half submerged in the water or missed planks, like pianos with keys missing.

In the water around the docks, the masts of old wooden ships stuck out of the water where the ships had sunk. Some ships still floated, but they were green with mold and the metal on them red with rust.

One large ship metal ship and ten smaller boats, some metal and some wood sailed into the harbor until they grew near the shore. The big ship's hull had once been green, but now its hull was red with rust and age. On the front of the ship a wooden statue of a mermaid was tied. The statue wore a smile, as if she was swimming through the ocean. On the side of the ship on both sides were painted the words, "Blak Plag."

A pilothouse sat on its deck with windows that looked out at the shore, and from them men gazed out as they piloted the vessel. A steady chug-chug sound came from deep in the belly of the ship, though it sounded rough and labored, as if the ship was on borrowed time. At the top of the wheelhouse, a pole rose into the sky. Fluttering from the top of the pole was a with a flag that showed skull and crossbones. Two more wooden poles stood on deck, one near the front and one in the back, for when they needed to use the sails. Old fashioned cannons lined the ship's deck. Next to the cannons stood barrels full of gunpowder, piles of old, rusty cannon balls and sticks used for packing the powder in the cannon's barrels.

Of the other ships, no two were alike. The only thing they had in common was they were all rusted and dirty and looked as if they would sink at any moment. Some were old fishing trawlers, others pleasure craft that had been remade into vessels for war. On the decks of the ships, dirty men in ragged clothes holding swords and muskets crowded together, all smiling with anticipation of reaching land.

At the front of the pilothouse on the large ship, Crooked Walk grinned and held onto the big wooden wheel. Dressed in old piratt clothes, he wore a three-cornered black hat and a long blue coat with gold trim. A tall man with a thin, pock-marked face, Crooked Walk's long gray hair and long gray beard made him look older than the thirty-five seasons he was. He liked to give the impression he was old, for it fooled those he fought with into thinking he would be easy to fight, and by the time they found out different, it was too late.

As Crooked Walk pulled his rusty old piratt ship into the harbor of Washington Deecee, he spied the lights of campfires on the beach. He long suspected this city was occupied and had planned to check it out and see what treasure he could find or mayhem he could cause there. Now he was cheered at heart to see he was right. He and his men were always looking for new places to loot, not only for trinkets and baubles but for weapons and food. He also liked to force the stronger looking men he found into joining his crew, for he was always losing someone in a battle.

The cranky old engine of the old ship coughed and wheezed. The piratts didn't know much about the strange machine that powered the ship, only that it needed a special water that smelled a lot to run. Every so often it would just stop making noise, and the ship would stop, whether from lack of the water or just because it was so old and rusted. Then they would have to haul the old sails out of the hold and raise them on the wooden poles they'd fashioned to two places on deck, one in front and one aft.

The sails would move the ship, but much slower than the noisy machine. One of the piratts, a crusty old man named Whale-beastie because he was fat and slow like one, somehow knew how to tinker with the old machine and get it working again. He knew where to put the water, and how to get more from a town if it was needed. He knew how to fix the machine too, most of the time. He'd go down below and bang on it with a metal stick, curse and turn little round knobs on it and open doors. Somehow, he always managed to get it going again. Whale-beastie was considered one of the most important members of the crew, and so he was treated better than most. He always got firewater whenever he wanted, and a bigger share of any loot.

Though Crooked Walk loved his ship, he hated having to rely on Whale-beastie to keep it running. In his dreams he would someday piratt a whole fleet of vessels, not just old rust-buckets like the ones he and his crew sailed on now, but nice, big ships with large cannons and decks and decks of room. He'd seen ships like the ones he dreamt about in some of the ports they'd visited, big ones as big as mountains with long guns that stuck out from the upper decks. They had white symbols on the side of the big metal tower in the middle of their top deck, ones like 72 or 68, and the decks themselves were so vast a hundred vessels like his ship could sit on them and not touch each other. How big a crew would he need to sail a vessel that big, he wondered? And would the old vessels even run again, after having sat for who knew how long? What kind of engines ran ships that big, and who knew how to make them run? Someday, no matter how hard it was, he was going to sail one, even if it took a thousand piratts to help him.

Behind Crooked Walks ship, the ten smaller ships each had a captain of their own, but they were all under Crooked Walk's command. They were not really captains like Crooked Walk was. They were just piratts he'd let take charge of the vessels for him. He could kill any one of them and they would not be missed. Crooked Walk was the real captain, ever since he had deposed that old snake, Captain Algon.

He often wondered what happened to Captain Algon. When Crooked Walk left him stranded on this very shore so long ago and sailed off with Algon's ship, Algon yelled and shook his fist and threatened to find him and get revenge. That was over five years ago. Crooked Walk barely remembered what Algon looked like. He doubted the old fool was still alive.

Limpfoot, Crooked Walk's first mate who was named for his deformed foot that he dragged along the ground, shuffled up behind him. Limpfoot may have had a bad foot, but he was a ruthless and coldblooded killer, with a heart as cold as the steel of the ship's deck. Crooked Walk had personally seen Limpfoot kill men and women right in front of their children and smile as he did it.

Limpfoot was only five feet tall but he was strong and wiry, and quick with a knife. Limpfoot's stringy black hair hung from his face like limp seaweed. Crooked Walk had never seen Limpfoot go near a bath, let alone water, and he knew the man had bug-beastie boarders on his body, and worse. He smelled too, so bad most men held their nose when he was in a room, but he was a good first mate, so Crooked Walk endured the stench.

Crooked Walk glanced at Limpfoot, put a hand to his nose and then pointed at the lights on shore. "See ye that building yonder?"

Limpfoot nodded, belching loudly. "Aye."

Crooked Walk frowned with distaste but then forgot Limpfoot's rudeness. "That be our target. It be lit up as if somewhat lives there and be making much merry. Treasure there be inside, and meats for the belly I wager, and in abundance. We come in like a roaring sea storm and kill all we meet, and we take it with no trouble. We'll put the fear of the Devil in them, by thunder."

"Aye," Limpfoot said in a bored monotone, and scratched his belly.

Crooked Walk glared at him in anger. "Don't just stand there like a mindless fool,ready the men, ye brainless sea urchin."

His insults didn't faze Limpfoot. In the same bored monotone, he replied, "Aye." Then he belched again and turned around to follow orders. Crooked Walk watched him leave, shaking his head and silently muttering curses at his first mate.

He yelled over his shoulder, "Stop the ship!" Then his words were repeated by piratts all along the ship, yelling them back to where Whale-beastie was by the machine below decks.

Then he turned the silver handle on the metal controller to his left from where the words said, "Forward" to where the words said, "Neutral." He yelled, "Weigh anchor!" And heard those words repeated too, from one piratt to the next until it reached the back of the ship. His eyes lit up and his heart soared at the thought of another night of pillaging and murder. These were the nights he lived for, and the only times he felt truly alive. Roasting some poor fool over an open fire while swigging down some sort of drink that made the mind silly. That was the life for him!

Crooked Walk looked out the pilothouse at the front of the ship through the moldy, cracked window. He yelled over his shoulder to Limpfoot, "Lower the boats!"

"Lower the boats!" Limpfoot echoed to the crew. They cheered and ran to comply shouting with enthusiasm. Crooked Walk grinned, excitement coursing through him. There was nothing better than a good town pillaging. He put on his fancy blue coat with its gold buttons. Then he picked up his sword and buckled it on, grabbed two pistols and shoved them in his belt and grabbed a bottle of firewater. He took a swig, grinned with darkness and headed onto the deck to start the fun.

CHAPTER 7

Foodcourt sat in the round shaped room in the middle of the place Misterwizard called the Capitol, behind the big, wooden desk in the comfy big blue chair with the gold seal on it. Somehow sitting there made him feel important, even smarter. Since he was short, though very strong, the chair seemed to swallow Foodcourt up, and it was almost like a bed for him. But it didn't stop him from sitting up tall and straight and frowning as if he was, in fact, the President.

The chair was smudged with rock dust and one of its arms was missing. The desk had a hole in the top on one side and two of the drawers were missing. The whole room, in fact, was trashed, with empty shelves and a hole in the ceiling. But somehow it didn't matter, it was still an important room, or at least had been once.

Across the desk in the middle of the room, Teavana

strolled around, picking up dusty, moldy books from the floor and paging through them. She moved her thin, long fingers over the pages and gazed at all the words on the pages. "How could anyone understand this?" She said. It's nothing but lines and more lines."

Foodcourt frowned, for Teavana was taking him out of his President dream. "I don't know," he said, slightly irritated. "Misterwizard is going to teach us all one day, if we ever stop having battles with all the crazies and gangers and wildies."

Teavana turned and looked at him. She smiled, for he sat up with a serious look, obviously enjoying his fantasy of being in charge. "You'd like to be President, wouldn't you, Darling?"

"And why shouldn't I be, Teavana?" He asked, sitting up taller. "I'm Johnny's father, and I've done a lot for this tribe."

Teavana walked over and sat on the desk, which promptly creaked loudly and looked like it was going to collapse. "You'd make a wonderful President, but you must remember, Johnny is the one the people want."

"Of course, I know that," Foodcourt said, waving his hand towards her. "But if, you know, Johnny were to decide he needed someone to back him up, say a helper or something."

"A Vice President."

Foodcourt and Teavana looked towards the voice and were both delighted to see Misterwizard standing in the doorway. He had changed from his shorts and Hawaiian shirt into a pair of green army pants and jacket. He looked ready from travel, with a backpack on his back. He looked odd, a short little round man with a short white beard and bald head in the army clothes, like an escaping gnome.

"Ah! Misterwizard!" Foodcourt said. "I was just trying it out, you know, seeing what it was like." Foodcourt exited the chair quickly, like a schoolboy caught doing something he shouldn't.

"Enjoy it as much as you like, dear Foodcourt." Misterwizard grinned and narrowed his eyes with mirth. "You may be closer to sitting in it than you think. Meanwhile, I must leave for a short spell."

Teavana stepped towards Misterwizard, a look of concern on her face. "Where are you going, Misterwizard? Is everything all right?"

"Oh, yes, most assuredly. I just want to catch a little fresh air and take in a little of the local scenery. I'll be back before you know it. But just in case it takes me a little longer than I anticipate, please don't tell Johnny. He needn't concern himself with the wanderings of an old man when he has the weight of a new country on his shoulders."

Foodcourt, being a smart man, sensed something was wrong, but he didn't say anything, just frowned and kept his thoughts to himself.

Teavana picked up a book. "Misterwizard, I was hoping you'd start teaching us, the way you did Johnny and Starbucks. When will we know how to read the strange words in these things? I want so much to be able to find out what they say."

Misterwizard walked over and took the book from her. He smiled at it with affection and turned the pages, gazing at them with pleasure.

"Ah, the written word. Books! How lovely they are, and so full of knowledge, romance, intrigue and adventure! My intentions were to start classes in reading, writing and mathematics for both the adults and their progeny as soon as we were settled in our new home. I planned also to lecture on the subjects of history, politics and the basic tenets of democracy. Eventually I hoped to make teachers of some of the quicker learners, such as you and Foodcourt, so they in turn could accelerate the learning process and multiply my efforts. However, as you know, things have been anything but serene since our arrival in Washington D. C."

Foodcourt and Teavana stared back at him, not understanding half of what he said, as usual. "Aren't things quieting down now, Misterwizard?" Foodcourt asked. "We beat the Wildies and their crazy king, didn't we? And we haven't seen any of the Gangers in a long time."

Misterwizard put the book back on the shelf and frowned, as if deep in thought. "I'm afraid the situation is still a bit chaotic, if we were to realistically examine it without the filter of sentimentality. Though we scared the Wildes away for the moment, they most definitely wil return and redouble their efforts to eradicate us. And now there is a new threat in the strange antagonists of our new-found allies, the Rat People, who we know virtually nothing about. And I would be reluctant to count out the Gangers just yet either. Something tells me, they lurk in the shadows and will return to cause us more grief before we are finally rid of them."

Misterwizard's words did nothing to cheer Foodcourt or Teavana. They looked at each other somberly.

"Will we ever have peace, Misterwizard?" Teavana asked, folding her thin arms across her chest. Misterwizard walked over and put a comforting arm around her shoulders.

"Most indubitably. Do not despair. Something deep inside that I cannot explain tells me we are destined to succeed. We will forge a new government and bring order back to this land. But it will not be easy and will not happen without growing pains and some suffering."

Finally, Foodcourt couldn't contain himself any longer. He looked Misterwizard straight in the eye and with his jaw set in a determined way said, "Something's happened, hasn't it? That's why you're going."

Misterwizard sighed and nodded. "You are a wise and insightful man, Foodcourt. I believe the Tribe has always underestimated your intelligence and value, and I did as well. Your dogged determination to travel to Australia disguised the fact that you have a keen mind and a good heart. Yes, I'm afraid something has."

Misterwizard picked up a large blue book with the words "Law and Justice Vol IX Chapter 11" on it and idly thumbed through it as he spoke. "Little Sephie has gone missing. Her mother and father are stricken with grief. I don't know if she has simply wandered off and gotten lost, or... "

Misterwizad couldn't finish his sentence, not only because of the horror of what the rest of the sentence meant, but also because emotion choked his words. He closed the book and set it down on the edge of the table.

"I promised Microsoft and Abercrombie I would go looking for her, and not return until I found her."

Foodcourt and Teavana shared glances of sorrow. Then they looked sadly at Misterwizard again.

Misterwizard gazed at them intently. "Please, you must keep Johnny from finding out. If he does, he will be stricken to the heart, just as I was. He would immediately go out on a quest looking for her, and he is needed here to help the Tribe, especially if I am gone."

Foodcourt and Teavana nodded.

"I will try to keep his mind occupied," Foodcourt said. "With any luck, you'll be back with the young lass before he even notices you were gone."

"Let's hope that is the case," Misterrwizard said.

They all headed to the door, Misterwizard to set out on his quest, and Foodcourt and Teavana to find a way to keep Johnny occupied until Misterwizard returned.

CHAPTER 8

Garr was short but strong with two heads and a thick body like a gorilla-beastie. Like all his kind, his skin was gray and thick, the color of dried mud. He stood in the dark, dank tunnel and watched the strange white people run away. His slow mind told him only that the meat was getting away. He tried to run after them, but his big, thick stumpy legs could only move so fast, and if he moved too quickly, his head hurt from the effort. His huge, gray body rippled with muscles, and his one large red eye dripped water, like it always did when he was hungry. His ear holes, for he had no ears on the side of his head just like the rest of his kind, felt squishy, for water had gotten into them.

He looked over at the others. They slowly stomped forward through the murky water as fast as they could, trying to catch the thin white people, but they were as slow as Garr, the fat ones even slower. Next to Garr, Ha, a short, fat female with long, stringy gray hair, frowned, unhappy. Ha's mouth was big and her nose holes crooked. She didn't have any missing arms or legs and was the most attractive female in the clan, so everyone liked her.

"Meat go," Ha said.

Garr nodded. "Where meat go?" His head on the left said.

All the Glag stomped over and stood in a group. They saw the last Undergrounder disappear up the side tunnel.

"Arr!" Sak, a tall thin female with only one eye said with distress. "Gone!"

"Go too?" Gum, a young one of only ten seasons, only five feet tall but with three arms, two on his right side and one on his left, said. He was still too young to know everyone did what they wanted, and nobody listened to anyone else. He would learn. The only rule was, every Glag for him or herself.

Gar turned both heads and peered up the strange, dark opening. Something inside told him it was a scary place. Bad things would happen if he even got close to it. Better to wait for white food to come back. He turned around and sloshed back down the dark tunnel, not answering Gum.

Gum watched as slowly the rest turned and followed, like slow moving sloth-beasties, slogging through the ankle-deep water. Gum just waited, his hungry belly telling his brain not to give up so easy. He turned and looked at the strange dark opening again. He looked at the white food village. It was abandoned now, the tents empty and forlorn looking. Then he saw something that looked very interesting.

He slogged over to a pot full of water sitting on a stick over some coals. A tasty aroma came from inside. Gum's heart beat faster. Did he really find some tasty food that the rest of the clan missed? To Gum's delight, he saw meat floating in the pot. He reached his hand in. The water was hot, and it burned his hand, but his skin was thick and his brain too slow to notice. He pulled out a hunk of meat. It looked delicious!

Glancing back at the other Glags, he saw with pleasure that they were too far away already to see what he was doing. Their gray forms had almost all disappeared into the black inkiness of the dark. Smiling happily, he opened his mouth and shoved the meat in. A heavenly taste filled his mouth. It was thick and juicy and tasty. He munched on the meat, chewing it with relish. It tasted even better than the white food did! He closed his eyes, suddenly having the best meal of his life.

He swallowed it down in one big gulp and licked his big, gray lips. He opened his eyes and took one more glance at the direction his clan had gone. They didn't know! He couldn't believe his good fortune! Most of the time being one of the youngest, he'd be the last to eat and end up chewing on bones with hardly any meat on them or scraps of meat that fell accidentally from other Glags' mouths, but this time he was different!

He used both his right hands to grab some more out of the pot. There was a lot inside, but he would eat it all. He hurried and ate fast, afraid the other Glags would return and see what he had. Then they would not only steal it from him, but probably kill and eat him too for not sharing.

When the last of the meat was gone, he made sure by

moving his top right hand through the hot water. He smacked his lips and rubbed his belly with the hand on his lower right arm. Then he picked up the boiling pot with his upper right hand and left hand and drank the juicy meat flavored liquid inside. It ran down his chin and all over his body, but he didn't care. He was in ecstasy.

He put the pot down and burped loudly. He wiped his mouth with the back of the highest of his two right hands and turned to head back. Where did the white food people get such tasty meat? If they gave him more, he would do anything, even promise not to eat them anymore. He slogged back towards the others, sad, sure he would never have another meal as good again. Soon he too was swallowed up by the darkness.

Back at Lord Algon's castle, confusion and terror slowly gathered, like a coming storm.

"What's that idiot yelling about?" Facegash said, looking out another window at the Wildie below with a cloth pressed against his bleeding cheek. Lord Algon thought fast, even as his mind threatened to shift into total panic. How could he use the piratts to get rid of the Gangers? He smiled, an idea coming to him.

"Arr, me allies have arrived. They be called piratts. They are them that hunt on the seas, preying on any townsfolk they cross paths with. Ye and yer Gangers should go meet them. They be very happy to meet you, of that I've no dobut."

Facegash studied Lord Algon's face for treachery. Lord Algon knew Facegash was not stupid, and he held his breath to see what Facegash would do.

Facegash's mind whirled too, like a man involved in a deadly game of cat-beastie and mouse-beastie. He wondered if Lord Algon was lying to him. The man outside didn't sound as if he was hailing an ally coming to call. Still, Facegash and the Gangers might be able to make a better deal with the piratts than they had with Lord Algon. Maybe he could see the end of the pompous, old food and finally find someone who knew how to win without turning tail at the slightest sign of danger.

Facegash smiled and nodded. "I should meet them. Maybe with their help, you can finally win a battle without turning tail like a chicken-beastie."

Lord Algon ignored the insult. The man outside ran in. Lord Algon knew he had to silence him before he gave everything away. He hurried over to the man and spoke before he could utter a word.

"Silence! Go fetch Hardhitter and tell him to gather the troops to meet our good friends."

"Good friends?" The man said, his eyes wide open in panic and confusion. "Good friends? It be the-"

Lord Algon put a hand on the man's mouth, stopping him from continuing. "Do as I say! Now!"

The man nodded vigorously and turned to run back out. Lord Algon grinned leisurely at Facegash. Facegash stared back, a knowing smile on his face.

"Let's go meet these friends together, shall we?" Facegash said.

"Ye go out, and I be joining ye presently," Lord Algon replied. "I want to put on me battle uniform, so I look me best."

"You do that," Facegash said, heading for the door. "And we'll be waiting for you."

Lord Algon didn't like the way Facegash said the last sentence. He watched Facegash leave. When Facegash was gone, he let his face show his panic again. What should he do? If it really was Crooked Walk, he would surely try and kill Lord Algon. He'd also be very interested in seeing the little kingdom Lord Algon had managed to assemble and want to take it over. Somehow, Lord Algon had to use the Gangers and his own Wildies to get revenge on Crooked Walk. As he quickly donned his battle gear and grabbed his sword, he tried hard to think of just what his plan would be.

Ripper walked through the scattered debris in the dark, musty old office. Broken desks and rusty old chairs lay on either side of him. Dust filled the room, and he coughed. Moldy old books with torn and twisted pages lay all over the floor. He kicked some of them as he walked down the aisleway between the rotted desks and they skidded away, making fluttering sounds like wounded bird-beasties.

Ripper heard a loud thump, thump, thump. He turned around looked. The weird metal man was following him! His eyes popped open wide and fear crept up his insides. "Why are you following me?"

The metal man walked stiffly, raising one leg and then slamming the foot on the ground, making the thumping sound, then raising the other. It stopped five feet away from him.

"I await proof you are an ally," it intoned its flat tinny voice. "If you are not an ally, then you are an enemy. All enemies and wild infestations shall be destroyed!"

Ripper gulped hard. Maybe it wasn't such a good thing he'd found this metal man after all. He tried to think of something to tell the metal man. Something told him he needed to do it fast.

"Look, I lied, I am the President."

The metal man stopped and turned its black eyes to look at Ripper. "You are President Winkle Watson?"

"I said so, didn't I?"

"Why did you lie?"

"I wanted to make sure who you were first," Ripper said, making the lie up on the spot, hoping it was good enough. He didn't have time to come up with anything better.

"Then you know where the Secret Location is."

Ripper backed up a little more, to put some distance between the two of them. "I can't go to the Secret Location with you following me. You have to wait here."

"Explain." The metal man stood perfectly still, but something told Ripper it could move fast when it wanted to.

"Well, it's a secret, isn't it? If it's secret, you shouldn't know where it is."

"I have been programmed with the knowledge of the location of the secret codes."

Ripper saw a glimmer of hope. Maybe this thing wasn't too bright. "Prove it. Tell me where they are, so I know you're not an enemy."

The metal man stood still for a moment, as if deciding what to do. Ripper held his breath, hoping, wishing, almost praying, though he didn't really know what that was, having never heard of religion before.

"The Secret Location is in the Auxiliary Weapons

Room, third floor, room 310. It can only be accessed through the wall panel between room 310 and room 308."

Inside, Ripper yelled with glee. The metal man was that stupid! His spirits soared. How lucky could he get?

He leaned on an old desk and smiled with dark pleasure. His swagger came back. "Good answer. I see you are an ally. Good thing, too, or I'd have to, well do something bad to you."

"What could you do? You have no weapons."

"Just something. Don't you worry about it."

Ripper started walking again, hoping the metal man would not follow, but once again it started clomping after him. Ripper turned and held up a hand.

"Stop! I command you to stay here!"

It worked! The metal man stopped moving. Ripper chuckled. This was getting fun.

"You have to do what I say, don't you?"

The metal man turned its round head to look at him and its red eyes blinked off and on. "I will obey your commands for the present, until such time as you prove yourself to be an enemy. Then I will destroy you."

Ripper smoothed a hand over his black hair nervously. "You really like saying that, don't you?"

"it is my purpose. Destroy all enemies of the United States and President Winkle Watson. Give all control to the President. All who rebel during this time of emergency must be neutralized. It is for the good of society."

Ripper turned and starting walking again. "Yeah, whatever. Pretty soon, you're gonna be destroying some rebels all right, and one of them is named Johnny Apocalypse. You're gonna rip him apart limb from limb, while all his friends watch."

Ripper almost made it to the door on the other side of the room when the metal man spoke again. "You have once again raised suspicions that you are not President Winkle Watson. Your speech patterns and tenor do not match my records."

Oh great, now what? Ripper thought.

"You now have thirty minutes to speak the password of the day. Then I will assume you are not President Winkle Watson and will find and destroy you."

The cold hand gripped Ripper's heart again and a cold sweat broke out on his forehead. "You're bundles of fun, you know that?"

"Twenty-nine minutes, thirty seconds."

Ripper ran from the room. He had to find that password, fast.

CHAPTER 9

Crooked Walk climbed down the rope ladder into the largest wooden boat, the Captain's boat. Around him the din of yelling piratts filled the air, all waving their swords and guns in the air. Crooked Walk gave the signal by pointing his sword towards shore, and the piratts on the oars pulled on them. The boat began its slow sail towards shore. It was a merry crew headed in to land, full of bloodlust and thought of murder.

As the boats grew close to land, Crooked Walk peered at the fires on the beach. Next to them, dark figures crouched. *Having their night-time meal,* Crooked Walk thought cheerily, *with no idea that soon they will be running, their minds filled with terror.* The thought made him so merry he smiled, and even chuckled. He couldn't wait to see the people on the beach begin to panic.

Just as he hoped, the figures on the beach did just as

he expected. They stood up, pointed and ran up the beach to escape. It was a scene he'd witnessed time and time again. It was so easy pillaging and killing, almost too easy. There were no soldiers to fight anymore, just rabble who wandered the empty cities. It was sad, really, boring even. He longed for a good foe to fight, someone who would get the blood boiling, maybe even give him the fear of death.

The boats hit the beach with a scraping sound as their wooden hulls slid up onto the sand. Instantly the piratts poured out and ran inland, swords raised high and screaming battle cries. Crooked Walk followed at a more leisurely pace. He was the Captain and had a certain dignity to maintain.

He heard a scream somewhere in the darkness. Some of his piratts must have caught some innocent landlubbers and were torturing or killing them already. It made him smile. The piratts ran down the dark streets, past the old, broken down, empty buildings and rusted hunks of metal on the sides of the roads. Crooked Walk followed, not turning to the left or the right but going straight down the middle of the road. His goal was the lit building in the distance, for there was where he figured any real treasure would lay.

The piratts searched each old structure, smashing down the old, rotten doors with their feet or throwing something through a window and breaking it then running inside. Most times they would run back out after finding nothing. Occasionally lucky ones would find loot, or even better, people living there, and then screams of terror would break the night silence as the piratts dragged the helpless victim out onto the street to start the fun.

Crooked Walk reached a metal archway in the middle of a stone fence. He quickened his pace, for past the archway lay the lit building he'd seen from the bay. Soon, they would find some treasure, he was sure of it. Surrounded by his first mate and a group of his piratts, he passed under the arch and into the strange grassy area filled with stones stuck in the ground. Something inside told him the dead lay beneath the stones. He smiled. The depressing and gloomy scene made him feel even more merry. More dead would join them, soon enough.

Ripper laughed as he ran down the dark hallway. He thought how stupid the metal man was, and how easy it was to fool him. He could tell that once he found the password it was going to be easy to control it. It would be his slave. His mind whirled with the thoughts of what the thing could do. It looked strong and dangerous. Just think what it could do to Johnny and the Tribe if he let it go and told it to kill everything that moved!

He passed by doorways, some open, exposing more rooms full of rotted desks and chairs and broken windows where the gray light of the Red Eye shone in. Other doors were closed. Those he had to open so he could look inside. He had to find the Oxillary Weppon Woom, whatever that was. He had no idea what it looked like, and since he couldn't read the ancient words, he had to hope he could tell by looking at it when he found the right place. It was a weapon room, right? Which meant it had to have a big, heavy door. But the metal man said you got the code from a small panel into the next room.

What a headache! Why couldn't it just tell him which room it was? The place was huge, and the doors seemed to go on forever. From outside the building was like a circle but with square sides and an open space in the middle, and now as he ran down the hall, he realized he'd come back to where he started. Now what?

He turned and was annoyed to see the metal man standing at the end of the hallway. What annoyed him most was the spark of fear seeing it instantly generated inside him. This metal man was really giving him the creeps, and he didn't know how long he could hang around it before he lost his nerve. He had to keep it together. He couldn't lose the great chance luck gave him of finding the metal man.

"I thought I told you to wait."

The metal man stood still, its tall dull gray metal skin glinting dully in the early morning light coming through an open doorway next to it.

It spoke in its flat, monotone voice without emotion, but somehow threatening just the same. "Twenty minutes five seconds. Do you have the password?"

Oh, oh, Ripper thought. This annoying monster was unpredictable. Ripper thought as fast as he could. He got the feeling he had only a few more chances before it decided he was an enemy and did... what? Tore him to pieces?

Finally, he thought of something, an idea like a piece of wood a man drowning in the sea grabs to keep him afloat. "I found the passageway, but it was jammed. It wouldn't open. I need you to open it for me."

With glee he watched the metal man turn and clomp down the hallway. The boards under its feet creaked from its weight. They were old and rotted, Ripper was sure the metal man would fall through the floor at any second. Was it really going to go to the passage and open it for him? Could it really be that dumb? He followed it at a safe distance, hope making his heart beat faster.

The metal man tramped along, making loud banging sounds with its flat metal feet and raising dust from the floor every time he stepped. It seemed to walk forever, though Ripper realized they'd only past five doors. Then it walked up some stairs. It took forever walking up them, and each time it put its weight on the next step the boards creaked dangerously. What if the dumb thing fell through the stair and crashed to the floor below? Surely if it took longer for the metal man to come all the way back, that wouldn't count as part of his time, would it? Ripper didn't want to find out.

It reached the next floor and slowly walked down the hall. Then as Ripper groaned, it started up another flight of stairs. Ripper followed it, beginning to really hate the slow moving, metal contraption. Finally, on the next floor it came to a large green metal door with silver handles and a round dial. It raised its hand and with its three fingers and thumb, rotated the round dial. It really was going to show him the way!

Ripper laughed to himself. *Piece of cake,* he thought. He followed the metal man into the room. This room had metal walls and racks of metal shelves with large, dusty books on them. The place smelled of rotted paper and Ripper immediately hated the room. It somehow depressed him, as if the thought of all those books he couldn't read made him feel inferior.

Ripper watched as the metal man clomped down the middle aisle past the racks of rotting books. A poster on the wall, faded almost white and with half of it shredded by age, showed a woman holding a finger to her lips. Next to her were some of the ancient words that Ripper couldn't read.

The metal man walked over to a small square panel on the wall. Bending over at the waist, it put one finger to the panel and pushed some buttons. The panel slid downward and part of the wall slid sideways revealing a hidden room!

The metal man turned and backed up, so Ripper could enter. With a huge smile of excitement on his face, Ripper walked up and peered into the room. What he saw made his heart leap for joy. The room was full of racks, and on every rack lay weapons!

At least, Ripper was pretty sure they were weapons. Some looked like the ones Misterwizard had used, other were metal and long and had all kinds of gadgets coming off them. It was like Ripper's favorite dream coming true. He couldn't wait to discover just what each of them did.

The metal man spoke from the other room, and even though his voice had no inflection, Ripper could feel the threat in his words. "You said the passageway was inaccessible."

"It was, Stupid," Ripper said, walking past the strange weapons, feeling them with his fingers. "I'm not as strong as you. Now wait her while I, see if the password is inassessible." Ripper didn't know that the word meant, but he wanted to sound like he knew what he was doing. He was still afraid the monster would kill him if he made a mistake.

So excited he could barely breathe, Ripper gazed at all the different guns and explosives. Rifles of some sort and rows of Misterwizard's green bombs. Green helmets and jackets hung on racks too. Handguns filled a glass cabinet. And on the floor sat a large, long, green metal box with something inside it. Ripper had hit the jackpot.

Johnny, Starbucks, Deb and Super headed down the hall on their way to see the barker, when Carny stopped them.

"Johnny, I need to talk to you. It's very important. It's about something I saw during the battle yesterday."

"Can't it wait, Carny?" Johnny said impatiently. "I'm going to do something very important right now."

"This is more important, Johnny!" Carny said stubbornly.

"I'll talk to you about it later." Johnny strode off, leaving Carny looking at him in annoyance.

"Sisters," Johnny said, and Starbucks, Super and Deb laughed. They all approached the door to the exam room where Johnny's new barker lay. Starbucks, Deb and Super all looked at Johnny, who wore a smile of joy tinged with caution on his face.

"You sure you want to go in there?" Starbucks said. "It might be sick, like the weird beastie we saw once with foam in its mouth that acted crazy."

"What if it's waiting by the door to attack you?" Super asked.

"Maybe you'd better wait for Misterwizard, Johnny," Deb added. "It might be dead."

Johnny smiled. He knew somehow that none of those things was going to happen. Something told him he was about to meet his new best friend.

"You guys wait out here. I want to meet him alone for

the first time."

"It's your funeral," Starbucks said, raising his eyebrows.

Johnny glanced at the others one more time, then cautiously opened the door and walked inside. Starbucks, Deb and Super stood in the doorway and watched, nervous and excited.

The room was cold and dark, and at first Johnny didn't see the barker. Then after his eyes adjusted, he saw it, standing in a corner. It was awake and looking at him.

Fear tingled inside Johnny and a fleeting thought ran through his mind that maybe his friends were right. Maybe it was crazy, or mean, and he was about to be bitten or worse. He pushed the feeling down though and steeled himself. He slowly walked towards it, watching it intently to see what it would do.

"Hey, fella. How are you doing?"

The barker stood still, looking at him. Johnny stopped a few feet away. The barker just stared at him.

"So now what, fella?"

The barker ran towards Johnny, and he steeled himself for what was going to happen next. The barker leapt on Johnny's chest, knocking him to the ground. Then it licked his face.

Johnny laughed and turned his face away from the wet onslaught, but the barker kept licking and wagged its tail. Johnny petted its head and held it, feeling its warm, soft fur. His heart filled with happiness and love for the big, shaggy black and white ball of fur.

The others walked in smiling and gathered around. They all knelt next to Johnny and started petting the barker. It wagged its tail harder and licked their hands.

"Wow, he really is friendly!" Starbucks said.

"It's so pretty," Deb said, stroking the barker's head.

"Boy, if all barkers were like this one, we'd all have one!" Super said, stroking the barker's back.

The barker rolled off Johnny and they all surrounded it, petting it and admiring it.

"What are you going to call It, Johnny?"

Johnny hadn't even thought about a name for it yet. As he held it around the waist, feeling its tail hit him in the back, he thought about it. Then he came up with it.

"I'm going to name him Deecee, after our new home."

"Deecee!" the others shouted, and then laughed.

"Do you like that, Deecee?" Deb asked, looking at Deecee's face. Deecee licked at her, and she smiled.

"I can't wait to show him to Sephie!" Johnny said. "She's going to be so excited!"

"The whole tribe is!" Starbucks said. "They're all going to want one. I want one!"

"Come on, let's feed it," Deb said. "It looks hungry."

They all stood up and walked out, and Deecee obediently followed, laughing with its mouth and wagging its tail. It was now a part Johnny's little gang.

Slon and the rest of the Undergrounders stood just inside the door into the subway tunnel. Loki and his parents Bott and Pak stood just behind Slon. All of them peered into the darkness with fear, even though they now held not only their swords but guns Misterwizard and Johnny gave them to defend themselves. Even Loki had a gun strapped on his hip, though his mother didn't approve.

"Here the bright light in the sky won't hurt us," Slon said, holding a rifle in his hands and looking back towards the door to the outside with sadness.

"But what about the Rat People?" Pak said, her right hand on Bott's shoulder and a look of fright on her face. "They will kill us if we go back."

"And our new friends?" Bott said. "We must learn to live in the light and leave this terrible place for good."

"I know that!" Slon said, irritated. "But it will take time to live in the light."

Slon peered down the dark tunnel. "This is our home. Our things are here, our memories."

"Bad memories," Bott said. "Memories of starving and fear of the Rat People."

Pak said, "Bott is right, Slon. We must leave this place for good."

Slon took a few steps down the tunnel towards the darkness. Then he looked at Bott, Pak and the rest of the Tribe and nodded. "I agree. But for now, we go back and collect our belongings. Then we will see what we can do to live in the new world."

"I bet they have much more wonderful things above," Loki said, his eyes bright with joy. "A whole world of wonderful things. Good food, and nice things to wear, and who knows what else!"

The rest of the Undergrounders all spoke their approval and nodded in excitement. Slon turned and smiled at Loki, the excitement affecting him too. But then he turned his smile into a frown and glared. "You are just a little boy, and do not need to think you can give counsel on the fate of the tribe. When we start listening to little boys, we will all be doomed."

Bott stepped forward, angry. "Do not forget, Slon, it was Loki who brought the angels to us. He saved us. You would do well to treat him better."

The rest of the Undergrounders smiled and nodded in agreement. Loki once again looked for Harp, and this time he saw her. Her long, soft face wore a smile directed at him. Then she waved her long, white hand at him! Loki felt a strange joy fill his heart, like butterflies.

Slon waved a hand. "I know that, and don't think I am grateful." He looked at Loki, waved a hand at him and said, "You will go down in history as a great hero to our people. Happy now?"

Loki grinned, delighted to hear this. Bott and Pak looked pleased.

Slon looked back down the tunnel towards their village somewhere ahead in the darkness. "Still, unless you have a way to keep from the bright light burning out your eyes, I see no way but to live here until we find a solution."

"Who will go and see if the Rat People are still there?" a woman with long stringy white hair and big, round eyes said. "If we all go, we might all die."

"I will go," Loki said, suddenly full of a courage that came from nowhere.

The crowd murmured their approval and smiled at him. Harp looked at him, her eyes warm.

"You are just a boy, Loki," Pak said. "I won't allow it."

"I am a hero!" Loki said puffing out his chest and looking important. "And I am not afraid."

"Let him go," a frail, thin man in the crowd said. "He has already shown himself to be brave and daring. He is a good lad, with a good heart."

"You all just want him to go risk his life, because you

are all too afraid!" Pak said angrily.

"I think Slon should go," another man said. "After all, he is the leader."

Slon's face went even whiter, and he looked frightened. "I have to lead the tribe," he said, his voice growing high and strained.

"My son is smarter and braver than any of you," Bott said. "And for that, you should all be ashamed."

"Then why don't you go?" A short round woman who looked like a snowball said.

"I am perfectly willing to go," Bott said. "Me and my son will show all of you how brave we are!"

While they were still arguing, Loki snuck off past Slon and ran down the tunnel. But just before he disappeared, he heard a soft, feminine voice behind him, one he instantly recognized. It made him stop right away and turn around.

It was Harp. She stood alone in the tunnel, looking at him sadly.

"Loki. Don't go. I don't want anything to happen to you."

Loki felt his insides go all gooey, and his heart pounded. "I have to go, Harp. But I'll be back."

"I'll be waiting," she said. "Be careful."

"I will."

"I love you, Loki."

Loki suddenly felt as if the was light as a feather. He never felt so happy before. No matter what he faced ahead, he knew he wouldn't even care now. He also knew he had to make it back.

"I love you too, Harp."

Loki didn't want to leave now, but he reluctantly forced himself to walk away. Harp watched him until he was swallowed up by the darkness.

Still arguing, the Undergrounders suddenly realized he was gone. They pointed and talked excitedly.

Pak looked worried and held Bott's hand tight. "Be careful, my son," she said, staring off into the darkness.

Lord Algon ran outside his castle into the graveyard into a scene of utter chaos. Wildie men and women ran everywhere, looks of terror on their faces. Chasing them were piratts, holding swords and knives. Some even had the new magic weapons. When had they gotten those?

Fear gripped Lord Algon. There was no way he could fight these tough, dangerous piratts alone. He would be crazy to try. He decided the best plan was to find a place to hide until he could mount a defense. Fierce hatred and loathing filled his heart as he thought of how Crooked Walk had once again ruined his plans. He looked around for Hardhitter and saw him hiding behind a large statue of a being with wings. He called to him, trying to do it quietly.

Hardhitter heard him and looked up. He motioned for Lord Algon to join him. Lord Algon crouched low and ran to him. He knelt down behind the statue next to Hardhitter.

"What be the plan?" Hardhitter said. "These piratts be fierce and terrible, and they've the same magic weapons as the Newcomers."

"To rally somewhere we must, to mount some kind of counter attack," Lord Algon said. "Spread the word to meet at yonder big building with the pointy top." He pointed to an old abandoned building in the distance that had once been called a "church."

"You do it!" Hardhitter said. "I'll not venture out and risk me life at thy bidding."

"Do what I say," Lord Algon spat back, "or by god Nucleer I gut you myself!" He raised his sword and walked towards Hardhitter, angry enough to do what he'd threatened.

Hardhitter and Lord Algon glared at each other, and finally Hardhitter relented. "Aye. But ye better have a plan. These here piratts look not ready to play games."

Hardhitter ran off, looking terrified. Lord Algon watched him, relieved that at least something had gone right. A plan? He didn't have a plan. His plan was to stay alive, that was his only plan.

He heard shouting and turned his head to look. What he saw filled him with hatred and anger so strong his stomach hurt. It was Crooked Walk and a gang of piratts. They strode towards his castle, big grins on their faces. They held torches! They were going to loot it, take all his precious treasures, or worse yet, maybe even burn his castle down!

He watched with sadness as they walked inside. His whole kingdom was dissolving before his eyes, and there was nothing he could do about it. He wondered if all his woes were because he hadn't prayed to the great god Nucleer enough. He never really believed in that nonsense, but now he wasn't so sure. He remembered a day not long before the Newcomers showed up when all the Wildies were kneeling before the statue of Nucleer. The statue was black with streaks of green, a man on a horse-beastie holding a sword in the air. It sat in the middle of the graveyard, and Lord Algon always thought it was silly to think it anything but a hunk of steel. On that day, he scoffed at it and walked away. Now he wondered if it was the statue of a god and he had made it angry.

It was too late to anything about it now, he told himself. Crouching low, he ran towards the building with the point at the top, as fast as he could, leaving his castle with a heavy heart.

CHAPTER 10

Wolf Fang and Sephie reached the bridge across the river. Wolf Fang held a rope tied to Sephie's waist and he tugged on it roughly to keep her moving. The men who had been with Wolf Fang left to scout the road ahead and report to Lord Algon. They'd been gone for a while, but Wolf Fang didn't care. He liked being alone much more than he preferred the company of men.

"Keep moving. We're almost there." He tugged again.

"I'm so tired. Can't we rest?"

Wolf Fang scowled impatiently. "You'll get to rest soon. Maybe permanently." He grinned at his dark joke.

Up ahead he heard the sound of shouts and the clink of sword on sword. What was going on now? He stopped and waited, listening. Sephie sat on the ground and closed her eyes, for she was exhausted.

"Hey, bug-beastie."

Wolf Fang turned towards the sound of the voice. Lady Stabs stood next to him. She hit him hard across the head with a board. He yelled and fell, dropping the rope. Sephie saw what was happening and grinned with relief and joy.

Lady Stabs ran over to Sephie and cut the ropes tying her hands with her knife. "Run, Sephie!"

Wolf Fang recovered, and he leapt to his feet, blood dripping from a gash on his forehead. He snarled with fury and pulled out his knife. Sephie struggled to her feet and ran, but she was so tired all she could manage was a fast walk.

Wolf Fang glanced around to find Sephie. He spotted her hobbling down the road towards an old abandoned building on the side of the street thirty feet away.

He had to get her back, but first he had to deal with the intruder. Lady Stabs swung the board again, but Wolf Fang stepped back, grinning. Last time she struck he was caught off-guard. This time he was alert and ready to fight, and things would be different.

Wolf Fang leapt towards Lady Stabs, full of anger and hatred. He stabbed at her, trying to kill her quickly before Sephie could get away. Lady Stabs took out her knife and leapt back, inches away from Wolf Fang's sharp blade. Wolf Fang leapt forward, trying to get closer, but Lady Stabs jumped back again. She was frightened. She'd been in fights before, but never with someone as tough and used to killing as Wolf Fang. She knew she was in the fight for her life.

"I'm going to make you pay for interfering, you stupid Ganger female," Wolf Fang said.

"I'm not a Ganger anymore. And talk is cheap, creep," Lady Stabs shot back. "I'm going to teach you to kidnap little scrabblers, making them suffer and be scared."

Wolf Fang sneered. "Poor little scrabbler," he said. "Just wait until you see what I do to her next."

Lady Stabs scowled herself. This man was a pile of scum. She had to kill him and find Sephie before something else happened to her.

The combatants circled each other in the light of the Yellow Eye, two dark figures holding knives doing a dance of death.

Wolf Fang pretended to jump towards her, and she leapt back. He laughed, enjoying the deadly game. He had no doubt he was going to win. He could see her death in his eyes. She was strong and courageous, but no match for his strength or fighting ability. He had to make her death fast, though, before the little scrabbler managed to hide so good he couldn't find her.

Lady Stabs knew she was no match for Wolf Fang too, but she knew she had to try. She'd die before she let the evil man take Sephie again. She watched Wolf Fang carefully, not giving him an opportunity to get close. She knew every minute she delayed him gave Sephie more time to run and hide.

As is reading her mind, Wolf Fang said, "I don't have time for this. You die, now!'

Wolf Fang leapt forward. Lady Stabs yelled and backed up as fast as she could to avoid his deadly blade. She didn't realize she was at the edge of the bridge. Before she could realize what was happening, the back of her foot caught on the ledge. Yelling in surprise she fell backwards, arm out, into the open air. She plummeted down and splashed into the cold, rushing river.

Wolf Fang laughed evilly. "Better still! Let the river kill you!"

He turned and scanned the horizon for Sephie. She was nowhere to be seen. He cursed darkly and ran after her. He had to catch her before she managed to get too far away. If it took him too long to find her, she could hide anywhere in the crumbling ruins. He might never get her back again.

Cursing, he ran to the first building, a two-story structure so destroyed it was nothing but an outside shell. The top floor was gone and only the front wall remained, with square holes where the windows had once been. Wolf Fang ran inside the door to find only a big pile of rubble. Sephie wasn't anywhere to be seen, but there was really no place for her to hide. The side and back walls of the building had collapsed, and the ground was just a pile of bricks and trash.

How did she get away so fast? He cursed the woman who ambushed him, not knowing Lady Stab's name. He hoped she didn't know how to swim and had drowned. It would serve her right from not minding her own business. Wolf Fang decided once he'd found Sephie and given her to Lord Algon, he'd come back and find the woman's body. Then he'd cook and eat her, just for his own pleasure.

He heard a sound outside on the street. He turned and walked back outside. A Wildie ran down the street, looking terrified.

"What be happening?" Wolf Fang yelled to him. The Wildie stopped and turned to look. He saw Wolf Fang, but the fear on his face didn't go away.

"Piratts be attacking! And they be much worse than

the Newcomers! They've boarded the castle and be looting everything!"

"Where be Lord Algon?"

"I know not. Neither he nor Hardhitter first mate be seen. It be every man for himself!"

The Wildie took off running again. Wolf Fang cursed again, this time with disappointment. Why did Fate keep ruining his plans? Now there was not only the Newcomers and their ghost friends to fight, but piratts as well. There were way too many people all trying to get control at the same time. It was becoming very annoying.

Wolf Fang walked out onto the street. He decided he might as well forget about the scrabbler for the moment. Since Lord Algon was nowhere to be found, there was no value in brining Sephie to him. Wolf Fang's reward disappeared like a cloud on a day when the Red Eye shined bright.

The piratts gave him an idea, however. He wondered if they were willing to take on new members. He thought he would fit in well with them, for he was a cut throat and a scoundrel just like they surely were. He smiled and decided to go observe these piratts, and just see how he could find a way to profit from their arrival.

Wolf Fang slowly made his way back towards the bridge, keeping in the shadows. With any luck, he would still find the scrabbler, and maybe the piratts would want her. She could be his fee to join their crew. He crept from old abandoned car to next car, then to the sidewalk to hide in the shadow of the nearest building, listening for any sounds.

Inside the first old, abandoned building Wild Fang searched in a small cave in the rubble, Sephie peered out, relieved the bad man had finally gone. But now, she was all alone, among the Wildies, Beasties and Gangers. She didn't' know what happened to Lady Stabs, and she didn't have any idea where she was.

Ripper walked through the dark room that smelled of oil and metal. As he passed the racks of guns and other strange weapons, his heart floated inside him, full of a dark, cruel glee. He was going to be able to kill anyone he wanted. He could kill the whole Tribe, blow them all to little bits and watch their bloody pieces fly in the air. Best of all, he could kill Johnny.

He stopped and touched a long rifle on a metal rack. The dark metal of its trigger glinted in the darkness and was cold to his touch. He couldn't remember feeling so happy before. Somehow, among these objects of death and destruction, he felt strangely at home, as if he'd finally found a place where he belonged.

So why did he still have that annoying, maddening feeling of doubt in the pit of his stomach, the one that kept telling him, 'it won't be enough; Johnny will still find a way to win." Was he so used to Johnny beating him that no matter what the odds were he was programmed to lose? Surely all these weapons, all this firepower would cement his victory. And the metal man! He had the metal man too! There was no way he could lose! So. stop feeling like Johnny will somehow win anyway, he told himself angrily.

A new fear crept over him, one that told him, "you'd better hide all this before Johnny finds it. Then he'll use it against you!" Ripper began to wonder if the constant fighting and losing was driving him mad. He had to win this time. He had to.

In annoyance, he realized the metal man was stood in the room watching him. It renewed more fear in him, the fear that the thing was going to kill him if he didn't find its stupid password.

"I am waiting. Retrieve the password. You have ten minutes, thirty-two seconds."

It was still counting! Ripper's breath caught in his throat. He ran down the narrow passage past the racks of weapons, frantically looking for anything that looked like a 'password.' He didn't even know what a password should look like. He hoped it wasn't in the ancient words, or he was doomed. He couldn't read them!

He reached the end of the racks to find a metal desk by the far wall. Sitting in a chair in front of it and with his head on the desk lay the remains of some ancient soldier. His uniform was green. His skin was shrunk in, leaving almost nothing but a skeleton. His gray hair hung on his skull like spiderweb. His eyes were gone, nothing left but empty sockets, and his mouth lay open showing crooked teeth. Ripper didn't want to admit it, but the old corpse scared him.

A block of colorful small blocks was pinned to his uniform on the left side of his chest, some with little metal stars on them. His hands lay on the table on either side of his head, as if he was just lying there, asleep. And then Ripper saw something clutched in the corpse's hand. Desperate hope sprang up inside him. Could the corpse be clutching the password?

Slowly, reluctantly, Ripper approached the dead man, almost afraid it would jump up at the last moment and grab him. He looked at its eyeless sockets. A bug-beastie crawled out of the left one, and Ripper thought he might get sick. Quickly he grabbed the piece of paper from the dead man's hand, hoping it wouldn't just fall apart.

He turned to see the metal man right behind him. *This was it,* Ripper thought, the moment when he would either live, or die. He held the paper up to the metal man, his heart pounding so loud he could hear it in his ears.

"Here it is, Stupid."

The metal man took it from him. Ripper backed up, ready to run if the metal man made any sudden moves towards him. He wondered if it decided to kill him if he could grab one of the strange weapons and kill it first but gave up the idea quickly. He didn't know how to use most of the weapons yet and wouldn't have a second to figure it out before the monster killed him.

He was pretty sure he couldn't outrun it, either. Something told him if the monster decided it was time to kill him, Ripper wouldn't make it two steps before it did just that. All he could do was wait and wonder if he'd made a big mistake coming in the strange building at all.

Johnny and his gang walked down the main hall of the Underground Bunker, all watching Deecee as he padded along next to them. "He's sure a happy guy," Super said, rubbing Deecee's ear.

"How'd you find him, Johnny?" Starbucks asked.

"It's kind of a long story. Right now, I want to show him to Sephie and Misterwizard."

"Let's go upstairs," Deb said. "I bet that's where they are."

They headed towards the stairs up to the Museum, but just before they reached them Foodcourt and Teavana met them. Johnny's parents both looked at Deecee with nervous smiles.

"So, this is the barker you were talking about," Foodcourt said, looking Deecee over. Deecce smiled back at him and wagged his tail. "My, he's a fine beastie."

"He sure is," Johnny said with pride. "Isn't he the best thing you ever saw?"

They all surrounded Deecee again, and this time Foodcourt and Teavana stood in front, petting Deecee.

"He'll make a great companion for you, Johnny," Teavana said as she petted Deecee's head.

"I can't wait to show her to Sephie," Johnny said. "She's going to be so excited!"

Carny walked up again. "Johnny, can you talk now?"

Foodcourt and Teavana frowned and glanced at each other. Then they stood up and faced Johnny.

"Johnny," Foodcourt said, looking uncomfortable, "I'm afraid you can't see Sephie just now."

Johnny frowned, curious. "Why not?"

"Well Johnny," Teavana started, and then looked at Foodcourt, trying to come up with something to say.

"Johnny, I need to talk to you!" Carny said, putting her hands on her hips.

"What about Sephie?" Johnny said, ignoring his sister.

"She went on a little adventure with Misterwizard," Foodcourt said, putting on his best fake smile. "She wanted to see the sights of the museums, the strange things from the world before, the baubles and doo-hickeys and such."

"Yes!" Teavana said, brightening. "He was going to

tell her all about the history of them and like that."

"Johnny…"

"Hmm," Johnny said, disappointed. "That's too bad. I guess I'll just have to show him to her later."

"Come on!" Deb said, smiling brightly. "Let's show Deecee to the rest of the Tribe!"

Johnny smiled again, though it wasn't nearly as big as before. "Okay."

"Fine!" Carny said. "Be that way. You'll find out on your own." Carny stomped away.

"Carny! Wait!" Johnny watched her stomp away. "I'm sorry. I was, well…" He should have said rude, but for some reason his pride wouldn't let him say it.

"I'll talk to her, Johnny, though we were all a little rude to her," Teavana said.

"We were all just excited about Deecee," Deb said. "We didn't mean any harm."

"I'm sure they're all going to love Deecee!" Teavana said encouragingly.

Johnny and his gang headed up the stairs, with Deecee padding along behind. Foodcourt and Teavana waited until they were gone. Then their smiles disappeared. They hugged and looked sad.

"I hated lying to Johnny like that," Teavana said.

"So did I. Let's just hope Misterwizard finds Sephie soon."

Johnny and his gang reached the top of the stairs and walked into the basement of the Museum. Deecee barked, and the sound echoed off the marble walls. Instantly all the members of the Tribe appeared on the marble stairs to the main floor, looking down at what made the sound.

Johnny, his friends and Deecee looked up at them.

Johnny knelt next to Deecee. "Friends and Tribe members let me introduce you to our newest member, Deecee. Say hello, Deecee."

As if on cue, Deecee barked. Everyone in the Tribe laughed and smiled, except for Cinnabon. She pulled Wheaties closer to her and said, "Are you sure that thing's friendly?"

Johnny chuckled and rubbed Deecee's head. "Are you friendly, boy?" Deecee smiled up at Johnny and waved his tail. Even Cinnabon had to stop frowning and she even smiled a little.

"Johnny let's take him on a walk," Deb said, smiling brightly. "We can see what tricks he knows."

"Sure, that sounds like fun!" Johnny, Deb, Starbucks and Super left, with Deecee tagging along beside them, his face gazing up at them.

CHAPTER II

As soon as she hit the water, panic filled Lady Stabs' mind. She'd never been in the big water before, and it terrified her. Now here she was, into the middle of it. She was sure she was going to be dead soon, that the water would swallow her and never let her go.

The first sensation as she plunged beneath the surface was a numbing cold. The next feeling was one of utter confusion. She couldn't tell which was up or down. Water surrounded her everywhere, swirling, cold, wet water, bubbling and churning. She flailed her arms, not even sure what to do. She opened her eyes. All she saw was deep blue water everywhere and bubbles floating upwards.

Finally, she was able to make out the shape of rocks on the river floor and one white wall on her right side. That told her which way was up, but how to get there?

The river moved fast, and it pulled her along at what seemed like a frightening speed. She'd never swam before and had no idea what to do.

Her natural buoyancy lifted her to the surface and her head popped up out of the water. She gasped for breath and then sank below the surface again. Her heart pounded as she flailed her arms, finally getting the idea she should push against the water to go up. Once again, she bobbed up out of the water. She looked around and saw she was moving swiftly along, past a white wall on either side of her. The wall rose three feet above the water and ended at a ledge, three feet across, and then there was another wall about ten feet high. Beyond that she would see the buildings of the city against the night sky.

She had to get to the side of the river, and quickly, before the water killed her. She moved her arms and kicked her legs, all the while speeding downstream. Finally, she made it to the wall. But how could she get up on it?

Almost as if to answer her, she looked ahead and saw a set of steps leading down into the water. She had to stay near the wall until she reached them and not be pulled back into the middle. She could barely keep herself from being sucked under again, and something else was happening that scared her even more. She was growing tired. She didn't know how much longer she could keep struggling before she simply had to stop. Then she knew she'd be sucked under for good, and that would be the end.

Lady Stabs couldn't remember a time when she was as scared as she was at that moment. Water was terrifying when it grew in strength and power. She never realized how dangerous and scary it could be. She paddled desperately, her breathing coming in ragged gasps, tears in her eyes.

Then she was at the stairs! The speed of the river threw her onto them and she grabbed the surface, clinging to it for dear life. She was out of the water! She sobbed with relief and shook, freezing cold, totally soaked, but alive. She looked down at the terrifying river speeding past her and desperately wanted to get away from it, but she was too tired and had to get her strength back. It was like staring into the face of a monster, but not having the strength to get away from it.

Finally, she thought she was rested enough to slowly crawl up the steps, one at a time, terrified she was going to slip and fall back in the water. The steps were wet and slippery, her water squished between her toes in her shoes.

Shaking and sobbing, she made her way up the steps. When she reached the top, she crawled over to the wall and sat down, utterly spent. Exhausted, she fell asleep. Her last thought before unconsciousness took her was, *I have to get back and save Sephie!* But she was too tired. Her eyes closed and soon she was in a deep slumber.

Johnny and his friends led Deecee out of the Museum and onto the big, grassy Mall. There they took turns running away from Deecee and laughing as he chased them. They raced Deecee from the front of New Sanctuary all the way to the remains of the old Capitol, weaving in between the Wildies shacks. Deecee, was so fast he ran circles around Johnny and his friends. Finally, Johnny, Starbucks and the girls had to lay down, out of breath. Deecee jumped on them and licked their faces as they pushed him and petted him, laughing and enjoying the soft, green grass.

"He's a great dog-beastie, Johnny," Starbucks said, smiling and rubbing behind Deecee's ears. "I'm going to have to get me one!"

"I want one too!" Super said. "But mine's going to be big and fierce."

"Do they have little ones?" Deb said. "I'd like one that I could carry around."

"None of them would be as good as Deecee," Johnny said, smiling with pride. "He's the best dog-beastie in the whole world."

Suddenly Deecee's head jerked up. His eyes grew intense as he stared into the distance at something.

"What is it, Boy?" Johnny asked.

They all looked in the direction Deecee looked. Sitting on the grass to their right next to a pile of rubble in the street sat a tiny rabbit-beastie.

Deb pointed at it. "Look! Deecee saw a rabbit-beastie. He sure has a keen sense of hearing."

Before they could react, Deecee leapt up and took off after the rabbit-beastie.

"Deecee, come back!" Johnny jumped up to follow, but Deecee was so fast he was halfway across the grass Mall before Johnny had barely started running.

"Let's get him before he runs away!" Starbucks said. Soon all four of them ran after Deecee.

The rabbit-beastie saw Deecee and took off in a flash, with Deecee right behind. They both disappeared behind a building on the other side of the Mall.

"Deecee!" Johnny said, afraid he was going to lose his new friend.

"Here we go again, searching for somebody!" Starbucks said, as all four of them ran off after Deecee.

Sephie crawled out from hole in the pile of rubble she'd been hiding in. The Red Eye slowly sank over the horizon and the oncoming night was cold. She didn't have a coat. She shivered and looked around. The broken walls of the building she was in rose up and looked like white skeletons around her, the square window holes eyes watching her. She didn't dare cry out for help, for that evil man might be nearby, and she didn't want to let him know where she was. What should she do?

She stepped gingerly through the stone rubble in the middle of the room where the remains of the roof that had collapsed on the floor. Her feet made a shuffling sound on the rocks. It scared her, and she stopped and then tried to walk more quietly. Why did that rotten man grab her, she wondered? And was he really gone?

She reached the doorway that led onto the street and stopped. The door was gone. Very carefully, she peered out at the street. Dark shapes loomed everywhere, full of shadows, all menacing and unfriendly. Was she all alone now, with no one to help her? Would she have to live the rest of her days by herself, looking through the old buildings for food and fighting off wild beasties? Would she have to hide every time a bad Wildie came by, hoping he didn't see her and kill her, or spend her life running from bad people who wanted to hurt her, maybe even eat her?

After waiting for a while and not hearing any sound, Sephie finally ventured outside. She looked both directions. She saw dark shapes on the street and knew they were the old junk cars. The strange, stick like things next to the buildings that rose up really high and then curved down over the street with little glass domes at the end of them, those were always there too. Misterwizard told her once they were called, "streetlamps," though he never really explained what that meant. Here and there she saw short square boxes with tops that looked like some kind of metal monster. Johnny told her once they were called, "mailboxes," but he never told her what they were for either. There seemed to be so many strange things from the world before that were mysteries. *Life before must have been very complicated,* Sephie thought.

Sephie steeled up her courage and put on a brave face. She would be courageous, just like Johnny. She wouldn't be afraid. She'd make Johnny proud of her. Hadn't she just escaped from the bad man, all by herself? "Yes, I did," she told herself with pride. "And I'll find my way back home and Johnny will be so surprised!"

She smiled, buoyed by her little speech, and walked slowly, cautiously down the street. *Which way to go?* she thought. She didn't have a clue. She could wander for days and just get further and further away. Then she remembered Lady Stabs. What happened to her? Sephie thought back, replaying the fight between the evil man and Lady Stabs that she'd seen from her hiding place. She remembered now. It seemed like Lady Stabs suddenly disappeared when she fought the evil man on the bridge. Sephie walked onto the bridge to where the fight took place, going to spot where she saw Lady Stabs fall. She looked down and saw the fast-moving river. With horror she realized Lady Stab must have fallen into the moving water! Concern for Lady Stabs filled Sephie's mind. The water looked scary and fast. Did Lady Stabs know what to do if she fell in? She decided the first thing she had to do was make sure Lady Stabs was safe, even if it meant going further away from her home. She decided she'd follow the river and look for her. Lady Stabs might be clinging on to something, waiting for Sephie to rescue her! She ran back off the bridge and began walking down between the buildings, trying to stay as close as she could to the edge of the river without risking falling in herself.

Suddenly she heard the scraping of feet on the ground. Someone was coming! Fear sprang up inside her. It could be the bad man coming back! She looked around for a new hiding place. She saw an old rusty car, just a shell of rusted metal, but with a big enough space she could hide. Quickly she ran over to it and crawled inside. She crouched down low, so she wasn't visible from outside the car. The metal was hard and sharp, and it hurt her knees and hands. It was dirty too, leaving red dust all over her. Still, she lay down as close to it as she could, knowing that the old pile of junk was her only protection against whomever was coming towards her.

Ripper waited while the metal man studied the slip of paper, or he assumed it studied it. It held the paper in front of its face and peered at it with its black eyes. He couldn't remember being so scared of dying before in his whole life. *This is it,* he thought. *Either I'm going to see all my dreams come true, or I'm going to die right now. Then Johnny will win.*

The monster's gold face looked sinister in the dark, cold room full of weapons and old costumes, as if the monster belonged there, but Ripper was an intruder. Behind the monster the racks of weapons lay on either side, and Ripper wished he had time to grab one of them, anything off a rack to defend himself in case the monster decided to kill him.

The monsters lowered the paper down. Ripper felt his insides turn to goo and he tensed up. He even closed his eyes tight and winced, waiting for the first blow.

"This is the correct password. I am at your command, President Watson."

Ripper opened his eyes and wilted in relief. "Yeah!" He raised his hand and jumped up and down, yelling. The metal monster watched him without moving, emotionless. Ripper sat down on the ground, weak from the tension. He felt like a rag doll, weak and without any strength. He sat against the side of a rack and just stared at the metal man for a few minutes, giving himself a chance to recover from the fright. Finally, when he felt he had regained some strength he stood up and all his cockiness returned.

"Okay, Stupid. From now on, you take orders from me! Got that, you, weird freaky monster?"

"I am at your command, Mr. President."

Ripper decided to give it a test. "Lift your right leg."

The metal monster dutifully raised its leg straight out. "How high would you like me to lift it?"

"To your head, Stupid," Ripper said.

"I can only functionally lift my leg three feet high. Would you like me to remove it?"

Ripper laughed. This was going to be fun. "Put your leg down, you look stupid, Stupid."

The metal man did it. Ripper walked around him, grinning. He stopped behind the metal man, and the metal man turned around to face him.

"Now do a dance."

"What dance would you prefer, Mr. President?"

Ripper scowled. "I don't know, Stupid, just pick one."

"I will do a waltz," the metal man said. Then it started dancing in a small circle, its arms out as if holding a partner. Ripper laughed so hard he almost peed his pants.

"Man, do you look silly. Okay, stop, Stupid."

The metal man stopped and turned to face Ripper again.

Ripper's mind raced at a thousand miles an hour. What should he tell it to do? Go find Johnny and rip his arms off? Go find Johnny's girl and kidnap her? Or find that annoying old man and kill him in front of Johnny. That would really hurt Johnny, Ripper knew. *There were so many possibilities!* Ripper looked around and had a great idea. "Listen, you know how to use all these fancy weapons?"

"I am knowledgeable in the operation of every weapon in history, from the 1400s to modern warfare."

Ripper waved his hand impatiently. "Okay, okay, but these here. You can teach me to use them?"

"Affirmative."

"Great!" Ripper picked up a rifle, all black with a funny looking cone on the front with holes in it. "What is this?"

"That is an AK-47 automatic assault rifle. Also known as Kalashnikov's rifle, it is gas operated rifle developed in the Soviet Union by Mikhail Kalashnikov. Its effective range is 350 meters and has a barrel length of 415 millimeters."

Ripper chortled with glee and jumped from one foot to the other. This was beyond his wildest dreams! This monster could train him to use all the weapons in the room! But what would he do next?

He stopped and thought about it. He would get Facegash, and together they would take over Lord Algon's army and kill Lord Algon. Then with the metal man's help and all the weapons, it would be on to Johnny. The thought of what would happen then made his heart warm with cruelty.

He thought of something else. "Hey Stupid, how well can you fight? Can you really kill someone?"

The metal man faced the opposite direction from Ripper. It turned its head to look at Ripper without moving its body, simply turning its head a full circle so its head faced its back. Ripper scowled and looked freaked out at how weird it looked.

"I have the ability to physical strength to kill a human being in many ways. I have been tested and found capable of killing humans at a rate of thirty per minute, depending on the resistance met and the proximity of the target. I can crush windpipes, break bones, rip arms and legs off and sever vital arteries. I can administer an electric shock that can stop the heart of a human after five point two five seconds. I have the ability to throw human bodies approximately one hundred feet in the air or at a velocity of twenty feet per second. I have a top speed of thirty-seven miles an hour. I can lift objects up to five hundred pounds in weight."

"Okay, shut up already!" Ripper said. He almost felt like crying. It was too good to be true, like his best dreams becoming reality, only they were better than he could have ever dreamt them to be. Ripper smiled dreamily, feeling giddy and weightless. He felt as if some evil god smiled down at him, telling him it was time for him to get his revenge, to show the world how terrible and fierce he was, to show them he was meant to be in command. He really was going to be King of the World! He looked at the metal man.

"Look, from now on, Stupid, turn around when you want to look at me. That thing of just turning your head around is creepy."

"As you wish, Mr. President." The metal man turned its head back to the front and then moved its whole body to face Ripper. Ripper looked at him thoughtfully.

"Look. From now on, your name is Mister Stupid. Got that? When I call you Stupid, you say, 'Yes I am, Master. What is your bidding?' Try it now. Hey Stupid."

"Yes, I am, Master. What is your bidding?"

Ripper bent over with laughter. He was having too much fun. It was time to put his plan into action. He walked towards the door out of the room and motioned for the metal man to follow.

"Okay. First, you're gonna help me find something to eat, even if you have to kill and cook it yourself. Then you and me are gonna go through these weapons and you're going to teach me how to use each one, one after another, got it Stupid?"

"Yes, I am Master. Will you revive the others now?"

Ripper froze, his mouth open, in total surprise and shock. No, he thought. It was too good, too amazing. Did he really hear what he thought he heard? He turned around and stared at the metal man. "What do you mean the others? Other like you?"

The metal man stared back at him. "Affirmative. There are twenty more G-49 series A.I. Goliath Initiative Robots in the Pentagon Command Fallout Shelter below the basement of this facility."

Ripper couldn't believe it. Twenty more. A whole army! Ripper shook his head, making sure he wasn't dreaming. Then he thought of something. "Do I have to give each of them a password too?"

"Negative, President Watson. You produced the Password of the Day, they are at your command."

Ripper's head swam with joy. He wasn't just going to be king of the world; he was going to be god.

CHAPTER 12

Johnny, Starbucks and the girls ran down the street next to the Mall, the same street where the girls had their adventure earlier, looking everywhere for Deecee. They couldn't see him anywhere. Somewhere in the gathering darkness, Deecee barked. The sound echoed off the broken buildings around them, making it impossible to tell where the sound came from.

"That way!" Starbucks said, pointing. He ran in the direction he pointed, and the rest followed, hoping he was right.

They ran into an old broken building with no door, no roof and only a broken half wall in front. Inside, piles of rubble filled the middle of the room.

"He isn't here," Deb said, disappointed.

Deecee barked again, but he sounded even further away. They all turned and ran towards the new sound.

Super frowned at Johnny as she ran. "That dog-beastie sure is fast. You need to get a rope to tie him up or you're going to be chasing him a lot!"

Johnny nodded, thinking to himself how he just hoped he'd find Deecee so he could do it.

"I just hope he doesn't manage to fall in the hole we did," Deb said. "I don't want to go through all that again."

Suddenly they heard a sound that started their hearts fluttering with alarm. I t was the growl of a large cat-beastie. They looked at each other, all thinking the same thing but no one wanting to say it. If Deecee heard the cat-beastie, he'd turn and attack it, and probably get killed.

They ran faster towards where they thought Deecee was, hoping to get there before the cat-beastie did.

Johnny looked angry. "If that cat-beastie touches one hair of Deecee's fur, I'm going to rip it to pieces."

Deb smiled, amused. "Listen to you, not even scared of the cat-beastie. Just wanting to protect your dog-beastie."

As they scrabbled over piles of rock, Johnny thought about what she said. She was right. He didn't even feel like he cared if he got hurt, if it meant keeping Deecee safe. He loved the dog-beastie now, more than anything. He just wanted to make sure he didn't get hurt.

Up ahead they saw an animal. It wasn't Deecee. It was the cat-beastie, a thin one with spots and a long tail.

"Hey!" Johnny yelled at it and ran towards it, his sword raised. The others watched, amazed at Johnny's ferocity. The cat-beastie turned towards Johnny, crouched on the ground, laid its ears back and snarled fiercely.

Johnny didn't even hesitate. All he cared about was making sure it couldn't hurt Deecee. He ran up the cat-beastie and stabbed it. It howled and scratched at him, raking Johnny's arm. Johnny, a grim look of anger on his face, stabbed it again and again, like a crazy Wildie. The others ran up to help, but they didn't even need to. Johnny had killed the cat-beastie.

"Wow!" Super said, smiling. "You really are courageous."

"We all knew that," Deb said, linking her arm in Johnny's. Then she looked down at his scratch with concern. "Johnny, you're hurt!"

"It's nothing," Johnny said, pulling away from her. "Come on, let's find Deecee before he finds something else to get into trouble with."

Johnny strode off. The others followed, after glancing one more time at the dead cat-beastie.

Misterwizard walked quietly, making sure to keep his footsteps soft so he could hear the slightest sound. He was used to taking long trips, for back when he and the Tribe lived in Philadelphia he took many treks from Castle to explore the countryside. It was on one of these trips that he found the underground bunker in Washington D. C. and came up with the plan to move the Tribe there. He knew, even when he wasn't listening for the sounds of a lost little girl, to keep quiet, for many dangers lurked in the dark in the wastelands.

Wild beasties roamed the land as well as Wildies. Often the Wildies were sad, pathetic wretches simply trying to scratch out an existence alone in the wasteland, but occasionally he would run across a dangerous one, the type who stole and robbed other Wildies or even killed them and ate them.

It was full night now. The moon, or the Yellow Eye as the Tribe called it, shone full and bright, casting a whitish light over the buildings and on the rusted hulks of the cars. To Misterwizard's left, the span of an elevated road ran, half of it destroyed. Trees grew beneath it as Nature reclaimed the world. Misterwizard thought of how once he'd passed a full-grown tree once, growing right in the middle of the road. He'd eaten apples off it and was mighty grateful for them at the time.

Misterwizard saw something lying in the road. It was small and green, and looked like a piece of cloth. Misterwizard's heart leapt with fear and sorrow, for he knew what it was. He walked up quickly and picked it up. He held it to where he could see it in the light from the Yellow Eye. It was Kermit, Sephie's toy. Misterwizard stood still, full of sadness, for this surely meant Sephie had come this way. But what happened to her? Was she walking alone, or was she kidnapped? And what could possibly make her drop her favorite toy? The possibilities all seemed like terrible ones.

Misterwizard stuffed Kermit in his backpack and kept going, his heart heavy with what he might find ahead. Then he stopped again. Up ahead, a dark shadow crept down the street. The way the figure moved, Misterwizard instantly could tell the person was up to no good. Misterwizard crouched down next to an old car and watched for a moment. The figure snuck around as well, moving from car to car. Misterwizard watched as the mysterious stranger crept from the dark shadow of an old bus across the street to the cover of an old mailbox on the other side of the street. Misterwizard was sure whomever it was, they were one of Lord Algon's allies. He decided he would capture the person and see if they knew anything about Sephie's disappearance.

Keeping an eye on the stranger, Misterwizard followed as closely as he dared, watching what the stranger did for his chance to surprise them. The stranger moved along the sidewalk, next to the crumbling buildings, leaping expertly over piles of rubble, always staying in the shadow of the buildings.

Misterwizard, being older and less agile, hurried to keep up, worried he might make more noise because of his need for haste. Fortunately, the stranger seemed intent on what was ahead of him and didn't suspect someone might be following. As Misterwizard grew closer, he could see it was a man, tall and strong, with black hair and beard. The man wore a dark cloak with a cowl and looked like a dark spirit of the night. Misterwizard could tell by the dark scowl on the man's face he was not a good man, but one definitely evil and dangerous.

Misterwizard crouched down in the doorway of an old stone building with a curved archway. Ten feet in front of him, the man also crouched as if waiting for something, or studying the view ahead to decide where to go next.

Misterwizard took a fast inventory of the things he'd brought with him. Bombs, a gun, a sword, and some food supplies. He'd never suspected he'd be wanting to subdue someone, or he would have thought to make some sleeping powder or knockout drops. Misterwizard hated violence, but he realized sadly his only option might be to knock the man out and tie him up. The thought that the man, despite his looks, might not be a bad man at all, caused Misterwizard pause. He hated the thought of doing harm to someone who didn't deserve it. He hoped he was right, and the man was at least in league with Lord Algon, which would make him the Tribe's enemy.

Now is the moment, thought Misterwizard. "Time to bolster your courage and fortitude," he told himself. "Speed and stealth are your allies, and the element of surprise will give you victory."

Slowly, Misterwizard crept forward, holding his sword high in the air. His intention was to hit the man with the Bottom of the sword. He took one step at a time, hoping his tired old joints wouldn't creak and give him away. He reached the spot right behind the man. In the light of the moon his eyes shone like wild white orbs and despite his short stature, his beard and round shape made him look like a strange wild man as he rose the sword high in the air.

Wolf Fang made it back to the bridge and could see it ahead. Having retraced his steps almost back to New Sanctuary, he didn't find the girl anywhere. Now returning in the hope she'd simply stayed put because she didn't know which wat to, not finding her put him in a bad mood. Disappointment dampened his spirits, for he hadn't heard a sound from the scrabbler. She could have wandered anywhere and been eaten by a beastie or caught by a random Wildie. She might be in some cooking pot already, or in the belly of some sleeping beastie.

He abandoned the idea of the getting her back and began to think of what else he could do to impress the piratts. A terrible but wonderful idea came to him. If he could bring them Lord Algon, they would surely be so impressed they'd not only let him join, but maybe put him in a position of leadership. It would be hard to find Lord Algon, though. Knowing what a coward and a weasel-beastie Lord Algon was, Wolf Fang knew the king would be hiding himself well. Why did everything have to be so difficult? Couldn't Fate just once make things easy for Wolf Fang?

He froze. Was that a sound he heard? He slowly turned around and looked behind himself. There stood a large, round shadow with wild, white eyes. And it was holding a sword over its head, about to bring it down on him! Wolf Fang moved to react, but he was too late. Just as the figure came into view and his shocked mind realized it was the strange old man from the Newcomers, he felt a sharp pain, and everything went black.

Misterwizard raised the sword high, his arms shaking from the effort. At the last moment the man turned and looked at him. Misterwizard brought the sword down as hard as he could, harder then he'd really intended because of the excitement. He heard a painful and unpleasant crack sound and the man's eyes closed. The man fell over onto the ground.

Misterwizard, his arms on fire from the effort,

collapsed onto the ground as well. He huffed and puffed, more from fright then from effort, and stared at the limp figure in front of him.

When he'd finally gathered his strength again, Misterwizard stood up clumsily and examined the unconscious man in front of him. The man's cowl had helped soften Misterwizard's blow, but still Misterwizard saw a lump forming on the man's head. He would have a good headache for a couple of days at least, but he didn't seem as if Misterwizard had killed him.

Misterwizard noticed the man's knife, a wicked looking dagger with a curved blade. This made Misterwizard happy, for it gave him more confidence the man was up to no good. Misterwizard took the knife away and searched the man's pockets for any other weapon. Finding nothing, he thought about how to bind the man, so he couldn't escape or fight back. Misterwizard removed the man's cloak and used it as rope to tie the man's arms. Underneath the cloak the man wore a black shirt, black pans and black boots. Misterwizard sat the man against the wall of the nearest building, sat on a nearby junk car, and waited for him to wake up.

Slowly the man regained consciousness. Misterwizard waited, chewing on a piece of bread he'd brought, one he'd made in his own oven back at Castle long ago. He washed it down with water from a jug from his backpack as he watched the man slowly begin to stir.

The man groaned from the pain of the bump on his head. Slowly his eyes opened, and he saw Misterwizard. He scowled with pure hatred and struggled to get free.

"Cease your efforts to gain freedom of motion and sit passively, or I will be forced to once again apply the painful force you recently experienced," Misterwizard said.

"What be ye talking about, ye old fool?" The man spat out, but he stopped struggling.

"I will ask you to assist me by relaying to me battle intel from who I assume is your commander, Lord Algon," Misterwizard said, taking a bite of bread and pointing his jug at the man. "You will respond by giving me what knowledge you have acquired about your Lord's plans and defenses. Depending on whether I ascertain you have answered me honestly without any attempts at subterfuge or efforts to delude me with patent falsehoods, I will decide your immediate future."

Wolf Fang's head hurt, and the old man's babbling made it hurt worse. "When I get free of these here bonds ye shall die old man for putting a hand on the great Wolf Fang. And also for assaulting mine ears with thy idiotic babbling."

Misterwizard smiled. This man was evil. He felt much better about hitting him.

"Do you know the whereabouts of a young girl, as you would call her, a scrabbler. Her name is Sephie, and she's six seasons old. She has blond hair and a very cute smile."

Wolf Fang grinned. So that was the old man's game. He'd come looking for the little girl. "Alas, I fear a beastie ate her," Wolf Fang lied, "and I watched it do it with pleasure. She screamed and cried, but it didn't move me heart an inch. I just watched and laughed good and hearty."

Misterwizard instantly grew furious and his face turned red with anger, though his heart felt a stab of sorrow. This was a very evil man indeed. Could he be telling the truth? The thought struck Misterwizard like a physical blow. Something Misterwizard told him the scoundrel was lying, just to cause Misterwizard dismay and disheartening. Or was Mistewizard simply hoping that was so?

Misterwizard's face darkened with fury, and he looked uncharacteristically dangerous. "If I discover your gruesome description of events is accurate, my scurrilous villain, I may do something I contrary to my beliefs and inclination. I may, in short, take revenge for her loss by removing your head cleanly from your shoulders."

Wolf Fang, rather than being frightened, found himself amused at Misterwizard's threat. He grinned, which made Misterwizard so angry he had to force himself not to carry out the revenge right at that moment.

Misterwizard grabbed the Wild Fang's arm and roughly dragged him to his feet. "Rise, evil miscreant. You will assist me in searching for the wayward child, even if it takes the rest of your miserable existence. If you believe in any sort of religion, you may want to utilize whatever method you employ to speak to your deity and ask them to intervene on your behalf. For if I find Sephie in the condition you have described, you will most assuredly follow her to whatever lies beyond the grave."

"What be ye sayin,' ye old fool?" Wolf Fang said, frowning.

"Get up!" Misterwizard snapped, getting irritated. "We will search for Sephie!"

"Aye. Why can't ye speak plain?"

Loki walked slowly, trying to keep quiet, crouching down in the darkness. Even though he was so scared his heart seemed to be trying to fly out of his chest, a pleasant feeling spread through him at the thought of coming back home to his village. The darkness soothed his sore eyes, and the damp coolness of the tunnel felt familiar and inviting.

He passed the hole where the god Lincone lay. He scowled at the statue with contempt, now that he knew it was not a god but simply stone. He couldn't believe how long he and his people had worshipped the worthless thing, giving it offerings and even precious food. Thanks to Johnny and the angels, his people were finally free of bondage to the silly superstition. The thought of living in the big, amazing world above excited him so much he couldn't wait to get back out there and see what kind of wonderful things he would see. All his people had to do was learn to see in the light. Then they would be truly free.

He reached the main tunnel and stopped just on the other side of the silver bars. He squinted hard and peered around, trying to see anyone lurking in the dark. In his mind, one of the Rat People waited around every dark corner, just behind the nearest rock or tent to snatch him the moment he got too close. He saw dark shadows ahead, and realized they were the tents of their village. It seemed quiet however and there didn't seem to be any of the Rat People around.

His legs shaking from fear, Loki slowly, ever so slowly, climbed over the metal rails and shuffled forward, turning his head right and left to spot the slightest movement. He reached the ledge that dropped down to the lower area where the metal rails ran and where the village was located. He could see better now, for his eyes had totally adjusted to the dark, just like when he lived there. He studied every dark corner and passage. He studied the village. The whole area looked deserted.

The tents of the village lay in disarray, some leaning to one side or the other, some squashed all the way to the ground. Cooking pots, clothes and furniture lay all over, evidence of the Rat People pawing through the village. Seeing the destruction made Loki angry. The Rat People destroyed their homes without any care about the people who lived there. But Loki realized he and and his people were lucky only their homes were destroyed, and no one was killed.

Loki wanted to run back to his tribe right away and tell them everything was okay, but he decided he should make a thorough search of the village first, just to make sure. If he told everyone it was safe and they came back only to find the Rat People waiting at the other end of the village, it would be a disaster.

He dropped down to the tracks quietly and padded over to the first tent near where the tunnel narrowed again. His heart had finally stopped pounding and now it just thumped every few seconds with a dull fear, though he felt as if it was ready to pound hard in fear again at the slightest good reason.

Loki noticed the cooking pot with the good meat was on the ground, turned over. All the good meat from the wolf monster the angels Deb and Super had helped bring them was gone. *The Rat People found it,* Loki thought, sadly. He would miss that meat, it was tasty. Loki walked down the passage between the tents. He stopped at each one and peered inside, frowning unhappily at the mess left by the Rat People. At each tent he stopped and hesitated, his heart pounding hard again for a few seconds waiting for a Rat People to jump out at him, his mind as tense as a bowstring. As he discovered each one empty, his heart would slow down again, but only until he got to the next one.

Loki reached the last two tents of the village with a sense of utter relief, and finally began to relax. It looked as if the Rat People really had left, gone back to whatever hole they crawled out of. *Maybe,* he thought, *the meat of the wolf monster had satisfied their hunger for the moment.* He walked quicker, losing his fear. Then what he feared most happened. From the last tent, he heard sound.

Freezing in terror, Loki fumbled with the gun Johnny gave him, trying to pull it out of the holster strapped to his waist. He was so thin, he had to tie the holster belt with a rope, and now, just when he needed the gun, the belt fell around his ankles. The gun wouldn't come out either, it was like it was stuck. Not that pulling it out would do Loki much good anyway. Johnny gave them all a lesson on how to shoot, but it was so long ago, Loki had forgotten almost everything Johnny said, and none of the Undergrounders had gotten any time to practice.

Loki finally got the gun to come out. It was heavier than he expected and the steel of it felt cold in his hand. The gun's barrel seemed so long, he wondered how he was going to point it at anything and hit it. He looked at the round thing in the middle, remembering how Johnny said that it was where the 'bullts' went. You did something to load them, stuck them in somehow, and then you turned the round thing. What was it Johnny said? You pulled something back, and then you pointed it at what you wanted to hit. Then you did something.

What was that? He tried hard to remember what to do, but there was so many things.

Giving up, he held it the way Johnny showed them, by the handle at the Bottom. As he peered ahead at the tent where he heard the noise, he remembered how to shoot.

"Put your top finger in this little hole," he remembered Johnny saying. "But only when you're ready to shoot then point at what you want to shoot, pull back on this lever, and hold the gun steady."

Loki held the gun out in front of him with both hands, but his hands shook so much the gun weaved up and down. His knees shook so much he was afraid he was going to fall down. Then he waited, the gun weaving up and down and side to side.

A banging and a shuffling came from the tent. Something was inside, searching through the tent for anything of value. *It had to be one of the Rat People,* Loki thought. Could Loki really fire the gun and hit it? What if he missed? It would be on him in a second. Maybe he should just turn and run as fast as he could and tell the people it wasn't safe.

The more he thought about it, the more running seemed like the smartest idea. He was just about to do it, when the thing inside the tent emerged.

A short, black round creature walked out, carrying a piece of moldy cheese. It was a Rat People all right, just like Loki was afraid of. Loki's eyes widened it fear as he saw it had two right arms and hands. He'd never actually seen a Rat People up close, the only time he saw them was from a distance as he ran away. It was gray, the color of the mud on the ground, with no ears or nose, just holes. Its eyes were red and wet, and its mouth held sharp little teeth.

It looked like a scrabbler near Loki's age. Loki became so fascinated looking at it that he forgot it was walking towards him until hit was only a few feet away. He realized It was too late to run now. He held the gun out and tried to point it at the intruder. Closing his eyes, he pulled the lever back with his thumb. Then he pulled the hammer towards himself, just the way Johnny taught him. A loud explosion followed, and the gun jumped in his hands, flying upwards. The force of the blast threw Loki fell backwards and he fell onto his bottom, sure he was going to be eaten at any second.

CHAPTER 13

It grew dark and the Yellow Eye, fully open, shone high up in the night sky. Johnny and his friends walked glumly down the street, back towards New Sanctuary. They'd searched all day and still not found Deecee.

"I'm sure he'll show up again, Johnny," Deb said, though she didn't sound very hopeful.

"Sure, he will," Starbucks said. "He knows where you live now. Once he gives up searching for the rabbit-beastie, he'll come back. You'll see."

Johnny tried to smile, thankful for the words of encouragement, but could only manage a slight upturning of his lips. "I hope you're right. I just found him, and I already lost him."

They came to a place where they could see New Sanctuary again. Thegap, Deb's father, ran up to them on his short stubby legs, puffing from the effort. He wore an excited look and his face was flushed, as if he'd been running.

"Johnny, come quick! I was watching from the wall and I heard something all the way from over at Lord Algon's castle! There was shouting and gunfire! I think he's in a battle, and it's not with us!

Johnny and his friends looked at each other with annoyed expressions.

"Here we go again," Super said.

They all followed Thegap and ran as fast as they could back to New Sanctuary.

Lord Algon sat in an old dusty chair covered in red velvet on the raised platform at the front of the large, main room of the building with the pointed top. He looked across the platform at the larger room below where a large crowd of his Wildies sat on long, wooden benches. A wooden stick on a wood base with another stick attached near the top making a cross stood just at the edge of the platform in the middle. He had to look around it to see his Wildies, which Lord Algon found very irritating because the sticks didn't seem to serve any useful purpose other than to be in the way. The Wildies all looked tense and afraid as they looked towards the distant sounds of shouting and gunfire outside in the distance.

How had things turned so disastrously wrong? Lord Algon thought. It was only a little while ago that he tasted the sweet flavor of victory. Now the only thing he tasted was the dull, sick taste of fear. He had to think!

How to turn things around? The piratts and Crooked Walk were way better organized, better armed, and definitely more fearless than Lord Algon and his Wildies. Maybe it was time to align himself with the Newcomers. Together they could fight the piratts, and when the piratts gave up and headed back to sea, he could simply betray the Newcomers again. The idea had merit, but somehow, he suspected that the Newcomers' leader Johnny was not a fool and would not be easily taken in. The realization sent Lord Algon into an even deeper gloom.

With a heavy heart and the dull ache of bitterness, Lord Algon finally admitted it was time to sneak off and let his people fend for themselves. He'd find a new place where he could start a new kingdom, and one day come back for revenge. All he had to do now was to find a way to distract the piratts long enough to escape. He smiled, full of bitterness. And the Wildies would be do it for him, whether they knew it or not.

Lord Algon stood up and all eyes turned towards him, looks of hope on their faces. He strode forward confidently, as if he had a plan and wasn't in the least bit afraid. He smiled confidently and stood behind the long stick with the platform on it, realizing that was exactly what the wooden thing must have been made for.

"Avast mateys, lend an ear to what I say. Be we lost? Do we turn tail and run at the sight of these robbers and thieves who've come to our shores to take what rightfully belongs to us? The answer be no!" Lord Algon raised a fist in the air and scowled with conviction. "This be our land and that be our castle they're looting. But we be more in number than they, I says. We be stronger, and with more fire in our bellies than a thousand of them there piratts."

He turned to look in the faces of the Wildies in the first few rows, whose faces showed fear, but also the glimmerings of hope. "Did we not fight the Undergrounders? And before they come along, there was the Baggers and the Wanderers and the Roving Beasties, and we fought them all off too!"

He looked out at the sea of faces, a warmth filling his insides at the thought that they were believing him. *They really were stupid sheep,* he thought. He shook his fist.

"And we be not going to our graves without we be puttin' up a fight! Now, here's a plan. If we fight them what's closest to us, we can capture them and clap them in irons. When we have enough of Crooked Walks mates, he'll have no choice but to parlay with us. Then we simply declare a truce, giving him the seas and us the land, and tell him not to bother us again!"

The Wildies didn't look too convinced, but they smiled anyway, as if wanting to believe him. Lord Algon turned to see Hardhitter sitting in the corner, holding his head in his hands.

"Ahoy, Hardhitter!"

Hardhitter looked up at Lord Algon with a look of fright and misery. Lord Algon scowled at him. "You be leading the first attack."

Hardhitter shook his head so hard it looked like it was going to fall off. "Nay, milord. We need be striking our colors and raising the white flag of truce. "

Lord Algon gritted his teeth in anger. Hardhitter was more of a coward than Lord Algon was, which irritated Lord Algon mostly because it meant Hardhitter was worrying about his own skin more than he was Lord Algon's . Lord Algon had to convince the lowly worm to lead the Wildies in a useless attack so he himself could escape. Someday, he vowed, he'd pay Hardhitter back for thinking about himself first instead of Lord Algon in Lord Algon's moment of need. Even as cowardly as Lord Algon was, he still found the cowardice of Hardhitter disgusting to look at.

"Ye do as I say, or I'll split yer gillet right here. Don't doubt who's still captain of this here crew. This be no time for yellow cowards and wilting hearts." *Except me,* Lord Algon thought with dark humor.

Hardhitter's knees knocked, and Lord Algon thought Hardhitter looked like he was about to cry. Hardhitter's lower lip quivered, and his brow creased. Lord Algon knew if he didn't get Hardhitter to act soon, the man would soon turn into a pile of jelly and be worthless.

Lord Algon marched down the two steps to the floor and grabbed Hardhitter by the arm. Pulling him up roughly he dragged him to the back door. He threw open the door and was just about to push Hardhitter outside when he heard the strangest sound he'd ever heard before in his life. He paused and listened, and so did Hardhitter and all the Widlies, who heard it too. A pounding came again and again in a steady rhythm, and with each crash the earth shook. It felt to Lord Algon like a thousand giants marched towards them, each one stepping in unison with the others.

Lord Algon and Hardhitter looked at each other, more frightened even than before.

"Now what betides?" Hardhitter said in a high-pitched voice.

"Go see ye what's the cause of this new racket," Lord Algon said, pushing Hardhitter out the door. Lord Algon had no intention of checking the scary sound out himself. But Hardhitter was finished. He shook all over, closed his eyes and fell to the floor. He curled up in a ball and lay still, babbling in fright. Lord Algon realized with disgust the worthless coward would be of no more use.

Lord Algon had no choice but to find out what the sound was himself. He knew he had to, for even if he planned on escaping, he had to know what new threat faced him. Leaving Hardhitter on the ground crying, he stepped out the door as if in a trance. The steady pounding came from the opposite direction of his castle and the marauding piratts. Lord Algon crept along the side of the building until he could see beyond it to the streets and buildings on the horizon. Then he ran as fast as he could, down the dark street, not caring if a Wildie or Beastie saw him. He ran like a man possessed, someone running away from the worst terror he'd ever known. He ran down block after block until he was so tired he had to stop running and catch his breath.

He looked up and saw the something bizarre, something so strange and alien to his mind he began to wonder if the strain of the last few days had made him finally go totally insane, for what he saw looked like it came straight out of a nightmare.

Sephie heard noises outside the old rusted car she hid in. She trembled, afraid the evil man who had kidnapped her had returned. She couldn't remember being more tired, scared or hungry before. She just wanted the nightmare to end, to climb into her bed at New Sanctuary with Kermit, pull the covers over her head and sleep forever. And she was lonely too. She wanted to see Johnny or

Mistewizard so badly and began to wonder if she ever would again.

She raised her head until she could see outside. She looked every direction, at the dark, cold street. She saw shadows in front of darker shadows, the strange old contraptions from the world before. None of them seemed to be moving, or did they move as soon as she looked away? She couldn't really see very far, even though the Yellow Eye cast a weak light on the street.

She heard voices! There were two people, and one of them was definitely the evil man who had kidnapped her. She couldn't hear the second voice well, it was too faint. But something about it seemed familiar. The voices grew closer! She scrunched herself back down as far as she could, hoping they wouldn't see her in the dark.

Out of the corner of her eyes, she saw two dark figures walk by her down the street. She stayed as still as she could, trying to be as motionless as the old junk car she sat in. Her heart beat hard against her chest and she dared not breathe. She finally had no choice, and gulped in air, hoping the strangers didn't hear it. Then they were gone. She sighed with relief, but tears welled up in her eyes. She was still as alone as before, with no idea where to go or what to do. Maybe she should just give herself back to the evil man. At least he knew where he was going.

She climbed out of the old car, careful not to scrape herself on the sharp edges where the car was torn and rusted. She looked herself over. She was coated with orange dust, and it had ruined her nice dress. This made her want to cry even more, but she forced herself to be strong. She didn't know how long she could keep from crying but knew it wouldn't be long.

Then she heard something wonderful, something that made her so happy she almost cried tears of joy. It was Misterwizard's voice! He was the other stranger! He must have come looking for her! Sephie sobbed with happiness and ran towards the sound of his voice. She had to catch up to him before he left, or she'd be lost again!

Without being able to stop herself she yelled, "Misterwizard!"

Ahead she saw two dark figures against the dark night sky. She could instantly tell by his short, round shape that one of them was Misterwizard. Now tears of joy fell from her eyes, but she didn't care, concentrating on running to Misterwizard instead. They were on the bridge, heading to the other side. They were so far away! She had to hurry! She ran as fast as she could, but she was so tired and weak. What if she couldn't make it? She had to, she thought. She put every effort into getting her tired legs to respond, though they felt limp and weak like string.

Finally, she realized if she didn't do something, they'd get away. She raised her hand and in the loudest voice she could manage yelled, "Misterwizard! Misterwizard! Come back!"

Misterwizard knew he and the evil man drew near to Lord Algon's castle. Ahead, he heard a loud ruckus, shouting and even the sounds of gunfire. Just what was going on?

"Stop, miscreant," Misterwizard said. "Do you hear

the pandemonium occuring in the distance?"

Wolf Fang stopped and stared ahead, his eyes bored. "Aye. I be not deaf, old man."

"Can you illuminate me as to what incites this new altercation?"

Wolf Fang turned and looked at Misterwizard, trying to keep his attention. He didn't want Misterwizard to notice he'd been working hard to undo the knot in his cloak that held his hands tied.

"Why ye not speak plain, instead of in riddles?

"Let me speak more simply, for simple minds. What is going on ahead of us?"

Wolf Fang stopped messing with his knot, now that Misterwizard was staring directly at him, and tried to look as if he was thinking about the answer. One thing he knew, he hated this old man, because his fancy words made Wolf Fang feel stupid and inferior.

"Give us a moment to think on it, matey. Surely if I ponder a bit I can recall what I heard. Now what was it Lord Algon said t'would be occuring?" He looked up at the sky as Misterwizard watched him warily.

"Could you be stalling for some felonious reason, dark and repugnant prisoner?" Misterwizard said, narrowing his eyes with suspicion.

Wolf Fang thought about what to say to waste more time, for he almost had his hands free. Then he saw something, or actually someone, running up the bridge towards them. It was the annoying little girl! She would be the perfect distraction.

"Well, well, looky yonder at what be comin.' Perhaps the beastie spit her back out again, finding her distasteful."

Misterwizard turned to look, giving Wolf Fang the

chance to work feverishly on the knot holding him bound.

Misterwizard saw Sephie and his face transformed with joy and relief. She was alive! So much happiness filled him he almost started crying himself, which he would have done without the slightest feeling of embarrassment. A big smile spread on his face and he turned towards her. "Sephie!" Forgetting about his prisoner, Misterwizard ran for her, arms wide.

"Misterwizard!' Sephie ran towards him, arms open, her face wet with tears. She ran right into his arms and he swept her up. Misterwizard hugged her tight and spun her around her face pressed tightly against his, both smiling in utter happiness.

Sephie sobbed and Misterwizard put his hand on the back of her head, comforting her. He closed his eyes, grinning from ear to ear.

"There, there, little Sephie. Everything is all right now."

"Nay old man, I be afraid it be not."

Misterwizard turned to see Wolf Fang free and standing behind them. He had snuck up to Misterwizard and taken a gun out of Misterwizard's backpack. Misterwizard had been too distracted to notice or feel him do it, and now Wolf Fang pointed it at Misterwizard's chest.

Sephie pointed at Wolf Fang. "He's a bad man, Misterwizard. A very bad man!"

"You are totally correct, Sephie, in your assessment of his character. He is definitely a man with no moral values or empathy for is fellow man."

"Belay that talk!" Wolf Fang said. He was in charge again, and now it was time for some revenge. "I be calling the shots now. And first thing ye do is stop that annoying blabbering. Next, ye hand that little lass to me. She be my prisoner once more. "

Sephie looked at Misterwizard's face, her full of fear. "No, Misterwizard, don't let him have me again! I don't want to leave you again!"

Wolf Fang sneered. "Don't be frettin for your old man freind, young scrabbler, you'll get to see him, until his very end." He scowled darkly. "Now get over here, or I'll put new holes in both of ye right now!"

Misterwizard knew they were in a bad situation. He had no doubt Wolf Fang would kill them without the slightest hesitation. He also knew Wolf Fang was not the brightest enemy Misterwizard had ever encountered. He could defeat him, but it would take ingenuity and luck. But at that moment, he saw no alternative to letting Sephie go.

Misterwizard gazed deep into Sephie's eyes. "Listen to me, Sephie. I promise you, it's going to be all right. But for now, do what this evil man says. I promise I will save you, and I won't leave you ever again."

Sephie nodded, trusting Misterwizard completely. Misterwizard leaned forward and whispered in Sephie's ear. "When you're next to him, you stamp on his foot really hard. That will distract him long enough for me to give him what he deserves."

Sephie nodded, a dark grin on her face, happy to be in on the secret plan. Misterwizard set her down and reluctantly she walked over to Wolf Fang. He grinned savagely and grabbed her arm. He pulled her to himself and put an arm over her chest, pinning her to his legs.

Misterwizard watched him somberly. "There is no necessity to harm her, deleterious felon. She is only a child and can do you no harm."

"I be the one deciding what's to be done, and I told ye to belay that type of talk 'fore I put a stop to it for good."

Sephie looked up at Misterwizard's face. He looked back at her. And then he nodded.

With all her might, Sephie raised her foot and brought it down hard on Wolf Fang's foot. He howled and looked down as an intense pain shot through his foot and up his leg.

Misterwizard didn't waste any time but threw down his backpack and rummaged through it. Grabbing an old-fashioned flare gun, he pointed it at Wolf Fang. Sephie saw what Misterwizard did. She squirmed out of Wolf Fang's grasp and ran away. He looked around, searching for her. Then he saw Misterwizard pointing the flare gun at him.

"I loathe violence and detest causing injury to any living creature, but in your case, I am willing to make an exception." Misterwizard shot the gun. A bright ball of orange light burst out of the barrel and traveled forward in an instant. It hit Wolf Fang squarely in the chest He screamed in pain and fright and fell backwards.

Almost at the exact spot where Lady Stabs fell in, Wolf Fang tripped and fell into the river. Misterwizard and Sephie ran up to the edge and looked down, just in time to see Wolf Fang disappear under the surface, a bright orange flame still burning on his chest. Swiftly the river carried him downstream, and in a second, he was gone.

Misterwizard through the empty gun away and knelt down in front of Sephie. She ran back to his arms and he pulled her close She smiled at him happily. "I knew you'd come for me, Misterwizard."

Misterwizard grinned. He pulled Kermit out of his backpack. "I think someone else is glad to see you too."

Sephie's smile grew even bigger and her eyes opened wide with joy. She grabbed Kermit and held him close, happy to be reunited with her favorite toy. "Kermit!" Tears came to Sephie's eyes again, but this time they were tears of joy.

Misterwizard picked Sephie up and put her on his shoulders. "I suspect I have one tired and hungry young lady on my hands. Shall we go home, do you think?"

"You bet!" Sephie said, holding on to Misterwizard's chin.

"Your wish is my command. You're the leader of this expedition. Off we go!"

Misterwizard set off, with a very happy and tired Sephie on his shoulders. But suddenly Sephie put a hand up in the air. "Wait!"

Misterwizard stopped and turned his eyes upwards to try and look at her. "Yes, Commander?"

"We can't leave, Misterwizard."

"Illuminate me, dear Sephie, on the reason, please."

"We have to find Lady Stabs. She's our good friend too. She fell in the river trying to rescue me. We have to try and find her."

Misterwizard nodded, happy that Sephie showed so much concern and consideration for someone else. "A kind and thoughtful decision for your first executive order, Miss President. You will indeed make a good leader someday."

"Thank you, Misterwizard," Sephie said proudly.

Misterwizard set her down. "If we are going to go on a quest to find our friend and not return to New

Sanctuary, we need to refuel and restore our batteries to give us strength. I will prepare us a short repast while you tell me all you know about Lady Stab's disappearance."

Misterwizard and Sephie sat on the ground near the bridge on the side of New Sanctuary. As Misterwizard took out some food for them to eat, Sephie told him all about the fight between Lady Stabs and Wolf Fang.

CHAPTER 14

Loki stood up, surprised nothing ate him while he lay on the ground. He looked around wildly for the Rat People he saw. It was nowhere to be seen. Did he kill it, he wondered? Or had he just imagined it was there at all? He held the gun out in front of him, unaware that to use it again he would have to reload it and it was at present useless. He peered at the tents in front of him and at the dark hulk of the old subway train beyond them. The flaps of both tents at the end of the village lay open and he could see inside each one. He looked at old boxes for chairs, ribbons hanging on the walls for decorations and tables made of suitcases, just the usual things. He saw no Rat People anywhere.

What should he do? he thought. If he told his people it was safe and a Rat People was still there, it might attack someone and then it would be his fault. But if he'd only imagined the Rat People in the first place, he would look foolish for making them all wait. He decided that no matter how scared he was, he would do a complete search of the area again. If he didn't find anyone, he would call the area safe.

He walked inside the tent on his right. It belonged to a couple of Undergrounders named Hok and Wee. Hok and Wee were older than Loki's parents and pinned to the tent were pictures of their children Woo and Bat. The pictures were hand drawn using mud from the ground, but they were very beautiful. A lot of work went into making them, and Loki could tell a lot of love. Loki was friends with Bat, even though Loki was a few seasons older. The two boys played in the tunnels sometimes, until Bat grew too scared to leave the village.

Loki felt funny looking through people's tents, as if he was a thief, but he told himself he was doing it for the good of the tribe. Hok and Wee had nothing but a rock for a chair and two old suitcases tied together for a table. On the suitcase table sat a piece of cardboard fashioned into a plate, and on it lay some meat. Loki recognized it as the good meat from the beastie the angels killed. So, a Rat People had been there! It sat on this very rock, eating. Loki felt better, knowing he hadn't imagined the Rat People, but worse too because it meant the creatures could still be somewhere near.

He finished searching Hok and Wee's tent and walked across the path to the tent on the other side. This tent belonged to Mah and Tor. They were even older than Hok and Wee, so old they walked with sticks. Their home had much more junk inside, from a lifetime of collecting. Loki searched through their possession with a tinge of jealousy, and his feelings made him feel guilty, but he couldn't help it. His family didn't have any of the nice things they possessed.

He saw a real bench from one of the long metal cars, and a piece of glass lying on a real wood table that showed your face when you looked at it. On the wall, a plastic stick hung with a round yellow circle at its top and pink petals all around the circle. It was very pretty, though Loki had no idea what it was.

Then Loki saw they even had a real chair with real cloth on it! The chair had four wooden sticks for legs and a seat made of some beautiful blue fabric that was very soft to the touch. The fabric had little dots of yellow all over it. The chair even had sticks on the sides to put your arms on. It was the nicest thing Loki had ever seen.

The more Loki looked around, the guiltier he felt. Then he grew angry and forced the feeling away. He was doing something for the tribe no one else had the guts to do, so he deserved to enjoy himself a little. No one was around, of course, so he smiled and sat in the chair. It felt so soft and comfortable on his bottom and back. He could imagine sitting in it for hours and never wanting to get up.

Then he heard a rustling behind him! The Rat People was hiding behind the chair! Like a bullet shot out of the gun Johnny gave him, Loki shot up as fast as he could. He jumped up so fast he fell right down onto his belly on the ground. Yelling, he turned over and looked up.

There behind the chair, two round, red eyes peered at him over the top of the chair. The eyes looked as scared as Loki felt, but Loki didn't care about that. He fumbled around, trying to find the gun on the ground, for he dropped it when he fell.

The gray creature spoke in a scared but deep,

guttural voice. "Me go."

Loki, unable to find the gun, froze. He didn't dare breathe and thought about how long it would take him to crawl out the tent and run away before it could grab and eat him.

"You stay, or I shoot you!" Loki said, even though he didn't have the gun. He hoped the Rat People didn't realize that fact, and he didn't think that the Rat People might have no idea what a gun was anyway. Loki stared at the Rat People from the ground and it stared back from behind the chair.

"You white food. You tasty?" Gum said.

"You'll never know," Loki said, trying to sound tough.

"Hungry not. Eat lots pot," Gum said.

"Good," Loki said, slowly inching backwards. "Then you can just go back to wherever you things come from."

"You meat," the Rat People said. "You talk."

"Of course, I talk, Dummy," Loki said. "I'm people. You don't eat people, stupid."

"Dummy not. Gum," Gum said.

"You look like a Gum," Loki said.

"Called you?" Gum said, raising his head enough so Loki could see he was smiling in a friendly way. Gum pointed a big, round gray finger at Loki.

Loki smiled back, despite being scared to death. "Loki. Not white meat." Loki had crawled backwards until he was almost to the opening of the tent. He figured he could jump up and run away before the Rat People could reach him. He stopped though, an odd sense of hope stirring in him.

"We could be friends, you know, if your people didn't try to eat us, that is."

Gum didn't reply, just stared back for a moment, and

Loki wondered if the Rat People understood him. Then Gum spoke.

"Friend not need. Meat need, lots."

Loki frowned grumpily. "Suit yourself then. We're going to kill all your people if you come back and bother us again. Tell your people that."

Gum didn't seem fazed. He stared back. Then he said something that sent chills up Loki's spine.

"Hungry now."

Loki jumped up, grabbed the gun from the ground and ran outside the tent. He ran as fast as he could back down the main street towards his waiting tribe, feeling the Rat People's hands on his back the whole way.

Ripper followed the metal man as it plodded along stamping its feet in rhythmic pounds on the dusty wooden floor. Ripper couldn't remember ever being so excited in his life. He still couldn't believe it was real. He really was going to beat Johnny! At long last he would get the revenge he'd dreamt about since way back when Johnny humiliated him at Sanctuary. He would pay Johnny back for the tiger-beastie scars on his face and shoulder. He'd pay Johnny back for making Ripper chase him halfway around the world. And he'd pay back his sister Carny too, for slashing him and leaving another scar. He'd take his time making sure they both suffered, days, maybe months.

He owned a metal man army! Not only that, but he had a whole room full of fancy weapons! He didn't think he'd even need the weapons now that he had the metal men. He decided he'd leave them where they were, hidden where only he knew how to find them. Once he and the metal men had taken over, he'd come back. He'd have lots of time for the metal men to teach him and his men how to use them once Ripper was king of the world.

He couldn't wait to see the look on Johnny's face when he saw the metal men marching towards the Tribe, a whole twenty of them, whatever that meant. When Johnny saw how powerful and strong the metal men were, he'd realize he was doomed. Ripper just hoped he'd be close enough to see really see Johnny's expression. It was going to be the best moment of Ripper's life.

The metal man plodded along down the dark passageway, past old desks and chairs covered with mold and dust. Each time it stamped its foot, a cloud of dust rose in the air. Ripper coughed and covered his mouth with his shirt. Stupid moved so slow! Ripper walked along behind it, growing more impatient every minute. He thought of how minutes ago, he thought he was going to die. Now he was king of the world. He wanted the fun to start! Why couldn't the metal man move faster?

Ripper moved around to the metal man's side, hard to do because it was so big it took up the whole passage. He tried to look at its face. "Move faster, you stupid piece of garbage!" Ripper snarled. He kicked the metal man in the leg from behind, but it didn't seem to even notice.

"I am traveling at my optimum speed of two point five miles an hour."

Ripper found a gap in the aisle large enough and he ran to the front of the metal man. He walked backwards in front of it, staring at its face with anger as it continued to plod along.

"Didn't I tell you your name was Stupid?"

The metal man turned its head and stopped moving. "Yes."

"And what are you supposed to say?"

"Yes, I am, Master."

Ripper sat on the edge of a metal desk and folded his arms. "That's right. So, answer me that way when I talk to you, Stupid."

The metal man stood still, looking at him. "Yes I am Master."

Ripper pointed a hand at its legs. "Why can't you move any faster, Stupid? You're supposed to be this amazing machine."

It replied in its emotionless voice, the red orbs in its eyes staring straight forward. "I am currently moving at my top speed of 2.5 miles an hour. The metal joints in my legs and feet and my weight of eight hundred pounds will not allow movement at any other speed. If I attempt to move faster, I will lose balance."

"Don't talk back to me, Stupid, or I'll turn you into a pile of metal scrap! Now hurry up!"

"Yes I am Master. Do you want me to accelerate despite the danger of falling?"

Ripper grit his teeth and scowled. He hated anyone being right besides him, even a stupid metal contraption, especially when the stupid metal contraption that wasn't even alive made him look as if it knew more than him.

"No, Stupid, just keep plodding along like a moron so we'll be here all day waiting for you to go down two floors."

Yes I am Master. As you command."

The metal man continued plodding along at its normal slow pace. Ripper rolled his eyes and turned around. Then he let it pass him and followed behind it agan. He vowed after he'd killed Johnny and became king of the world, he would use a bomb to blow the metal man into pieces. It would be fun seeing its arms and legs fly off and its stupid head roll around on the ground. He hoped it could still talk and say, "Yes I am, Master."

They reached another stairway and the metal man turned and started down them. He walked even slower on the stairs, pausing between steps and dropping one foot at a time, then pausing again before moving the other foot. *Are we ever going to get there?* Ripper thought. He felt a strange urgency, as if something had to go wrong if he didn't hurry. Fear of Johnny was making him paranoid.

While he walked along behind the metal man, he had lots of time. What was he going to do first? His head swam with happy possibilities. He could go right over and kill Johnny, the very first thing. *No,* he thought. Surely something would happen. He hated the feeling of fear and reluctance he felt, but he couldn't stop it. Johnny would do something to spoil things, he felt it all over, in his bones.

Then he thought of it. He'd go kill that idiot Lord Algon first! Then the Wildies would rally around him and he'd have an army to fight Johnny with. That would make him win, wouldn't it? He felt disgusted with himself at his constant fear of a boy who was two years younger than him. Johnny was big though, and smart. Shut up, he told himself! You're bigger than he is, and smarter! But Johnny is courageous... It was like he had two people in his mind, one who was the confident, tough named Ripper the Ganger, and the other who was a spineless jellyfish-beastie named Ripper the Leader Nordstrom look-alike, cringing and weak and terrified of Johnny. He had an army of metal men and a room full of fancy weapons. What was he so afraid of?

Still, better safe than sorry, he decided. He'd take over the Wildies, get the rest of the Doomsday Prophecy back together, and then with his metal men wipe out the Tribe once and for all. Then he'd go after Johnny and his family last. Leave Johnny for the very end, when all his friends and family were gone. Surely Johnny would be helpless then. Surely.

They reached the next floor. To Ripper's dismay, the metal man started plodding down the hall, back its slow pace. Ripper would going to die of old age before they got there!

They reached another set of stairs and once again the metal man started down.

"Are we almost there?" Ripper's voice rose, almost as if he was pleading.

"The door to the Executive Fallout Shelter is on the next floor. It is located exactly thirty feet, three inches from this point."

"Who cares about all that nonsense? Just get there, you annoying piece of junk!"

They reached a concrete floor. It was darker, and the air was cool. The concrete hallway was much narrower than the halls of the floors above. Ripper couldn't see anything but the reflection from the glow of the metal man's red eyes. He stumbled along behind it, following by listening to the plodding of its metal feet. It grew so dark he couldn't see his own body. He touched the cold concrete wall and moved along slowly, his heart thumping in his chest. They reached a set of metal doors. Ripper only knew because the red glow from the metal man's eyes shone on them. A square pad on the wall next to the doors had figures on it. Ripper looked at the metal man nervously.

Oh no, thought Ripper. *Not another one of these stupid password thingies.*

"I already told you the password. You got to open this one."

"Yes Master I am. As you request."

The metal man raised its hand and pushed on some of the buttons with his finger. Ripper watched him with relief. Some of the buttons lit up, glowing yellow. The doors clicked and swung backwards as if by magic. Ripper peered inside. In the dark, he saw the shadows of more metal men, lined up in rows, as far as he could see.

He jumped up and down and giggled with happiness, his eyes wide. He felt almost insane with joy, and for moment forgot everything else but the sensation of pleasure at seeing the monsters at his command. The metal man turned towards him.

"Yes I am Master. Speak the command phrase and they will be activated."

Ripper's joy faded away and he groaned inside. He couldn't believe it. Another obstacle? Was that all the people in the old days did, make up passwords and phrases? He looked around and saw a metal bar on the floor. He thought about how much he wanted to take it and bash the metal man's head in, even though since the metal man was ten feet tall he'd have to get on a chair to do it. *Someday,* he thought, *but not yet.*

He sighed, suddenly tired. "Don't start that garbage

again. You do it, Stupid."

"Yes I am Master. A robot cannot give the command to activate another robot. You must issue the command. You are President Wilkie Watson."

He couldn't lose, not this close! *So that's what it called itself, a robot,* he thought. He'd still call it Stupid. "I told you to say the command phrase. Now say it, Stupid, before I smash your head in. And stop saying, 'yes I am, Master' anymore. It's getting annoying."

"As you command," the robot said, turning its head and looking at him. The robot turned and looked at the other robots. "Goliath Initiative activated. Seek and destroy all enemies of the President and eradicate any foreign infestation."

Ripper looked at the robots with a big grin, waiting for them to all come to life. But nothing happened.

"Why didn't they do something, Stupid?"

"I told you. Only you can give the command."

"You bet I will!" Ripper said. He stomped past the robot and into the dark underground shelter. Inside the air was even cooler and smelled old and damp. Boxes lined the walls around the room with writing on them. He saw that the room was huge with a large curved concrete ceiling. He looked towards the back and saw the robots filled half the room. The rest was full of boxes of all shapes and sizes, as well as metal cots with moldy old blankets on them.

The metal men all looked just like the first one. How would he tell them apart? He turned and looked back at Stupid.

"Are you the leader?"

"Define leader."

"Are you the head robot, Stupid?"

"There is no head robot. We are all under your command."

"Well, from now on, Stupid, you're the head robot. Got it? When I give a command, you tell it to the other Stupids."

"You are overriding my basic protocols of command and authority. Is this your intention? Confirm."

"Yeah, Stupid. From now on, you're my second in command."

Ripper looked around and saw the skeleton of a man from before the Great War sitting in the corner. He wore a green coat with little colorful ribbons on his chest. Ripper smiled. He walked over and pulled the jacket off the skeleton. He brought it over to the robot.

"Put your arms out straight, Stupid."

The robot stuck its arms straight out from its sides. Ripper put the jacket on the robot.

"Okay, put your arms down." The robot did. "From now on, your name is General Stupid, Leader of the Metal Stupids."

"Yes, Master."

"Okay," Ripper said, rubbing his chin and smiling with evil glee. "Let's wake up the army!"

He walked back inside the Shelter. General Stupid followed him.

Ripper tensed with excitement. Then in a voice that was almost a whisper he said, "Goliath Initiative activated. Seek and destroy all enemies of the President and eradicate any foreign infestation!"

The red lights of all the robots' eyes lit up at once. They raised their heads and looked at Ripper. A chill went through his body, and a shiver of fear. A fleeting thought came to him. What if the other robots didn't want to follow his orders? He dismissed the thought, calling himself a chicken. After all, General Stupid said they would obey, right?

The robots all spoke at once in the same, flat tone.

"What is your command, Master?"

Ripper smiled, his face dark with hate and revenge. "Do anything I say, got it? And from now on, kill anything I tell you to."

CHAPTER 15

Loki reached the far end of the tent village. He breathed so fast he felt faint, and a clammy hand gripped his fast beating heart. His legs felt wobbly, and he hoped he could make it up the ledge on the side of the tunnel that led to where his tribe waited before the Rat People caught him.

He hurried over to the ledge, threw the gun up onto it and leaned against it. He threw one leg up then slowly pulled himself up onto the ledge. He lay down panting so hard he couldn't move for a moment. He lifted his head fearfully and looked back at the village. Where was the Rat People Boy? He saw no one there, only the dark outlines of the tents and the dirt ground met his gaze. It was as if no one had ever been there for many cycles.

Had he just imagined the whole thing? He decided to not to take a chance. Now that he finally had his breath back, he quickly stood up and ran a few feet away from it. Then he looked back again.

Then he saw it. Two white eyes in that same big round head poked from around the edge of the nearest tent. Gum had followed him!

"Aha! I see you!" Loki said, pointing, fear making his voice shake. "You better leave, or I'll shoot you again!" Loki picked up the gun and pointed it in Gum's direction. The barrel of the gun moved up and down because of Loki's nervousness, and he knew if he shot, he wouldn't hit anything, but he hoped the Rat Boy didn't know that.

The Rat Boy poked its head out. It smiled gaily, showing big, crooked, yellow teeth. It hit its own chest with a fist. "Gum."

Loki smiled grimly. "I know you're Gum, Stupid. So, after wanting to eat me, now you want to be friends, is that it? You just want to fool me into getting close, so you can grab me. Well, I'm not stupid, you know, you are."

Gum laughed, a harsh guttural sound, as if it was the first time he'd tried it. "Gum," Gum said again, smiling happily, pointing at himself again. "Now Gum hungry."

Loki couldn't help but chuckle, though he knew he was in danger. "Go eat some dirt, then. Look, I'm going to get my tribe. When they get back here they're going to kill and eat you, so you'd better run away!"

Gum frowned, unhappy. It pointed at the black pot where it found the yummy meat before. "More pot!"

"So, you ate all our delicious food. Well, that's all you're getting. I'm giving you one more chance. Leave or I shoot."

"Loki." Gum pointed at Loki again. "Go Gum!"

Go AWAY!" Loki said, wishing the dumb Rat Boy

would just leave.

"Eat Loki Gum not. Eat GumLoki not."

"Fine. I won't eat you, and you don't eat me," Loki said, smiling grimly. "Now go home and tell all your people to do the same thing. Then we can really be friends."

Gum stared back, not understanding. Then he said, "Home Gum go. Come Loki!" He motioned with his hand for Loki to follow.

Loki couldn't help but chuckle again at how insistent and dumb the rat boy was. "Right. So your people can make a meal out of me. No thanks. You go, before I kill you. But we won't eat you. You look like you'd be very unpleasant to taste, not to mention bad for our health."

Gum looked disappointed. "Home Gum go."

Loki wilted with relief. "Good. Gum go home. Bye now."

Gum turned and left. Loki felt like closing his eyes and letting himself pass out from the exhaustion caused by the tension of the encounter but resisted the urge. He knew he had to get back to Slon and the others to let them know everything that had happened.

He turned and, suddenly more tired than he could ever remember, plodded back to his tribe. Then he smiled. He would be a big hero. He was his tribe's Johnny. The thought made him so happy his energy returned. He laughed and jumped as he made his way back down the tunnel.

Crooked Walk took his time, enjoying the cool night

breeze. Around him, his piratt gang ran from one of the strange stones to another, knocking them over with their feet or hacking at them with their swords.

Suddenly a group of foolhardy Wildies rushed at Crooked Walk and the five piratts surrounding him. There was ten of them, both men and women, and they ranged in age from twenty seasons all the way up to the ripe age of forty. Their hair stood up on their heads in ragged, dirty clumps and the eyes in their dirty faces opened wide with excitement. They rushed at Crooked Walk with swords and clubs held high.

Crooked Walk grinned happily at the prospect of a fight. Though he and the men with him were outnumbered, he'd fought much bigger odds, and he was a seasoned fighter. He had no fear of the ragged band coming at them at all, sure they were just like most of the other wanderers in the wastelands. Most had no clue how to fight or the stomach for it. If they did fight they were clumsy and weak and were easily frightened off or killed without much effort.

Crooked Walk raised his sword and strode towards the onrushing attack. "Aye, finally someone who wants to fight! Come spill some blood with me, ye scurrilous dog-beasties!"

Crooked Walk's men yelled with pleasure too and grinned as they faced the Wildies. The Wildies ran until they were five feet away. Then they stopped and brandished their weapons in a threatening way.

Crooked Walk chuckled so hard his belly shook, for the Wildies looked pathetic and more scared themselves than able to scare anyone else. Crooked Walk's men laughed as well and looked at each other, enjoying the sport.

But then the Wildies parted, leaving a space in the middle of them. As Crooked Walk watched curiously, another group of Wildies rolled a cage up towards them. Crooked Walk strained to see what was inside, but all he could make out was something very big, and very strong.

He instantly realized he'd made a mistake. These Wildies were not as stupid or as foolhardy as he'd assumed. He turned to his men to tell them to back up, but it was too late. A Wildie opened the door to the cage and the huge, black beast barreled out.

Crooked Walk's bravado turned to instant fright and the turned to run. In the corner of his eye, he saw the huge beast grab one of his men by the throat. As Crooked Walk stumbled backwards he heard the man's scream of absolute terror, and then the sickening sound of cracking bones.

Crooked Walk ran across the dark landscape, dodging the strange stones. He looked everywhere to find more of his men to help fight the monster. "Avast, mateys!" Crooked Walk yelled as loud as he could. "Come to the aid of yer Captain!"

The piratts nearby heard and turned to look his way. Not knowing why Crooked Walk called for help, they ran towards him, thinking there were men to fight. They didn't know he was luring them into a fight with a terrible beast to save his own skin. Soon ten of his men surrounded Crooked Walk. His heart pounded with fear, and he pointed at the black beast. It grabbed men and bit them as they screamed in agony.

"A thousand pieces of gold to the man what slays yonder beast!" Crooked Walk pointed. The men all turned and spied the horrible creature. The creature snarled and tore a man apart as men ran away in terror.

The men with Crooked Walk took one look at the monster and turned and ran the other direction.

"Ye cowardly dogs!" Crooked Walk shouted after them. Then he looked at the black beastie again, so scared he couldn't move.

The creature dropped the remains of the man it had just torn apart, opened its mouth to show its fierce, sharp fangs, and beat on its chest. It howled and glared around, looking for another man to destroy. It looked right at Crooked Walk. He did the only thing that came to mind. He fainted.

Ripper rode on the shoulders of the golden robot with the green jacket, a big cruel grin on his face. Its glowing red eyes stared forward as it plodded along, one foot after another. Ripper was a king on his mighty steed. He was Master of the World, and his heart soared with thoughts of revenge and the death he would soon cause. He dreamt of saving some of the Tribe and killing them slowly, in fun ways, making the entertainment last as long as it could. Maybe he'd save Johnny till the last, so he could see all his friends and family die first. The thought made Ripper's insides tingle in a dark, twisted way.

Behind General Stupid, the other robots marched in rhythm in three straight lines, each stomping the ground in unison. Ripper decided to see just what the robots could do. He raised a hand. "Halt!"

General Stupid and the other robots stopped moving. Ripper, loving the feeling of power commanding the strange mechanical machines gave him. He looked around. They stood in the middle of a street, with a long metal pile of junk with broken windows next to them, lying on its side.

"See that piece of junk?"

"Yes. It is the remnant of a Yankee Clipper model streetcar. Created in approximately 1984..."

"Shut up! I didn't ask you for a lecture, you idiot! I want you to blow it up!"

"As you wish, Master." General Stupid turned his body so that he faced the streetcar. Then he said, "For your safety, you should disembark before I fire. The proximity to my rocket might cause you damage."

"Okay, General Stupid, put me down for a minute. And hurry up about it!"

General Stupid lifted Ripper up gently with his hands and set him on the ground. Ripper stood back and waited, excited to see what happened. "Okay. Hurry up!"

General Stupid looked at the streetcar. He raised his right arm. His hand bent upwards revealing a hole in his arm where four pointed sticks with red noses sat. General Stupid pointed his arm at the streetcar. Suddenly one of the sticks sailed out of his arm with smoke trailing behind hit! As Ripper watch with delight and amazement, the stick hit the streetcar and exploded.

"Wahoo!" Ripper said, jumping up and down.

The streetcar flew up in the air as if a giant had picked it up and tossed it and pieces of it flew in all directions. Loud clanging and rending sounds filled the air as the pieces skittered down the street or hit nearby buildings. The streetcar came back down to the ground with a loud crash, a big hole in the middle gone. Its metal body was twisted, and smoke and fires filled its interior.

"That was awesome!" Ripper said. He looked around and spotted an abandoned building with broken windows across the street. An old metal sign hanging crookedly from the front said, "Orpheum Theater," in rusted and broken letters.

"All of you!" Ripper said, pointing to the building. "Destroy that building. I want to see what you can do!"

All twenty robots turned towards the building. They all shot their rockets at it. The front of the building exploded in a huge spray of metal and concrete, making a huge dust cloud. The whole front wall collapsed in the street, revealing the rooms inside as if it had been cleanly sheared off. The metal sign on the front of the building fell to the ground with a loud clang. Inside the building, small fires sprouted on all the floors, burning old desks and papers.

"Yee-haw!" Ripper said. Suddenly, he couldn't wait to get to Johnny.

"Okay, that's enough!" The robots stopped shooting.

"Pick me up, General Stupid! Somebody's waiting to meet us."

General Stupid picked Ripper up and set him on his shoulders again.

"March!"

The robots resumed their slow plodding. Ripper was so happy he felt giddy. He just wished the robots would move faster. Then he saw something ahead that made him even happier. He saw a person he could try his new power on, somebody to kill.

Gum walked down the dark tunnel, splashing through the ankle-deep water. Around him, Furry Food ran everywhere. His stomach grumbled, and the Furry Food looked tasty, but he didn't grab any. After the delicious meal at the camp of the Food People, a Furry Food didn't sound very appetizing.

He thought about the food Loki. He wanted to eat him, but something inside made him not want to eat him too. He didn't understand why he would not want to eat him when he was hungry. He wished he could figure out why but didn't know how. All he did know was that somehow, he wanted to be next to Loki and talk to him some more. He'd never had someone to talk to. All his people ever did was eat and fight with each other.

Gum knew he was getting close to home when he started stepping on old, dried out bones, the remains of old food. The ground from here on out was strewn with all kinds of bones, people bones and beastie bones, but mostly rat-beastie bones, for they were the easiest to catch. The familiar crunch of the bones under his feet made him feel good, and even safe, knowing his people were not far ahead.

The tunnel turned ahead to the left, and strange lettering on a sign that hung down from the ceiling said, "Blue Line-Next Stop Farragut West," though Gum had no idea what it meant. He only knew it meant he was very close to his home.

As his feet crunched on the bones and he followed the curve of the tunnel, he saw the familiar dark shapes in the distance, darker than the blackness that surrounded him. These were the metal caves his people had fashioned out of the long metal tubes, created long ago by his ancestors for their homes. The metal caves kept the constantly dripping water from falling on your head, as well as the dust that constantly drifted down from the top of the tunnel.

As he grew close, he heard shouting. He knew it was because they were all hungry and so were cranky too. No people meant they had only rat-beasties to eat, and everyone was sick and tired of Furry Food.

Even though Gum was happy to be home, he almost felt like running somewhere and hiding until the arguing was over. He hated it when people fought, it made him feel bad inside. He decided to go in anyway, and hope that he could just hide in a corner, unnoticed.

He walked into the large, ragged metal cave with its twisted, sharp metal edges that you were always careful not to touch. He saw Garr arguing with Sak. They stood face to face and yelled at each other. Around them, the other Glags stood behind one or the other, as if divided into two camps supporting one side or the other.

"Go food go. Starve we!" Sak yelled.

"Starve not!" Garr's right head said, as he pounded his fist on the ground. "Food find!" He looked angry with his left head, scowling.

"Food furry?" Sak pointed at a rat-beastie staring at them from a corner of the cave and spit on the ground. "Furry food sick!. Meat want!"

"Meat find!" Garr's right head said. "Lead you!"

"Where?" Sak said, putting her hands up and turning her one eye to look all around. "Where find?"

"Go!" Garr's left head said, as he pointed down the tunnel to where the Undergrounders disappeared. "Meat follow!"

"Place bad!" Sak said, shaking her head. "Said you."

"Furry food then," Garr's right head said. "Other no,"

his left head said.

Sak turned and stared with her one eye at Gum, and Gum didn't like the look in her eyes. When she spoke again, Gum knew he'd been right.

"Gum eat."

The whole tribe of Glag turned and looked at Gum. Gum decided it was a good time to hide for a while. He ran out of the cave as fast as he could, to his special place that no one knew about but him.

Lord Algon wondered if sometime in the last few days, he'd simply gone insane. He wondered what day it was when things first started to change? When was that, the day that the Newcomers showed up? Was that when he went crazy then? No, it was even before that, when he captured that wormy man who called himself Leader. He remembered feeling strange that day, as If something strange took place, and would never be the same again.

Now, as he looked at what was coming towards him, he was almost certain that he had to be crazy. Or else, how could he be seeing what he was seeing?

Coming towards him were ten feet high men of gold, walking stiffly towards him like dead men, but with steady, plodding steps. Somehow, they made his skin crawl, as if their coming heralded a slow descent into terror.

The strangest sight of all was the one in the front, the leader. It wore a green coat with weird colored bars on one side. And on its shoulders a man sat. Lord Algon swore he recognized him, but he couldn't put his finger on who it was.

Lord Algon babbled in fright, feeling his mind slip gears. So many bad things had happened in the last few hours his mind seemed like it was getting all gummed up and out of working order. He stood in the middle of a grassy field, staring as the golden men tramped closer and closer. He had no energy left. He felt dead, as if he'd already been stamped on by one of them and was now just a mashed down pile of dead meat on the ground.

The metal men reached him. The lead one in the weird green coat stopped. Lord Algon looked up at the man riding it. His mind, dulled by fear and shock, tried to drag out the memory of who it was he was looking at. He'd seen the man before, and the only thing he could recall was that the last meeting had involved fear as well.

Then he had it. This was the man at the very beginning of Lord Algon's miseries. That day that seemed so long ago, when he held Johnny, Johnny's friends and that worm of a man Leader. They were just about to invade the Newcomer's base after ransacking the yellow buses. He could see the scene in his mind's eye as if it happened only a second ago. An explosion, and then he looked and saw the Gangers for the first time. And there leading them was this man. At the time, Lord Algon thought he looked like an evil, dangerous man. Now he knew he'd been right. This was the real leader of the Gangers, and he was Bad News.

The man grinned at him, his face full of evil, deadly glee. "Beg for your life, worm, and maybe I'll spare you. Or maybe I'll still have General Stupid tear your arms off."

The golden man the man rode on raised its right arm. Two of the other golden men stepped forward in a threatening manner.

Lord Algon knew he was seconds from death. He fell to his knees, shaking with fear so badly he almost fell over sideways. "Have ye mercy, master. Spare me miserable life!" Was all he could choke out, as he wet himself and started to cry. The man on top of the metal man reared his head back and laughed. It was obvious the man knew he had power, more power and strength than anyone Lord Algon had ever met, and Lord Algon knew, this man was the new king of the land.

Even in his terror, the wheels in Lord Algon's mind turned, trying to find a way to save himself or escape. An idea came to Lord Algon. He didn't hold much hope for its success but trying anything was better than just dying.

"I be leader of a vast army, kind master. If ye be merciful to a lowly worm such as I, I will command them to follow ye. Together we will vanquish all thine enemies."

The Ganger leader didn't move, and Lord Algon's mind filled with dull terror. He willed the Ganger leader to listen to reason, and not just kill him.

Johnny, Starbucks and the girls joined the rest of the Tribe as they ran outside to see what Thegap was so excited about. Thegap led them to the top of the junk car wall. At the top of the wall, Thegap pointed out into the dark, towards a distant orange light in the distance on the other side of the black inky ribbon that was the river. Johnny and the others looked where Thegap pointed.

The orange light danced and bobbed, fires burning

somewhere across the river. Distant shouting and shooting could be heard from the same place, voices of fear and anger. As they watched a brighter light appeared and a loud distant thud echoed in the darkness, the sound of an explosion.

"Wow!" Starbucks said, peering into the darkness, looking at the distant commotion. "Something's sure going on." He looked at Johnny. "Do you think there's somebody new, Johnny? How many different bad people live around here, anyway?"

Johnny smiled grimly. "I don't know. It sure looks like Lord Algon is busy fighting someone."

Deb grabbed Super's arm and pulled her aside. Super looked at her with curiosity. Looking to see Johnny and Starbucks didn't see, she whispered to Super in a low voice.

"Super, I'm worried about Loki and the Undergrounders. You don't think it's them fighting Lord Algon and the Wildies, do you?"

Super frowned, not having thought of the possibility before. "I hope not," she said. "If they are, we should be there helping them."

"I want to go find out," Deb said, a look of determination on her face. Super could see Deb was serious.

"You should tell Johnny what you think, so he knows. We've gotten into enough trouble wandering off on our own."

Deb looked at Johnny and Foodcourt. They stood at the edge of the wall, staring off into the distance. "If we tell Johnny and Starbucks, they'll just tell us not to go. Loki's my friend. I want to make sure he's all right." She looked at Super. "You don't have to go. I'll only be gone no more than a few hours."

"Uh, uh," Super said, shaking her dark curls and wagging a finger at Deb. "We're a team, you and me."

Deb smiled and grabbed Super's arm. "Thanks. We'll tell one person, just in case."

"Who?" Super asked. They both looked around to decide who they could trust to keep their secret.

Deb pointed. "Carny. She'll keep our secret."

"Johnny's sister?" Super said, with little confidence.

"Carny's smart and courageous, just like Johnny. She'll understand."

Super shrugged. With a glance back at Johnny and Starbucks to make sure they weren't seen, Deb and Super snuck away down the ramp to where they saw Carney walking towards them at a fast speed, holding a sleeping Miracle in her arms.

As they approached her, Carny saw them and looked up. Even though she was in a hurry to get to Johnny, she couldn't help but reflect again how pretty Deb was with her long blond hair and soft blue eyes. She really was the most beautiful girl in the tribe, and Carny was glad she'd chosen Johnny. Super was beautiful too, with her long black curls and dark eyes. She noticed both girls wore leather outfits and carried swords, just like Johnny and Starbucks. The girls were becoming adventurers, just like the men they loved. It made Carny grin to think about it, and how much she'd seen the two girls change. Deb had been so shy, while Super never was, but both had grown bolder and more courageous than how she remembered them back at Sanctuary.

As Deb and Super reached Carny, they stopped in front of her, making her stop too. They smiled down at Miracle and touched his head and little hands. "He's getting so big already!" Deb said.

Carny grinned. "He does nothing but eat and sleep, so he ought to be."

"He's so perfect, with no missing ears or fingers."

Carny looked down at Miracle with joy. "Misterwizard says that means that things are changing, and the world is getting safer."

"Carny," Deb said, glancing one more time up at Johnny. "We need to go somewhere, and we don't want to worry Johnny or Starbucks."

Carny frowned, sensing they weren't telling her the whole truth. "What's this all about? Whatever you're planning, you should tell Johnny."

"All right, we admit it," Super said, tilting her head to the side. "If we told him, he'd never let us do it."

"Then maybe you shouldn't," Carny said, rocking Miracle back and forth.

"We're worried about the Undergrounders," Deb said. "Either they're the ones fighting, or they don't know about it. We want to go check on them and warn them that something is going on."

"You should tell Johnny before you go. He'll understand. And there's something you should know before you go anywhere."

"What's that?" Super said.

Quickly, Carny told the girls how she'd seen Ripper. The girls were as shocked and surprised as she'd been.

"That's terrible," Deb said. "That evil man still alive!"

"Which is even more reason why you two shouldn't be running around outside."

"Which is more reason we should make sure the Undergrounders are all right," Deb said.

Carny shook her head and grinned at Deb. "You're

just as stubborn as Johnny, you know that? You two are a lot alike."

Her words made all three of them smile, despite the danger.

"Look," Carny said, "I have to tell Johnny about Ripper. Let me tell him about what you're going to do too. He needs to know what's going on."

"He's got enough to worry about, and now you're going to tell him his worst enemy is still alive," Deb said. "We'll only be gone for a little while."

"This is a bad idea, ladies," Carny warned, as she held Miracle up to her shoulder. "Haven't you two been in enough trouble lately?"

Super said, "There doesn't seem to be a way to avoid trouble around here."

"Please don't tell him, at least until we leave. I really want to make sure the Undergrounders are all right."

"All right," Carny said, "but I really think you're making a mistake."

Deb and Super smiled one more time at Miracle and then left. Carny looked down at Miracle. "When you grow up, don't you be as stubborn or adventurous as your uncle Johnny or his friends. You just stay at home and be good. Do you understand?" Miracle didn't answer, just kept on sleeping. Carny smiled at him, her eyes filled with love. Then she looked up at the wall where Johnny was. She dreaded having to tell him about Ripper, Johnny had so much else to deal with, but there was no choice. She slowly walked up the ramp to reach him.

Johnny and the rest of the Tribe continued to peer out at the darkness and discuss what they thought was happening.

"Misterwizard picked a good time to go on a walk

with Sephie," Johnny said.

Cinnabon sat with her son Wheaties on the top of an old car, part of the floor of the wall. She and Wheaties were busy eating pieces of a chicken-beastie she had cooked. Without looking up or realizing what she was saying she blurted out, "Oh, he didn't go on a walk. He's out looking for her. She's lost!"

Johnny turned to stare at her, his face blank with shock and dismay. Foodcourt, who stood behind Cinnabon, grabbed the chicken-beastie leg from her hand and waved it at her irritably. "Thanks, Cinnabon! Can't you keep think before you talk just once?"

"What did I do?" Cinnabon said, looking innocent and offended. "Didn't somebody tell him already? Now give me back my dinner!"

Foodcourt instead started chewing on the leg himself, making her scowl with anger at him. Johnny looked at Foodcourt. "Father, you knew about this and didn't tell me? Where is she?"

Foodcourt and Teavana looked uncomfortable. Foodcourt stopped eating and dropped the hand holding the chicken-beastie leg to his side.

"I'm sorry, Johnny," Teavana said. "But after the big fight with Lord Algon, she disappeared. Misterwizard didn't want to worry you, so he asked us not to tell anyone."

Johnny's heart sank into a well of sorrow. Sephie, gone, and Misterwizard too! Worry filled Johnny's mind. *The battle had been such a long time ago,* he thought. If Misterwizard wasn't back yet, he must have gotten into trouble himself. The thought of either Misterwizard or Sephie being hurt struck Johnny like a knife in his chest. Even worse was the thought that somewhere they lay hurt or injured somewhere and Johnny had no way to know about it or help them. Or even worse, what if they'd been captured by Lord Algon?

"Which way did Misterwizard go?" Johnny asked Foodcourt.

"I don't know, son," Foodcourt said, waving the chicken-beastie leg around. "I saw him searching the buildings around here and then he was gone."

"Johnny," Teavana said, putting a hand on Johnny's shoulder, "Maybe Misterwizard has already found her, and they're on the way back home."

"That could be true, you know," Thegap walked up and said, his small round face beaming. "Let's not always assume the worst. Let's think positive. Sephie's a smart girl. She learned from you, Johnny. I bet she's a lot tougher than we think."

Johnny nodded. He tried to smile, but there was no joy in it. Foodcourt looked at the chicken-beastie leg, but he'd lost his appetite. Cinnabon kept eyeing it, still angry he'd stolen in from her.

In the distance, the yelling grew closer. "Johnny, I know how much you care for Sephie an how much you hurt right now. We all love her, and we're all worried too. But part of the reason Misterwizard didn't tell you is because he knew you'd want to go looking for her. With Misterwizard gone, someone needs to be here to protect the Tribe. I know it's not what you want to hear, but it there's a battle going on. We need you here to defend us."

Johnny scowled, not wanting listen. Being still only fifteen seasons, the boy in him wanted to get angry, but the man he was quickly put a stop to it. Foodcourt was only trying to help, and even more importantly, he was right. No matter how much it killed him, Johnny had to stay.

He nodded, and everyone saw and relaxed. Cinnabon smiled proudly. "See, it all worked out okay." She turned and glared at Foodcourt. "Now give me back my dinner."

Foodcourt rolled his eyes and handed it to her. She looked at it, saw there was nothing left but bone, and tossed it aside, glaring at him.

Foodcourt pointed at the orange glow lighting up the night sky. "What are we going to do, Johnny?"

Johnny's mind whirled in fourteen different directions. He had a hard time thinking about the battle. For once, he turned to Foodcourt. "What do you think, Father?"

Foodcourt, surprised and pleased that Johnny had asked, wrinkled his brow in thought. He raised a finger in the air and wagged it back and forth. "I think we should send out spies to see just what is happening. Then they can report back and let us not what to do.

"That's a great idea!" Johnny said. Many of the others in the Tribe nodded their heads in agreement. Foodcourt beamed, proud of himself.

Johnny smiled at his father. "I should ask your advice more often, Foodcourt."

Foodcourt chuckled. "Thank you, son, but you've proven that you're the real leader here. I'm just glad to help."

"Who should we send out to spy for us?" Starbucks asked.

"You already sent them, though you don't even know it."

Everyone turned to see who spoke. It was Carny, standing next to Johnny with Miracle in her arms.

"And I have something else to tell you Johnny, and this time you're going to listen."

Everybody chuckled, and Johnny grinned. "Okay, Carny. Sorry I didn't take time to listen to you before. What is it?"

Carny scrunched up her face in seriousness. "Ripper is alive!"

CHAPTER 16

Ripper stared down at the cowering Lord Algon and laughed. *How fortunes changed,* he thought, *and how it made the strong turn weak.* Only a little while ago, he thought he was going to die. He couldn't imagine how he was going to beat Johnny, and now here he was, king of the world, standing over a cowering man who had once been king of the whole land. He wanted to kill him, see him blow into a million pieces, but somehow, he knew he shouldn't, that Lord Algon might come in handy. It irritated him, how good he was at planning and scheming, so that he had to constantly hold himself back from just enjoying himself. But he knew he'd regret it if he killed Lord Algon and later found out he needed him. What Lord Algon said was true. If Lord Algon could get his Wildies to serve Ripper, it would mean more forces to attack Johnny. But he didn't need more forces, did he?

He had the robots! So why did he still feel so nervous, as if even the robots couldn't guarantee a victory against Johnny? Because Johnny was so annoyingly courageous and smart, that's why, and somehow, he'd find a way to win anyway. It made Ripper hate him even more.

So, he wouldn't kill Lord Algon, not just yet. Still, he could enjoy watching him cower for a few more minutes, enjoying the man's misery. He sat on General Stupid and watched Lord Algon write in terror, feeling warm inside. Finally, he decided he had to say something and let Lord Algon off the hook, though it killed him to have to do it.

"Stand up."

Lord Algon stood on weak legs that wobbled, his whole body shaking in fear.

"Come forward."

Lord Algon slowly shuffled forward, a wretched smile of hope on his face.

Ripper grinned. "Kiss General Stupid's feet."

"General Stupid?" Lord Algon said, not understanding.

"The robot, idiot," Ripper said angrily.

"Oh. Of a truth." Lord Algon got on his knees and kissed the robot's feet over and over. Ripper laughed so hard he almost fell off General Stupid's back. Then he looked down, grinning.

"Okay. Stand up."

Lord Algon stood up, a sickening smile of gratitude on his face.

"You will tell your Wildies that I am the Lord of these lands now. I am king. Do you understand me?"

Lord Algon nodded up and down quickly, almost as if his head had come unattached. "Aye, Master, ye truly be a man to be reckoned with, the lord of these lands. Me and me mates will serve ye till the end of our days, and that be the truth. Only… "

"Only what?" Ripper said, curious.

"There be a piratt attacking me castle as we speak. He goes by the name Crooked Walk, and he comes from a ship he stole from me. He be the one who betrayed me many long year ago, and now has come to bedevil me again, though I never done him a bit of harm. If ye kill him, then all me forces, and his too I'll reckon, be thine."

"Crooked Walk, eh?" Ripper said, happiness spreading inside him like the opening of a flower. Here was someone who he didn't have to save, someone he could kill with wild abandon. "Show me to this Crooked Walk. When I'm done with him, he'll wish he'd never been born."

The full, round yellow eye shone down on one of the strangest sights it had every illuminated in its long history. Twenty-one golden men of metal marched in unison, with a man riding one wearing a green coat, and another man in a blue cloak with long black hair tramping along beside them.

General Stupid stomped on down the street, it red eyes staring forward emotionlessly with Ripper astride him, arms around the robot's neck. Lord Algon walked beside them, a smile of surprised joy on his face, simply happy not to have been torn to pieces. He knew he was no longer the lord of the land, for there was now a much more powerful king, one with an army of golden men to serve him.

He almost felt sorry for the Newcomers and their leader Johnny, for Lord Algon knew how much Ripper hated them and that it wouldn't be long before he got his revenge. It made Lord Algon's blood go cold thinking about how the new king of the world planned on torturing and murdering Johnny and his friends. It also made him smile though, for when he remembered how Johnny had cost him his own throne, he knew he was going to enjoy watching him die.

Ripper looked at Lord Algon from his perch on General Stupid's shoulders. "Where's my Gangers? You better not have hurt them, or I'm going to take it out on you."

Lord Algon's eyes opened wide with fright, and he tried to remember quickly just what he had done. He was going to kill one in the Arena, but then someone shot his guard, and he stopped. Now he was glad they did. Then he thought of something; could it have been Ripper who protected the gangers? Lord Algon smiled, sure it was.

"Nay dear master, I've not harmed a hair on their heads, bless them. They joined us to fight the Newcomers and our common enemy this Johnny fellow."

"Where are they now?" Ripper asked.

"I know not, milord. Crooked Walk scattered us all like sheep-beasties when the wolf-beastie comes to call."

Ripper scowled. "He'll pay for that, too."

Ripper's words made Lord Algon smile, to hear he was going to get to see Crooked Walk suffer.

As Lord Algon walked along, he thought about asking King Ripper if he could ride another of the robots but thought better of it. He didn't want to be too pushy. After all, he was alive, and that was more amazing and unexpected than anything else that had happened over the last few days.

Ripper looked at Lord Algon again, almost as if reading his mind. "How far until we get to what's left of your tribe? And where's this sidekick of yours, what's his name?"

Lord Algon bowed and looked contrite, fawning at Ripper with a sickly smile. "If it please ye, my lord, his name be Hardhitter, though the name of a surety be ill fit to his nature. He be but a cowardly dog, who be good at nothing but groveling at the feet of a real man."

Ripper grinned, rocking back and forth with the motion of General Stupid's walking. "Just like his master, ay?"

Lord Algon's mind filled with hatred, but he dared not show it. He smiled and nodded innocently, taking the insult, though it took every ounce of his strength not to react. "Just as ye say, master, ye be wise and all knowing."

Ripper laughed, and Lord Algon burned with jealousy. He'd known the pleasure of being the king and laughing at other's misery, but now it was Ripper enjoying it, and all Lord Algon could do was watch and wish it was him.

"It better be soon. Or I'm going to tell General Stupid to break one of your arms, just for fun." Ripper turned and looked forward, and fear filled Lord Algon's mind and made it hard to breathe. He told himself Ripper didn't mean it, he only said it to scare him, but he couldn't totally convince himself it was true. The fear refused to leave and settled in his chest, filling him a cold dread. He found himself looking around frantically, hoping they would reach the old building with the spire soon.

With relief he saw the dark outline of the steeple

against the night sky up ahead. They were almost there! Good! It meant someone else to take Ripper's mind off Lord Algon for a while. *Ripper could torture as many Wildies as he wanted,* Lord Algon thought, *as long as he left Lord Algon alone.* He began to think the best course of action was to run away at the first chance.

As they reached the church, Ripper put up a hand. "Stop, Stupid." General Stupid stopped, and all the robots behind him did the same. Ripper turned to Lord Algon.

"Go in there and explain things. I'll give you five minutes."

"Yes, milord." Lord Algon ran so fast he fell and had to get up and start again. Ripper laughed and pointed, having a great time watching him be so afraid.

It wasn't long before Lord Algon returned, leading his first mate Hardhitter and a group of Wildies along with him. They all stared with wonder and fright at the silent rows of golden robots, and then at Ripper.

Ripper grinned and adjusted himself. Riding General Stupid beat walking, but the robot wasn't very comfortable, in fact he was hard as steel. Ripper decided if he kept riding the robot, he'd have to get someone to make him a soft saddle to sit on.

"Well, have you told them?" Ripper asked grumpily.

"Aye, my lord. They are all now sworn to thy service. Lead on. We look forward to fighting Crooked Walk beside thee.'

"Good, finally somebody to kill. General Stupid, march!"

General Stupid set off again, and the rest of the robots marched too. Lord Algon, Hardhitter and the Wildies waited until the robots had passed then they followed behind them, watching them with amazement.

In the distance, Ripper saw dark walls with a tall building in the middle.

"That be it!" Lord Algon pointed excitedly. "There be where Crooked Walk be plundering and pillaging. Only he doesn't have a clue what's about to befall him." Lord Algon grinned in delight at the thought.

"Well, let's show him!" Ripper said, smiling. He leaned his head to look at General Stupid. "General Stupid get your weapons ready. We're going to light up the night!"

Sephie walked ahead of Misterwizard, a determined and serious look on her face. She was in charge now, and Misterwizard just smiled and followed along, simply happy she was safe and unhurt. He worried about how tired she must have been, however. He tried to think of a way to convince Sephie to give up the search for Lady Stabs when he determined the search endangered Sephie's health with exhaustion.

Sephie, as if aware of Misterwizard's thoughts, yawned wide. She plodded along, determined to keep going until they found the Ganger who was now their companion and good friend. They had crossed the bridge, and now were on the side of Lord Algon's castle. In the distance, they heard shouting and gunfire. Misterwizard didn't like the thought they were growing close to the enemy's camp, and he kept one eye on the horizon, looking for any signs of Wildies or Gangers. He also kept his ears tuned to the sound of anyone approaching close.

"Sephie, you are a loyal and compassionate young heroine, and I am proud of your determination to find your missing comrade. However, even the most determined and stalwart hero must face the reality of his or her own physical limits at times. Not only are we both nearing the limits of our physical capacities, the search area we are traversing is discouragingly broad. If Lady Stabs escaped the watery clutches of the river, she most assuredly would have returned to the place most likely to reunite with you, New Sanctuary."

"She would stay here and look for me," Sephie said, stubbornly. "I can't just leave her. She's my friend. Johnny wouldn't go back."

Misterwizard chuckled at how Sephie used Johnny as an example. Johnny was Sephie's hero, and he could tell she wanted to be just like him. "All right, I will acquiesce for a few brief moments more. Then I will have to ask you to see the light of reason. Even Johnny sometimes has to temporarily halt a quest and resume it at a different time or in an alternate fashion."

Something banged ahead of them. Both Misterwizard and Sephie froze and looked towards the sound. Then they looked at each other. Without saying a word, they both ran to the cover of a nearby orange, twisted hulk with the silver symbol of a cat-beastie on the back. They squatted down next to each other and peered over the edge of the rusted metal at the dark.

A Wildie appeared out of the dark. He was an old man in dirty and in ragged clothes. He wore a scraggly and filthy beard, and he held a wicked looking piece of metal in his hand. He dragged the twisted, sharp end of the metal on the ground, making the scraping sound. He drank from a Bottle he held in his other hand and staggered, appearing to have imbibed quite a bit of the intoxicating beverage.

Misterwizard put his finger to his mouth to warn Sephie to be quiet, and she nodded. Then they waited for the man to pass by, hopefully without seeing them.

Suddenly the man turned and yelled. "Avast! Who be hiding in there? Come out, 'fore I run ye through like a stuck pig-beastie!"

Misterwizard and Sephie thought they were caught at first, but then they saw the man was looking in the opposite direction at another old car. The man reached in with his hand and grabbed at someone, but then he yelled in pain and pulled his hand back. Misterwizard and Sepbie could see his hand bled. Someone stabbed it with something. The man grimaced with anger and raised his metal stick to strike, but whoever was in the old car was too fast. The car was empty when the old man hit it.

"I'll teach ye some manners, ye scurvy dog! I'll eat ye for me supper!"

The old man ran around the side of the old car, and now Misterwizard and Sephie saw another dark shadow. It was a woman.

Sephie's eyes lit up with happiness. "Misterwizard! It's Lady Stabs!"

Misterwizard saw too that it was their friend. But she was in trouble, for the old man was after her, metal stick held high.

"Wait here," Misterwizard said to Sephie. Then he jumped up and ran towards the combatants. Sephie didn't listen, though, and she hurried to follow him.

When Misterwizard reached Lady Stabs, she was dodging the old man's stick as he thrust it at her over and over. Lady Stabs didn't see Misterwizard or Sephie, she was too busy fighting for her life.

Sephie ran up and would have ran past Misterwizard but he put a hand up to stop her.

"Leave her alone!" Sephie yelled, but the man didn't hear her.

"Stand still so I can gut ye like a fish-beastie!" The man snarled. Lady Stabs backed away from him, but she looked tired and dirty. Orange rust from the old car she'd been hiding in mixed with the water from the river to make her look orange from head to toe. She staggered and looked like she was about to fall. The man was almost on top of her!

Misterwizard scowled and took out a device from his backpack. It looked like a small blue gun made of plastic. He held in the direction of the man and pushed a button. Suddenly two strings shot out of the gun and attached themselves to the man.

The effect was instant. He tensed up and jerked around, like a puppet on a string. His teeth clenched together, and he spun around to face Misterwizard and Sephie. He dropped the stick, and then fell himself, eyes closed, unconscious.

Misterwizard and Sephie walked over and looked down at him. Sephie smiled at Misterwizard. "Wow, that was neat. What was that?"

Misterwizard smiled with mischievous glee. "That, my dear young lady, was known in the ancient days as a taser. Not lethal, but definitely effective at getting your opponents' attention."

They turned and looked at Lady Stabs. She looked back at them joy and relief on her face. Sephie ran to her and leapt into her arms and Lady Stabs grabbed her, tears in her eyes.

"Lady Stabs! You're all right!"

Lady Stabs sniffed and wiped a tear away from her eye. "I was just about to say the same thing about you! Oh Sephie, I'm so glad to see you!"

Misterwizard walked over with a big smile on his face. Lady Stabs looked up at him, happy to see him too.

"I see why you're safe now," Lady Stabs said, grinning at Misterwizard. "A real hero came to save you."

Misterwizard grinned happily. "From what I hear tell, that moniker fits you as accurately as it does any other individual."

Misterwizard helped Lady Stabs up and all three hugged and enjoyed a moment of victory. Misterwizard looked at Lady Stabs' appearance. "It seems you have had quite an adventure of your own, Lady Stabs."

Lady Stabs sighed wearily and nodded. "I will never come near that rushing water again, if I can help it. It almost killed me."

"I'm afraid we'll have to approach it at least one more time," Misterwizard said. "The bridge is the only way back to New Sanctuary."

"Okay," Lady Stabs said, nodding weakly, "but if I fall in again, I hope you can fetch me out. I don't think I'll have the strength to do it myself again."

All three walked back towards the bridge. Sephie held Lady Stab's hand and they swung their hands back and forth merrily. They were very close to Lord Algon's fortress now, and the walls of the cemetery stood like dark shadows behind them. Misterwizard glanced back occasionally , hoping another Wildie wouldn't find them before they put some distance between them and the fortress.

Sephie looked at the orange all over Lady Stabs and

giggled. "You're orange!"

Lady Stabs laughed too. "Don't hide in one of those old pieces of junk, if you can avoid it. They're filthy."

"I already did once. See?" Sephie lifted her arms and Lady Stabs saw that she too had dirt and grime all over.

"We both need a good wash. Sephie, how did you escape from that bad man?"

Sephie opened her mouth to tell her, but suddenly a strange humming sound filled the air. It was so loud that Sephie put her hands to her ears. They all turned to see what caused it.

"Look!" Sephie pointed at the night sky. A strange beam of red light filled the night sky and then disappeared. Then suddenly a bright orange light filled the sky and a building nearby exploded.

Misterwizard pulled Sephie and Lady Stabs closer as the light of the flames in the building reflected on their surprised faces. They ran and hid behind a streetcar and watched. They heard a whooshing sound and another bright light lit up the night for a second and another building exploded.

In a hushed voice full of amazement, Sephie whispered, "Misterwizard, what is it?"

Misterwizard stared at the burning buildings, his face grave. "I'm afraid I don't have enough data to give you an accurate answer at the moment, Sephie. I can, however, be fairly confident that it is not a positive development for our Tribe."

As they stood in the dark, huddled together, golden men walked out from behind a building and marched down the street. Tall and straight, they marched in unison, each one putting the same foot forward, then the next, as if they were all one man reflected twenty-one times over. They marched in the direction of Lord Algon's fortress, fortunately away from the weary travelers.

Misterward wasn't positive what they were, but he had his suspicions. One thing Misterwizard did know. Whatever the golden men were, they spelled danger for Johnny and the Tribe, possibly more danger than they'd ever faced before.

CHAPTER 17

When they reached the bottom of the ramp they looked up and were relieved to see no one noticed they'd left. At the bottom of the car wall, a car was set up with doors that opened on either side of it, so someone could go from one side of the wall to the other. They crept over to the car that had the unlocked doors, a rusty car that had once been red and shaped like a beetle-beastie. Its windows were smashed and the upholstery inside was gone, leaving only metal springs.

Deb opened the door on their side slowly, hoping it didn't creak. It did, but very softly. She stopped and listened. The conversations above them continued just as before. Satisfied no one heard, she crept inside the car. The old metal springs were rusty and stiff, and they hurt her hands and feet, but she crawled over them as fast as she could. Super climbed along right behind her.

"Look!" Super said. Deb looked hanging from a piece of glass attached to the front window was a little yellow man on a string. He was short, round and stocky, with black glasses and little blue pants. "He looks just like Misterwizard."

Deb grinned darkly. "Super, not now." Deb reached the other door. Slowly she pushed down the handle and the door swung open. Suddenly she fell out the door and tumbled onto the ground on the other side with a yelp. Super didn't notice. She was busy looking in the little piece of glass attached to the window.

"Look, I can see myself in this glass." Super looked around to see if Deb heard her and realized she was gone. She looked out the other door and saw Deb lying in the grass on the other side. "You all right?"

Deb stood up and brushed her leather pants and vest off. "Come on, will you?" Deb whispered.

Super crawled the rest of the way and made a more graceful exit than Deb had. Slowly they closed the door. They glanced one more time up at Johnny and the Tribe, this time from the outside of the wall. It felt strange to the girls to be outside, and kind of scary. They glance at each other, both thinking the same thing: what were they doing?

But then Deb crept along the car wall. Super took one look at the orange glow in the distance and then followed her. They crept along, staying close to the wall until they reached the far end of the wall where the cars piled up against the nearest building. Then they walked along the side of the building until they reached the street. This was the same street they explored with Johnny and Starbucks when they fell into the hole. They knew where the hole was now, about four city blocks away, but they had no intention of going back in it. They would keep going for another six blocks to where the door to the subway was Johnny opened and where the Undergrounders first left the subway.

"We need to get there as fast as we can," Super said, as they hurried down the dark, cold street. Deb didn't answer, but Super could tell she heard her.

Even though the Yellow Eye was full and round in the night sky, the looming buildings on both sides of the street blocked much of its light. Black shapes dotted the landscape, the cars and mailboxes and chunks of building lying in the street. Trees grew up everywhere as well, some right in the middle of the street, the beginnings of a new forest. Occasionally they would pass the much larger hulk of an old streetcar or a bus. The night was so dark the girls felt like they swam through a black inky river.

Deb stopped and grabbed Super's arm. She pointed to the left on the horizon. "Look!

In the far distance to the left they spied the orange glow of the battle. Super nodded. "We need to get to the Undergrounders and back, fast."

They walked faster.

"Uh, maybe this wasn't such a good idea after all," Super said, glancing around nervously.

Deb tried to look at Super but could only see her dark outline. "Funny, you're usually the brave one, and I'm the chicken-beastie."

"Maybe I just don't want to be eaten by some beastie or killed by a Wildie," Super said. It was so dark she almost felt as if she could feel the darkness around her. She put out her hands to make sure she didn't run into a car or one of the other pieces of junk in the street and fall.

Suddenly they heard a bark! They both stopped instantly and moved closer to each other for safety.

"What was that?" Deb's voice high-pitched and ghostly in the dark.

"A dog-beastie," Super said, her voice higher than normal with fear. "And it sounds hungry."

The bark came again. Deb spoke again, but this time her voice was happy. "It's Deecee!"

Super grinned too. Together they both peered into the darkness trying to see him.

"Good old Deecee!" Super said.

"Deecee!" Deb said, putting her hands to the side of her mouth. "Deecee! Here boy!"

Deecee barked again, but he sounded farther away. The girls both frowned in dismay.

"He's going away," Super said, disappointed.

"At least we know he's still alive," Deb said brightly.

"Yeah," Super said, brightening. "If we can find him and bring him back, just think how happy Johnny will be. He might even forget we left without telling him."

They both laughed and walked again.

"Deecee!" Deb called again.

Super looked around at the dark. "Uh, maybe you shouldn't be too loud. There may be other things out here in the dark, too."

"Yeah, maybe you're right."

Deb peered at the darkness, her heart suddenly pounding. "We'll just have to hope we can get closer to Deecee so we can call more quietly."

They walked on.

"Misterwizard, what are they?" Sephie stood close to Misterwizard and he put a protective arm around her. Misterwizard, Lady Stabs and Sephie peeked out from the side of a building near the bridge. Lady Stabs stared in mute horror, her eyes wide with alarm. Misterwizard looked grim as well, a dark gaze peering from under his bushy white eyebrows. He stroked his short white beard, his face dark with worry.

The golden men marched down the dark street. They didn't even stop when they reached an old rusted car, but simply walked over it, crushing it under their feet. As they passed by, the hiding trio noticed their red eyes that glowed bright in the darkness.

"They look like people, but they're all hard like metal!" Lady Stabs said.

Misterwizard nodded, beginning to understand what he was seeing. "I believe I know what we are seeing now, my friends. Unfortunately, they are not men at all, but machines."

"Machines!" Lady Stabs said in wonder.

"Yes. I believe they were referred to in the ancient language as androids. Other words for them were synthetics, cyborgs or automatons. But the most common term for them was simply robots."

"They're machines, Misterwizard?" Sephie asked. "How can machines look so much like people?"

Misterwizard chuckled. "The technology to build them is quite advanced. Though I've only seen them in pictures and story books and never imagined that they truly existed, it seems at the end of the Great War, America must have made great strides in artificial intelligence. Despite our rising terror, you must admit, they are amazing to watch!"

"And scary!" Lady Stabs said.

"They're terrible, Misterwizard!" Sephie said. "They made those buildings explode!"

"Yes, they seem to have formidable weaponry. We need to get back to the Tribe and formulate a strategy to combat this new threat, while the robots are occupied with our opponent."

The trio turned and quietly backed away to hide in the shadows of the nearest building, careful to make sure robots didn't see them. But suddenly Lady Stabs stopped, her mouth wide open in complete shock. Misterwizard and Sephie noticed and looked at her, wondering what was wrong.

Lady Stabs pointed her finger towards the golden monsters. "It can't be. I think I'm so tired I'm seeing things!"

Misterwizard turned his round face towards her and squinted at her in the dark. "Elucidate please, Lady Stabs."

"Look!" She pointed again. They all looked in the direction of her finger. Then Misterwizard and Sephie saw it too.

The lead robot had a green coat on with brightly colored pieces of cloth on its chest. And sitting on its shoulders, was none other than-

"Ripper!" Lady Stabs whispered, not believing her own words. "I must be having a nightmare."

Misterwizard's face turned grim. "If you are then it is one I am sharing with you. It is indeed Ripper. Alas, I saw him alive once before, during the battle with Lord Algon. I'm afraid he seems to be difficult to eradicate."

"Johnny killed him, Misterwizard, didn't he?" Sephie asked. "Did he come back from the dead?"

Misterwizard put an arm around Sephie and smiled at her. "Not in the least, Sephie. Besides being a scientific impossibility, I see evidence on his face and shoulder of his encounter with the tiger-beastie. Somehow, Ripper managed to survive."

"And now he's in command of robots!" Lady Stabs said, fear making her voice tremble. "Of all the people to find them and get them to obey him. What can stop him now, Misterwizard?"

"The situation does appear to put the odds significantly in his favor, but let's not lose hope just yet. We need to accelerate our departure from the proximity to the danger, however. Let us flee!"

Misterwizard led the way and all three ran towards the bridge. In the distance behind them the night sky lit up and the air was shattered by more explosions and cries of fear.

And then they heard men screaming in pain and the sounds of gunfire.

Loki ran back to his tribe of Undergrounders, happy to have made it back without getting eaten. They all turned and stared excitedly as he ran up, waiting to hear what he had to say.

Harp ran up and Loki smiled at her. She smiled back, both excited to see the other.

"Well?" Slon said impatiently. "Are the Rat People gone?"

Loki puffed out his chest, proud to be the courageous one who braved the danger. In a voice that he thought sounded like Johnny he said, "All except one. There was a small one, a boy I think. He was crazy in the head. But he's gone now."

Pak, Loki's mother walked over and smiled at him proudly. "You were brave to risk yourself for the tribe, Loki."

Loki looked over at Harp. He saw her staring at him, and he felt ten feet tall. He threw his chin up and smiled. "Thank you, mother. I was glad to do it."

"You see?" Bott, Loki's father said. "I told you he was the bravest boy in the world. You all owe him your lives again!"

Loki began to feel a little embarrassed, and wished his father wasn't pouring it on so thick. His face turned a little pink, making him look less pale.

"So," a thin, white man with white hair that stood up like icicles said. "Should we go back or not? Hurry up and tell us. I'm getting tired of standing here."

They all turned to Slon, waiting for guidance. And to Loki's great pleasure, Slon turned to Loki. "We must leave this place. But do you think we dare risk returning long enough to gather the things we love from our homes?"

Loki, feeling more like Johnny than ever, looked serious and said, "I think if we are careful and keep our eyes always watching the tunnel, we can go and get our things. The Rat People don't expect us back, so if we're quiet, we should be okay."

"Listen to me, people!" Slon said, as if he was the one

who knew everything. "We will go back, but we must do it quietly. We will keep our eyes on the tunnel and listen for the slightest sound. If we hear the Rat People coming, we must drop everything and run for the door to our new world."

"But what of the light?" an old, wrinkled woman, her white face ghostly as it appeared from behind a white shawl she wore said. "We still can't take the light."

"We will think of something," Loki said. "By the time we leave, Slon will have a plan."

Slon looked at Loki and smiled at him. They shared a moment of friendship and appreciation. Slon looked at the tribe of Undergrounders. "With Loki's help, we will find a way to live in their world without pain."

The Undergrounders all talked happily and started back towards their village.

"Quiet!" Pak reminded them, and they all nodded and started talking in barely audible whispers.

Loki walked at the back of the group. Suddenly he felt a soft, warm hand in his. He looked up to see Harp holding his hand and smiling at him. He grabbed her hand, and together, they walked back to their village.

Crooked Walk woke up from where he lay on the grass next to a stone statue of some woman with big wings like a bird standing on a square slab. He looked up at the statue's face and it seemed to smile down at him with affection. Its arms were open as if inviting him in. The statue made Crooked Walk's blood go cold, as if it was welcoming him into the land of the dead. Who would make such a creepy looking statue? And for what purpose? He couldn't imagine, unless it was to frighten away attackers.

He sat up and looked around the ground, surprised that he was alive at all. What happened to the big monster? All around him in the dark were more stone tablets with rounded tops stuck into the ground. He saw there were other statues on stone blocks as well scattered about, a whole stone statue army of the winged creatures. Were they silent guardians of Lord Algon's castle? Crooked Walk even began to wonder if some kind of magic brought them to life. He shivered at the thought, then laughed at his foolishness. The recent encounter with the monster was making him go silly in the head because of the fright.

He stood up, looking for his men. Then he froze, instantly terrified. The monster sat not ten feet away from, chewing on something. Crooked Walk thought he knew what kind but didn't even want to think about it. He had to sneak away quietly, or he knew he'd be the beastie's next meal.

When he thought he was far enough away not to be heard he turned with relief to run, only to see something even more strange and terrifying, though he had no idea what it was. An army of golden men ten feet tall marched towards him! The one in the lead had on a green coat with colorful ribbons on it. And on the shoulder of the lead metal man, a person sat. Suddenly Crooked Walk wished he'd never brought his piratts ships to this land, for something told him, he would be in the arms of the stone angel of death before the night was over.

He turned to run, but it was too late. The man rode on top of the leading metal man saw him and pointed.

This must be the leader of the golden men, Crooked Walk though. Crooked Walk froze in terror. He'd never seen such a terrifying sight before, and suddenly he wasn't the captain of a fighting force of piratts, but just the little boy who'd ran away from monsters when he was five seasons old and all alone in the streets of the small coastal town where he grew up. He wished he was there now, where he'd been hungry and alone, and frightened, but at least not sure he was going to die.

CHAPTER 18

Ripper didn't have General Stupid walk through the gate of the cemetery, he made him smash his way through the wall. It crumbled before the robot, like tissue paper. It made Ripper happy to see the look of dismay on Lord Algon's face as he destroyed the wall. When would Lord Algon realize it was no longer his castle and land? Ripper couldn't wait until he really showed Lord Algon who was king by killing him.

The robots followed behind Ripper and General Stupid, walking through the opening General Stupid had made. This disappointed Ripper, who wished they had each smashed the wall down on their own. He smiled though when he saw General Stupid smashing the strange stone tablets sticking up out of the ground with his feet as he walked. If Ripper hadn't planned on living in the castle, he would have enjoyed watching the robots destroy it. *Oh well,* he thought, *there would be enough other things to destroy.*

"So, where's this Crooked Walk?" Ripper yelled down impatiently. "If this is some kind of trick, I'm going to-

"Nay, me lord, he is here for a surety!" Lord Algon hastened to reply, his hands in the air. "He be surely taking up residence in my castle yonder."

Ripper nodded slowly. "Okay, here's how it's going to go. We find him, and then you and him are going to fight. You said he stole your ship and marooned you, well, this is your chance to get your revenge." Ripper smiled at the thought of seeing the old enemies fight it out for his entertainment.

Lord Algon frowned unhappily, understanding just what this fight meant. He was just a lackey now, fighting for Ripper's amusement, just like how he used to make men fight in the Arena for his own pleasure. Ripper was the king now, and Lord Algon was just another slave. It made Lord Algon seethe with hatred inside, there where was nothing he could do about it.

"And Algon," Ripper said. "This fight is to the death."

Lord Algon nodded, worried. Could he really beat Crooked Walk in a fair fight? He wasn't sure. It had been years since he really fought anyone, and the fact was he had grown soft and chubby from eating and drinking. He only knew that his life depended on it, so he'd better be ready to do anything he had to do so he could win.

As they walked, Hardhitter grinned at Lord Algon, making Lord Algon want to rip Hardhitter's eyes out. Hardhitter knew what Lord Algon was thinking and could see how frightened Lord Algon was.

"Ye best be showing this Crooked Walk what kind of a man ye really be now, your lordship," Hardhitter said mockingly. "Or Crooked Walk will be showing us your insides."

Lord Algon glared at Hardhitter with a look of pure hatred. "Aye, and once I am victorious, it will by you who better be watching out, for by thunder, I'll serve your liver up to our new king for a dainty on a plate."

Hardhitter frowned, instantly afraid, and Lord Algon smiled, once again proving what a real coward Hardhitter was. He vowed that if he survived, Hardhitter would die, one way or another and in as gruesome a way as he could manage it.

Suddenly Ripper pointed a finger at the ground ahead. "Is that him?"

Lord Algon looked, his heart pounding with the excitement of anticipation. Yes, there on the ground lay none other than Crooked Walk himself! What was he doing lying in the grass instead of lounging in the castle? Lord Algon couldn't figure it out, and it was another mystery that his scheming mind filed away for future reference. Lord Algon was always thinking, planning his next move, and he constantly filed away little bits of information that might make the difference in a fight.

Crooked Walk must have heard them. He sat up. At first, he looked up at the strange stone woman with wings next to him as if trying to figure out what it was. Then he looked at something else in the dark that seemed to scare him. Then he finally noticed Ripper and the robots, and his face turned white with fright.

Ripper raised his right hand in the air. "Stop!" All the robots stopped in unison and stood still. Ripper looked down at Crooked Walk.

"Are you Crooked Walk the piratt?"

Crooked Walk stood up on shaky legs and looked up

at Ripper and the huge robot he sat on with a frown of fright. "Aye," he said in a thin, shaky voice.

"Do you recognize this man here?" Ripper pointed at Lord Algon.

Crooked Walk looked to see who Ripper pointed at. As soon as he saw Lord Algon, he frowned with even more fear, wondering if Lord Algon had come to get revenge.

"Aye," Crooked Walk said, still in a shaky voice.

Ripper turned his upper body as he sat on General Stupid and looked at Lord Algon. "Now is your chance, Algon. Show me you're the tough piratt you claim to be." Ripper turned and looked back at Crooked Walk. "Whichever one of you survives gets to be my second in command."

Crooked Walk and Lord Algon turned and looked at each other as Lord Algon advanced. Hardhitter handed Lord Algon a sword, and someone else gave one to Crooked Walk. The two men squared off a few feet from each other, both scowling knowing they were in a fight to the death.

Ripper settled down on General Stupid's shoulders and made himself comfortable, ready to watch a good battle.

"Let the fight begin!"

Loki walked alongside Harp, holding her hand. He didn't care what happened to him just then. The pleasure of having Harp next to him and her hand in his meant he could be torn apart by wolf-beasties and still be happy and smiling. He glanced over to see her smiling back at him. He knew then that she was his girl, no matter what, and it made him happier than he could ever remember being before.

The Undergrounders reached the main tunnel. They stopped, peering ahead at the tent village with frightened looks, trying to spot any Rat People.

"Are you sure they're all gone, Loki?" His mother Pak asked in a scared whisper. "We don't want to get eaten."

Loki stopped too and peered ahead at the village. "They were gone when I left. If you want, I'll go check again real fast."

"Yes, you do that," Slon said, sounding official, but everyone knew he was really afraid to do it himself.

Loki grinned, feeling like Johnny again. He turned to Harp. "Wait here. I'll be right back."

Harp nodded, and Loki once again walked slowly alone to his village. He reached the ledge and dropped down to the lower area below where the village and the old metal trains lay. Suddenly he heard a sound beside him. He looked and with surprise saw Harp standing there.

"I'm going with you."

"No, it's too dangerous!" Loki said.

"I don't care. I want to be with you. If you can face danger, so can I."

It looked like he wasn't going to talk her out of coming along, so Loki nodded. He didn't like the thought that something might happen to Harp, but he was happy she wanted to be by his side.

Together they walked down the tracks to the first two tents on either side of the main path into the village. Loki held the gun steady, pointing forward. Now he felt more like Johnny, and he carried the gun with confidence, not wavering. He still didn't know that it had to be cocked to work again, but it looked to Harp as if he was a hero, and that was the important thing. He realized Harp didn't have a weapon. He stopped and pulled out his sword and handed it to her. She took it and held it steady. Something about the way she frowned with ferocity and held the sword made Loki like her even more; she had courage. She looked like one of the angels when they fought the wolf monster. Loki felt even more like Johnny, having his girl beside him.

Together the two, slim white figures walked slowly down the main path until they could see inside the first two tents. They both peered into one and then the other. There was no one there.

Loki turned and waved to the Undergrounders. They smiled and cautiously started towards the pair, still looking frightened.

Loki and Harp grinned at each other, two heroes protecting their people. They walked on to the next set of tents.

"I have an idea, Loki," Harp said. She picked up a piece of black silk from a table in the nearest tent. As Loki watched, she put it over her eyes and tied it at the back of her head.

"Look," she said. "I can still see, but it is darker. If we put on cloth like this, maybe we can go out in the light and it won't hurt our eyes."

Loki nodded, impressed. "That's a very good idea! You are very smart."

Harp took the cloth off her eyes and smiled at him, feeling good because of his compliment. "We just need to find enough for everybody."

"I bet we can," Loki said. "Let's finish checking out the village, and then we'll tell Slon about it."

Harp nodded, and they walked on, inspecting the rest of the village.

Johnny stared at Carny, his face blank with surprise. Everyone else was shocked and surprised too, and they all stood motionless looking at Carny. Finally, Johnny said, "Carny, are feeling all right?"

Everybody chuckled, but Carny scowled irritably. "Of course, I'm all right. And I'm not going Wildie in the head.

"I saw him too, Johnny," Foodcourt said. "He tried to shoot Misterwizard with a gun. I don't know why I forgot to tell you about it."

"I fought him," Carny said, looking disappointed, "but he got away."

Johnny grinned, impressed. "You fought him, Carny? That was brave."

Carny smiled but in a serious way. "He killed Buildabear and wanted to kill me. Even though Buildabear was not good, he was my mate. Ripper needs to pay for what he did."

"Tell me all about it," Johnny said, looking at both Carny and Foodcourt. "Where did you see him, and what happened?"

Quickly Foodcourt explained how he and Misterwizard saw Ripper when he shot at them. Then Carny explained how she fought him. She told how Thegap came to her aid but was too surprised to do anything.

"Ripper had a big scar on his face, Johnny, and his right arm didn't work so good. I think the tiger-beastie hurt him but somehow he survived."

Johnny looked at the orange glow in the sky. "Maybe it's Ripper and the Gangers. Maybe they're fighting Lord Algon."

"Then maybe they'll kill each other off!" Foodcourt said grinning hopefully.

"Wouldn't that be fitting justice?" Super said.

They all looked at the orange glow in the distance and listened to the distant sounds of shouting.

It was another bizarre scene the Yellow Eye shone down on that night. In the abandoned graveyard that used to be called Arlington where the gravestones of famous warriors from before the Great War dotted the grass, two strange new and strange combatants fought. Each armed with a sword, they faced each other. And watching the fight to the death silently stood twenty-one giant, golden men of steel in two rows. To make the scene even more strange, the golden metal man in front wore a green coat with ribbons on it, and on his shoulders sat a real man with black hair and scars on his face. To finish off the picture, a crowd of men and women in ragged clothes carrying knives, swords and clubs stood around the whole scene, watching.

Crooked Walk and Lord Algon circled each other, holding their swords high. Both scowled at the other, both seeing the other's death in their eyes. Lord Algon was the larger man, but he was soft from years of eating good food and being carried around. Crooked Walk was used to running and pillaging, and even though he was only a little over five feet tall, he was all muscle and sinew.

Surrounding them were not only Lord Algon's Wildies but Crooked Walk's piratts too, for they had heard the commotion and ran over to see what was happening. The remainders of Ripper's Gang, including Facegash, had come as well, so a mixture of three different warring parties stood shoulder to shoulder. There was one thing everyone understood, however, and that was that Ripper was the king. They all saw the tall golden men with him, and just like a pack of wolves knows when one is the dominant wolf, they all knew Ripper was the one with the power now. For the moment, they would all serve him, until someone stronger or more cunning killed him. Then they would serve the new leader. It was the way of wild animals and evil men, the strongest ruled.

The light from the torches held high danced off the faces of everyone there, gleaming off the golden sides of the robots and mixing with shadows and the dark, evil smiles on the faces of the men and women watching the fight. Crooked Walk and Lord Algon moved in a circle, staying just out of reach and watching the other warily.

"Oh, come on, fight already!" Ripper said, growing impatient.

Suddenly they heard a scream and the crowd parted hastily. Men and women ran in fear. Ripper looked to see what was going on, upset that he couldn't finish one fight without interuption. Crooked Walk knew what it was, and his eyes opened wide with fear.

"The beastie!" He turned and ran, right into a group of Wildies and they all went down in a heap. Lord Algon was smarter. He ran towards the robots and hid behind General Stupid, peering out.

The gorilla-beastie bounded into the open area where Crooked Walk and Lord Algon had been. It snarled and beat its chest, showing its dominance. It glared around, looking for someone to challenge it.

Ripper grinned with evil pleasure. Here was something he could kill.

"General Stupid!"

"I see it, Master. A wild infestation. Shall I destroy it?"

Ripper stared at the magnificent, dark beast with its black fur and savage face. He almost hated to destroy such a beautiful and terrible beastie. It would make a great pet if he could only tame it. If he could just cage it, it could provide hours of entertainment. With regret he knew he didn't have time, he had a fight to win against Johnny.

In an unhappy voice he said, "Yes. Turn it to ash."

General Stupid turned towards the gorilla-beastie. Sensing a challenge, the gorilla-beastie turned towards the robot and snarled. General Stupid raised his left arm and his left hand tilted up. Suddenly a hail of bullets poured rom the hole in his hand. The bullets tore up the ground in front of the gorilla-beastie and around it, some shattering stone tablets in the ground behind it. Men and women from all three armies dashed out of the path of the withering storm of bullets. The gorilla-beastie screamed and jumped backwards.

"Kill it, Stupid!" Ripper yelled.

But the gorilla-beastie was fast. In a moment, it leapt over the Wildies behind it before they could even react. As they all watched, it ran away and disappeared into the darkness.

Ripper glared down at General Stupid. "I thought you said you were good."

"Would you like us to pursue it, Master?"

"No, Stupid." Ripper looked around. Where are the two idiots who were going to fight?

While everyone was distracted by the gorilla-beastie, Lord Algon saw his chance. He spied Crooked Walk standing behind a group of Wildies, watching the beastie. With an evil and dark grin, he snuck up behind Crooked Walk. Crooked Walk didn't hear him, he didn't even turn around. Looking around to see that no one was watching Lord Algon put his left hand over Crooked Walk's mouth and pulled his head back. Then he took his sword in his right hand and stabbed Crooked Walk in the back. Crooked Walk screamed, but Lord Algon's hand muffled the sound. Crooked Walk struggled as Lord Algon held him. Then finally he slowly sank to the ground. Lord Algon stabbed him again and again, making sure he was dead. Then he grinned. He hadn't become king of the land without knowing how get rid of a few enemies.

He wiped the sword on the grass and spat on Crooked Walk with a scowl. "That's for stealing me ship and marooning me, ye filthy sea dog. And with that, me revenge be complete."

Just then Lord Algon heard the pulsating sound of General Stupid's machine gun and saw the gorilla-beastie leap over the heads of the Wildies. It landed right next to him! He screamed in fear and stumbled backwards, but the beastie was in no mood to fight. It bounded off into the darkness and was swallowed up by the shadows.

He heard Ripper talking. "Where are the two idiots who were going to fight?"

He saw everyone looking around. The Wildies in front of him saw him. They looked down and saw Crooked Walk lying dead on the ground. They turned and yelled to Ripper.

Ripper motioned for General Stupid to walk over, and the robot did. Soon a crowd surrounded Lord Algon and the body of Crooked Walk. Lord Algon smiled up at Ripper with confidence.

"He be dead. I am the victor, as ye can see."

The piratts in the crowd, including Limpfoot, looked on their dead captain with dismay. Then they joined everyone else as they all looked at Ripper, to see what he would say.

Ripper adjusted himself on General Stupid. "Man, this robot is uncomfortable."

Everyone chuckled, except Lord Algon, who was too worried about his future to have any sense of humor.

Ripper grinned. "So, you snuck up on him like a coward and stabbed him in the back."

Lord Algon frowned, worry clouding his face. "I-I-"

"Relax," Ripper said. "It's a sign of a real snake to stab somebody in the back when they're not looking. It's what I would have done. I'm impressed."

Lord Algon smiled, relieved. He lowered his sword and even chuckled a little. Ripper, being an underhanded rat-beastie just like Lord Algon, understood.

"The only problem is," Ripper said in a relaxed but sinister voice, staring at his fingers, "You might do the same thing to me."

Lord Algon moved a little closer and put on a look of

worry again. "Nay, me lord. I swore my allegiance to thee. Pray please believe me. There's not a false bone in all of me body."

Lord Algon knew he'd overdone it, and so did Ripper.

"Sorry, Lord Algon. There can be only one king. I just don't need you anymore!"

Ripper looked down at General Stupid. "General Stupid kill him."

"NO!" Lord Algon screamed, and it was the last thing he ever said. General Stupid shot his machine gun again, and Lord Algon's body was riddled with bullets. The bullets tore through his body, shredding it into a mass of flesh and red spray. When General Stupid stopped, there was nothing left of Lord Algon.

Limpfoot yelled to the piratts. "Back to the ships, mateys!" Then he turned and ran back towards the harbor. The piratts in the crowd took off after him. Ripper turned and watched them.

"Hey! Get back here! I'm your master now!"

But the piratts were already gone. Ripper turned to the Wildies and his Gangers.

"Nobody else better leave, or I'll cut you down too!"

A Wildie man with three teeth missing and short stubby hair said to Ripper, "We not leave thee, master. Where would we go? Ye be the king of this land now."

Facegash strode up and grinned up at his old leader. "We're all behind you, Ripper. I'm so glad to see you're back! I should have known Johnny couldn't kill you!"

Ripper smiled, happy. He'd lost the piratts, but he still had his army. He looked at the Wildies. "The first thing you're going to do is stop talking that gibberish and talk normal. That piratt talk you guys do gives me a headache. Got it? "

The Wildies all grinned at each other and nodded. The Wildie man with the missing teeth answered. "Glady, your kingship. Lord Algon made us talk that way. We didn't much like it either."

They all laughed. Ripper laughed too. It was a strange moment as two separate groups of cruel bad men shared a moment of togetherness. It was a good moment for Ripper, when he felt like he was king of the world. For a moment, he almost forgot all about Johnny and the Tribe.

"General Stupid put me down."

General Stupid knelt and Ripper climbed off. He made a face and rubbed his sore behind. "We're getting a pillow before I get back on you again."

Facegash turned to the Gangers and Wildies and raised his fist in the air. "All hail King Ripper! All hail King Ripper!"

All the Wildies and Gangers bent down on one knee and lowered their heads, including Facegash. Ripper put his hands up as they all repeated what Facegash said, enjoying the adulation. He couldn't remember a more wonderful moment in his whole life. Lately the good moments began to outweigh the bad. He began to wonder if things were finally going his way. The whole world was at his doorstep. He was king! He only had to do one thing first.

Facegash looked up at Ripper, happy his act had pleased his new King. "What are your orders, oh king?"

An old Wildie in the back with white hair and wrinkled skin said, "Can we take a break and get something to eat? It's been a long night of fighting."

"No!" Ripper said, his face clouded with dark intent. "We will rest in the rubble of New Sanctuary after we've destroyed it. And we'll feed on the dead bodies of Johnny and his Tribe."

He rubbed his rear again, wishing he had time to get a pillow, but there was no time to worry about comfort. "General Stupid let me on again."

General Stupid bowed down again and once again Ripper climbed on his shoulders. General Stupid rose up again. Ripper turned enough to see his troops behind him. "Now march!"

CHAPTER 19

Loki and Harp finished checking out the village, going into first one tent on one side of the path and then the tent on the other side. The Undergrounders followed nervously from far behind. When Loki and Harp reached the end of the village and saw there were no Rat People anywhere, they both relaxed. Harp held the cloth up to Loki. "Now let's go tell Slon about our idea!"

"You mean your idea," Loki said.

Harp looked at him and squeezed his hand. "Our idea."

They hurried back through the tent village to find the people returning to their own tents, talking cheerfully with smiles on their faces. The danger for the moment was over and they all could relax.

Loki's mother Pak walked up and put her arms around him. She kissed him on the cheek.

"You are such a brave boy. I'm so proud of you!"

Loki's white cheeks colored with red. "Mother, you forget yourself."

Harp giggled behind her hand, making Loki feel even more embarrassed. Pak glanced at her and then looked at Loki again. "Don't stop a mother from being proud of her son. I think your friend knows how brave you are too."

Loki finally gave up and smiled. He nodded at Harp. "She was brave too."

Slon walked up, looking like his old arrogant self. He was going to ignore Loki and Harp and walk on by, but Pak frowned at him and touched his arm.

"Don't you owe Loki a word of thanks?"

Slon shrugged. "He did what any Undergrounder should do, help his tribe."

Pak scowled at Slon with anger. "A little boy and his friend were more courageous than the leader of our tribe."

Slon scowled back. "Do not forget your place, Pak. I am still the leader, and you need to show me respect."

Pak nodded in a casual way. "I will show you respect. If I have to."

Harp nudged Loki with her elbow. He looked at her and she lifted the cloth up.

"Slon?" Loki said.

Slon glared at Loki, still angry at his mother. "What do you want?"

Loki decided trying some diplomacy was the best course of action. "We know you are the leader and do your best to help the tribe. Thank you for letting me help."

Slon smiled, pleased that Loki at least knew how to

respect him. He looked at Pak, who simply smiled back with humor.

"Thank you, Loki, for being willing to take orders and do what I asked." He turned to Pak. "There. I thanked him. Happy now?"

Pak walked away. Over her shoulder she said, "No. I will be when Loki is leader. He's going to be, someday."

Slon started to get angry again, but Harp spoke quickly to change the subject.

"Slon, may we talk to you? We need your wisdom about something."

This made Slon feel even better. He smiled again, at ease and looked at Harp with friendliness. "Of course, dear Harp. I didn't forget how brave you were to join Loki in his mission."

Harp smiled her most engaging smile at him. Then she held up the cloth. "We were trying to find a way this cloth could help us, so we could go outside in the new world. We thought maybe it could be used somehow to block the light. What do you think?"

Loki smiled at Harp, at how good she was at saying just the right thing.

Slon, flattered at her compliments and feeling important because she asked for his advice, took the cloth from her. He held it up in the darkness and turned it over and over, as if giving it a thorough examination.

"Yes, this might be useful. Hmm."

He turned it over and over, and Harp began to think he wasn't going to catch on. She decided to give him a hint.

"Maybe if we put the cloth over our eyes…"

"Yes!" Slon said nodding. "It might just help keep the light out enough to let us spend a small amount of time outside. Mind you," he waved the cloth towards Loki and Harp, "it might not work, and then it will have to be understood that you two suggested it to me."

"Of course," Harp said, nodding gravely. "But if it does work, well, it was all your idea, wasn't it?"

Slon grinned, very happy. "Yes, it would be, wouldn't it?"

Loki chimed in. "We could make enough for the whole tribe. We have enough cloth."

The wheels in Slon's head turned, a slow process. He scrunched up his eyes with the effort. "There are over many people in our tribe." He looked at Loki and Harp. "You do not know how to do this, but since I am a priest of Lincone, I know the ancient magic of counting. There are over tloo hunner people in our tribe. That would be a lot of cloth."

"Yes, but if we get started making them right away..."

Slon frowned, and Loki was afraid he might have overdone it, but then Slon nodded. "We will have to start right away. We don't know when the..."

He glanced with worried eyes at the darkness beyond the village. "The Rat People will return."

"We should get the whole tribe working on it right away, don't you think, Leader Slon?"

Slon nodded. "Yes. But I am very tired. I don't want to deal with something this petty."

"Put us in charge of it then!" Harp said.

Slon smiled at them. "You are good children, and someday you will be leaders. I will tell the tribe to listen to you, on my authority!"

Loki and Harp grinned at each other.

Slon turned around and spoke in a loud voice.

"Undergrounders, listen to me."

All the Undergrounders walked out of the tents into the middle pathway and looked at Slon.

Slon stood up tall to look official. "I have given Loki and Harp instructions. You listen to what they tell you to do, for they have my temporary authority to give you orders. They will explain how we will escape from the Underground and be able to live in the new world."

CHAPTER 20

Ripper tried to keep his eyes open as the rhythmic movement of General Stupid made him feel sleepy. He was afraid he was going to fall asleep, let go of the robot's neck and fall backwards onto the ground. Not only would it be highly embarrassing, it might also break his neck. He'd been awake for at least two days, ever since he wandered into the strange building where he found the robot. He cursed silently to himself. Here he was on the verge of his greatest victory, and he was going to miss it because he needed sleep? No way! He'd sleep after Johnny was dead!

His body didn't seem to be listening to him, however. His eyelids felt like old metal plates like the ones he saw everywhere on the streets, so heavy. He caught himself, eyes closed, snoring, and he woke up and shook his head to clear it.

And hungry! He realized the last time he'd eaten was early in the morning. It angered him to think the old Wildie might be right, and he hated how smug the old man would be when Ripper called for them to stop and rest, but he simply had no choice. Johnny or no Johnny, old man or no old man, he had to stop, rest and get some food. He realized his victory wouldn't be half as much fun if he was hungry and tired. He wanted to be good and alert when he watched the Tribe destroyed.

"Stop!" He yelled. The robots all stopped. "Put me down!" He told General Stupid, and the robot knelt, so Ripper could disembark.

The Wildies and Gangers following behind the robots ran up between them to see what Ripper wanted.

Ripper turned and stood up tall, happy to be the king and bark out orders. "We will stop and rest until the morning. Find me food and a place to sleep."

Sure enough, he saw the old man smile. Ripper decided he'd pay the old man back for that. When he was done killing the Tribe, he'd put the old man in the arena and see how long he lasted. The Wildies and Gangers all scattered to fulfill his orders. He turned to General Stupid. "Can you shut yourself off to save your, power or whatever?"

"Affirmative. I can reduce my power consumption to point five percent by transferring to standby status."

"Whatever. How will I wake you up?"

"You need only to speak again, and I will return to full operation."

"Good. You and your fellow Stupids go to sleep."

"As you wish."

As Ripper watched, the other robots shut off. How General Stupid told them to shut down, he didn't have a clue. It must have been some kind of magic. Ripper thought about how scary General Stupid and the robots really were, and how he knew nothing about them. He just hoped he didn't do something wrong and make them turn on him. The idea that he had no clue what might do that made his blood run cold. He had to be ready to run, just in case they did.

Foodcourt walked up to Johnny. Johnny turned to look at his father. Normally wearing a cheerful grin, Foodcourt's face was darkened by a look of seriousness. "Johnny, we should send out some spies to see just what is happening."

Johnny nodded, thinking about it. Behind Foodcourt, his mother Teavana walked up, her thin, wraithlike form almost looking like a ghost coming towards them in the dark. She put a hand on Foodcourts shoulder and he glanced up at her.

"Now, now, Johnny has done enough. Let someone else do the dangerous job for once."

Foodcourt grinned with excitement. "I'll go."

Teavanna shook her head, her long black hair seeming to float on the air. "No, Foodcourt. We need to help Carny. She has a baby now."

As if hearing her name mentioned, Carny walked up. "You don't have to worry about sending a spy."

Everyone near her looked at her with curiosity. She smiled at them then looked at Miracle, who was awake now. Miracle smiled back at her.

After she didn't say anything else, Johnny walked up

to her to ask her what she meant. She looked at him.

Just then, TheGap ran towards the front of the wall looking at something in the darkness, almost falling off the edge. He pointed towards Lord Algon's castle. "Johnny! Look!"

The whole Tribe turned and looked, including Johnny, Foodcourt and Carny. Then they all reacted with surprise and amazement at what they saw.

It was Ripper and the golden robots. Far in the distance they marched out of the darkness in three rows. And there on the lead robot rode Ripper. His eyes were half-closed, and he gripped the robot's head, holding on. On his right cheek, three deep gash marks showed her he'd fought the tiger-beastie. His right eye was damaged too and seemed to look around independently of the other. And he seemed to be favoring his right arm, holding it in a little as if it hurt him.

"What are those things?" Carny asked, her mouth open.

"They're not good, I can tell you that," Foodcourt said gravely.

"Johnny, look who's riding on top of the one in front."

Johnny nodded. "It's him, all right." Johnny scowled. "I should have made sure he was dead."

"He's a snake, and they're hard to kill," Teavana said in her soft, lilting voice, and everyone looked at her with mild surprise. She rarely said anything mean or harsh, so it seemed very out of character.

Then Carny smiled with joy, a total opposite reaction from before. She pointed, shaking Miracle who frowned. "Look who's coming!"

They all looked where she was pointing. Then they all

smiled with joy. It was Misterwizard, Sephie and Lady Stabs! They ran along by the side of the buildings to the left, hurrying towards the car wall.

"Yahoo!" Starbucks said. "They're okay!"

Johnny's heart filled with relief and happiness. He felt his eyes grow moist, and suddenly it was hard to breathe. He sucked in a ragged breath and tried to keep from crying in front of everyone. He was just so happy to see his friends.

"Hurry," Johnny said, in a husky voice full of emotion, "open the car so they can come in!"

Two members of the tribe hurried down the ramp to the door. One called up from the darkness. "Johnny, the door is already open!"

Johnny shrugged. Right then he didn't care. He hurried down the ramp along with everyone else to meet the wayward adventurers. Foodcourt stayed behind. "Johnny! What about Ripper and the things out there?"

Despite his joy, Johnny reluctantly realized Foodcourt had a point. There was not a lot of time to celebrate if Ripper and the strange machines he had with him were on their way. He called back to Foodcourt. "Keep an eye on them, Father. We'll be right back!"

Foodcourt nodded and peered out past the old Capitol building to the horizon where Ripper and the strange creatures approached.

Johnny hurried to join the crowd at the open car door where the missing members of the Tribe would enter. The first to crawl through was Sephie. Her mother and father stood next to the car door, tears of joy on their faces. As she emerged, she was covered in grime and rust and looked as if she'd rolled around in dirt. But she wore a big grin of triumph on her face.

Sephie's mother Abercrombie ran over and gave her a big hug. For a moment, they both held each other and cried with relief and joy as the rest of the Tribe watched, happy. Microsoft, Sephie's father, gave her a hug too. Then he looked at the Tribe with a big grin. Abercrombie finally let Sephie go. She stared at her appearance with a smile, wiping her eyes. "My, how did you get so dirty?"

Everyone laughed. Lady Stabs climbed out next and everyone cheered. Some walked over and shook her hand. Misterwizard climbed out next, and the cheer doubled in size. People jumped up and down, so happy to see Misterwizard back. He wiped dirt from his bald head, shook his round body and said, "Climbing through this vehicle is quite challenging for a man of my girth and lowly stature. Quite a tight fit!"

They all laughed. Sephie walked up to Johnny. Johnny knelt and looked into her eyes a big smile on his face. He was trying hard not to start crying himself, but having a hard time doing it. Sephie put her arms out and Johnny swept her up. He lifted her in the air and hugged her. Sephie didn't bother trying to hide her tears, but balled loudly, so happy to see Johnny again. She held up Kermit.

"Look, Johnny! I found Kermit again!'

Johnny nodded, too touched to be able to respond.

"Johnny, we had an adventure!"

Everyone laughed, including Misterwizard.

Johnny finally spoke, no longer trying to hide his emotion. "Did you?"

Sephie nodded, full of pride. "I was a hero, just like you, Johnny!" Sephie said. "I fought the bad guy and hid so he couldn't get me. Then I found Misterwizard and we saved Lady Stabs. Then the bad man was swept away by the river!"

She used her hand to demonstrate. "Wait until I tell you all about it!"

Everyone laughed and talked. Johnny said, "I can't wait to hear all about it."

He saw Misterwizard approaching and put Sephie down. The two walked up to each other and grinned. Then they hugged. Misterwizard's eyes were wet too, but he didn't even bother to wipe them. They let go of each other and stood back, smiling at each other.

"We seem to be having a plethora of these moments, Johnny, where we lose contact in the heat of battle, only to be reunited. I would venture to say, too many."

Misterwizard looked at Sephie, "this young lady was quite the bold adventurer!"

Sephie grinned up at them with pride.

"She maintained her courage and pluck in the face of danger that would make even the most stalwart heart tremble."

Johnny smiled at Sephie, proud of her as well. Sephie's mother and father smiled at her too.

"That's because I'm just like Johnny," Sephie said.

"How did you get so dirty?" Johnny asked.

"It's a long story," Sephie said with a sigh, and they all laughed.

"I lost Deecee, Misterwizard," Johnny said. "He ran off when me and my friends were out exploring."

"Hmm," Misterwizard said, scratching his ear. "I am sorry to hear that, Johnny. I am confident, however, that your canine companion will endeavor to find his way back. He was a very intelligent animal."

Johnny nodded. Then he remembered Ripper and his strange companions.

"Misterwizard!" Johnny pointed, as if towards the area beyond the wall. "Did you see what's coming our way?"

Misterwizard nodded, frowning again. ""Yes. I'm afraid, as wonderful as this reunion, is, it seems to be we come once again with distressing news of another coming catastrophe. It is a common vignette we seem to keep repeating, a most unpleasant form of déjà vu.' It's almost as if we are in a time loop, or a dimension of repeating negative possibilities. And yet, this repeating scenario may not be all that surprising, as we attempt to tame a land that has been unsupervised and ungoverned for so long."

Johnny nodded impatiently. He wasn't in the mood for Misterwizard's confusing talk.

"If you're talking about Ripper, I already knew he was still alive."

"Do you know about the gold robots?" Sephie asked, pulling on Johnny's sleeve.

Johnny looked at her and then at Misterwizard. "What's a robot?"

"Let's get going again," Deb said, eager to get out of the darkness as soon as possible. It reminded her of being in the dark tunnels of the Undergrounders and made her feel creepy.

"Which way do we go?" Super said.

Deb wasn't sure anymore. She peered in the darkness again, and thought she recognized the car she'd bumped into. "I think it's that way."

They both started walking again, this time holding each other's hand. Then Super bumped into something, something big.

They both stopped and looked up to see what it was. With shock, they saw it was a ten-foot tall man made of gold.

"What is it?" Deb and Super stared at the strange, tall figure, menacing and silent.

Super replied, "I don't know, but it's sure scary. Let's get away from it, fast."

Deb nodded agreeing. Somehow the giant metal man gave Deb the chills. Deep down inside, she didn't know how, but something told her they were going to regret finding the metal man and regret it badly. The thought of one of it coming to life and moving towards them made her want to run, regardless of where she ended up.

She grabbed Super's arm. "Super, let's get out of here, fast."

"I'm with that," Super said with conviction.

The girls tiptoed as fast as they could, their feet sounding way too loud. They reached a building across the street in the dark. They stopped and crouched by the side of it, wanting a moment to recover from the scary ordeal.

"We have to warn Johnny," Super whispered.

Deb shook her head, her long white hair flying around her face. "We check on the Undergrounders. Then we'll tell Johnny."

"But what if that thing is on its way to attack the Tribe?" Super said, motioning with her head back towards the frightening figure. "Johnny needs to know!"

They looked at each other. Deb frowned, knowing Super was right. She wanted so much to make sure her friends in the underground were still safe, but if she and Super didn't warn Johnny and something happened, it would be terrible. She'd never be able to forgive herself.

"Okay," Deb said gloomily. "You're right."

They started moving again. Then they heard a voice which sent a chill up their spines.

"Where be ye going my lovelies?"

They turned to see a Wildie man leaning on a chuck of broken rock next to a building. He pointed at gun at them. They'd been caught.

CHAPTER 21

What's a robot?" Johnny asked.

"Those things out there, I bet," Starbucks said, pointing to where the robots were on the other side of the old Capitol building just close enough to look like little metal toy soldiers.

Johnny replied, "And they're coming this way!"

They all ran back up the ramp to Foodcourt, who stood leaning forward, peering out into the darkness. Johnny reached him first. "Dad, what are the robots doing?"

"Robots?" Foodcourt asked, his face wrinkled with curiosity.

"Those things," Cinnabon said irritably from far back in the group where she stood, pointing a finger at the dark metal shapes in the distance.

"Oh, those!" Foodcourt said, smiling cheerfully.

"They stopped."

"Stopped?" Johnny said, squinting to see the robots in the distance.

"Yes, stopped," Foodcourt repeated.

Everyone stared at the distant robots and talked at once, wondering why.

"But I saw something else, Johnny."

"What's that, father?" Johnny asked.

"There's an army behind them, and they seem to have weapons like the ones we found in the Bunker."

"That's just great." Starbucks scowled. "What else does Ripper have, some Mushroom Monsters too?"

"Let us sincerely hope this is not the case," Misterwizard said, his round face grave. "From some undetermined but fortuitous event, we seemed to have been granted a slight reprieve."

"Misterwizard, just what is a robot?"

Everyone turned and looked at Misterwizard, interested to hear his explanation.

Misterwizard's face darkened, showing he was deep in thought. He stuck his index finger in the air and waved it as he spoke, as if lecturing. "As I explained to Sephie when we first saw them, robots are mechanical devices, just like automobiles or computers. These particular mechanisms have been fashioned to look like men and perform many of the same functions, such as walking, talking, and completing simple manual tasks like picking up objects or doing mathematical calculations."

"Are they dangerous?" Foodcourt asked.

Misterwizard nodded. "I suspect they can be, if armed with weaponry."

"Ripper's in charge of them, Misterwizard!" Carny said, pointing at the lead robot with the green coat, even though Ripper was no longer sitting on it.

"Yes, a most unfortunate turn of events." Misterwizard began pacing back and forth on the roofs of the cars making up the wall, and everyone followed his movements with their eyes. "We can assume Ripper would not bring the robots here if they could not do us injury. I suspect he believes they will be able to destroy us."

Murmurs of fear rippled through the Tribe. Johnny put his hand on his sword and looked down, deep in thought.

"Swords won't stop them, that's for sure," Foodcourt said as he looked at the one he held in his hand, his face grave.

"Would even bullets stop them?" Thegap asked, nodding at his rifle and then looking at Misterwizard for the answer.

Misterwizard stared out at the robots, scratching his beard, as he did often when he was deep in thought. "I suspect bullets will prove ineffective. I doubt they have either the speed or the size to penetrate the robot's thick armor plating. However," he pointed a finger in the air, "explosives should at least do some damage to their legs, rendering them immobile."

"We only have a few up here," Starbucks said, picking up one of the green balls with strange bumps all over it and a lever on the side. He held it up for Misterwizard to see. "Not enough to stop them all."

"We have more at New Sanctuary," Johnny said. "Let's get back and get ready, while we have a chance."

"Let's hope they'll be enough against the ones Ripper's army has," Foodcourt said.

Ripper walked out of the old building with the glass wall he'd slept in that night. Not the most comfortable place, it had shiny yellow floors and moldy food on shelves everywhere. But he found an old, smelly couch in a back room, and so had been able to sleep, though not comfortably.

He looked at the world outside the building. The Red Eye had just risen, and its pale light revealed a strange scene of golden robots standing in a row and men and women wandering about and making campfires. And guarded by three Gangers, two young ladies, one with long blond hair, the other with dark hair, lay on a mattress in the street, still asleep.

Ripper couldn't believe how his fortunes kept getting better and beter. Not only was he about to destroy Johnny once and for all, but Johnny's girl Deb and her friend Super had simply wandered into their path, letting Ripper capture them! Something had to be wrong. Things couldn't be going this well for him, could they? He kept thinking Fate was simply laughing at him, setting him up and lowering his guard before it gave him a good one-two punch in the gut.

But he'd just enjoyed a full night's rest and a good meal of deer-beastie one of his men had killed. The fears of losing to Johnny for the first time lessened, and he began to feel like he could breathe again.

Up ahead he saw the broken remains of the old Capitol building. On either side of it running to the buildings on the right and left stood the strange car wall the Tribe built. It would be his his first goal. The cars, stacked on top of each other and of different shapes and colors, looked like a crazy jigsaw puzzle. Yellow buses and taxis sat on top of red sports cars and trucks. The wall didn't look steady but looked like it was ready to tip over at any second. *Ripper would help with that,* he thought with an evil grin.

He walked over to Deb and Super. Super woke up and sat up, glaring at him.

"Morning, Sunshine," Ripper said, grinning at her evilly.

Super scowled at him and rubbed her hair with her hand. "You're dead, you know that, don't you? Johnny's going to make sure he really does it this time."

Anger filled Ripper's mind, and he balled up his fist. "You know, there's no reason why I have to keep you alive. Johnny doesn't care about you."

Super's eyes widened with fear, making Ripper feel good. "You hurt me, and my boyfriend Starbucks will rip your head off."

Ripper laughed. This girl had spirit. It was fun trading threats with her. He toyed with the idea that after the battle was over and everyone in the Tribe was dead, he'd force her to be his mate. He bet she would enjoy it, after she got over whoever this Starbucks guy was.

He grinned at her. "I won't kill you, just yet. Maybe I'll let you ride with me on General Stupid."

"In your dreams, freakazoid," Super said. "I'd rather you just kill me than be that close to your stench."

Ripper frowned, wondering if he did smell. He lifted his shirt and sniffed. He was pretty smelly. He decided after the battle, he'd have to put actual water on his body, though the idea scared him a little.

"Wake up the princess," Ripper said, pointing at Deb. "It's time to kill everyone she knows, including her precious Johnny."

Ripper looked at the men guarding the girls. "When they wake up, make them ride on two of the robots, near the front by me. And then follow along behind them. You lose them, I'll have a robot rip you two apart." The men nodded fearfully.

Ripper walked away, feeling Super's eyes full of hatred burning on his back. It actually made him feel good. He loved the hate of a good enemy, it made life interesting.

"Wake up, Stupid."

At Ripper's words, General Stupid's eyes began to glow again. A soft whirring sound came from somewhere inside his body. Then as Ripper watched, the eyes of all the other robots lit up as well.

"Kneel," Ripper said, yawning.

General Stupid did as he was told. Ripper sat once again on his shoulders, so excited he was barely able to keep from hopping up and down. This was it! His chance to finally see a look of terror and defeat on Johnny's face! Even better was going to be the look in Johnny's eyes, when he finally had to admit Ripper was the winner, and he was going to die. The thought made Ripper so happy he almost shed a tear.

"Turn around."

General Stupid turned around. Ripper looked at the wandering Wildies and Gangers, many still asleep on the ground or sitting by fires, eating rat-beasties and bits of other scraps for breakfast.

"Make some kind of sound to make my men listen," Ripper said, and a second later wished he hadn't, for

General Stupid set off an alarm that hurt his ears. He covered them and grimaced down at the robot's face. "Enough, Stupid!"

General Stupid shut off the alarm. Slowly, the Wildies and Gangers walked towards Ripper, past the waiting robots. When most of them had gathered, Ripper looked down at them, a king to his subjects.

"Today is the day we have been waiting for. Today, we destroy our enemies and make ourselves the true rulers of this world."

The Wildies and Gangers gave a ragged cheer.

"Listen very carefully. You all have stuff in your bellies, and you got a good sleep. You have fancy weapons from the robot's place. So now, I want to see everybody fight to the death, even if it takes all day and all night. When we get thee, I don't want to see anybody not fighting, or they join Johnny's tribe in dying. Everybody got that?"

The Wildies and Gangers all nodded.

Ripper grinned. "We have Johnny's girlfriend, and his best friend's girl too, so this is gonna be easy. Johnny will have to surrender, or he knows what'll happen to 'em."

The Wildies and Gangers smiled evil smiles.

"And then when he does, we kill 'em all anyway!"

The crowd cheered. Ripper raised a hand. "Nobody kills Johnny, his sister Carny or the old man except me. Got it?"

The Wildies and Gangers nodded and muttered their understanding.

"All right. Let's go to war!"

The army cheered, and Ripper told General Stupid to turn around. "March! Destroy everything that doesn't move!"

General Stupid began to slowly step forward again, and the rest of the robots followed. The Wilides and Gangers ran along beside or behind the robots, yelling and shaking their weapons in the air.

In his mind he played Lord Algon's death over and over, the pleasure like a fine glass of wine he'd just drunk. It felt so good to kill people! And then he'd scared that gorilla-beastie away, it was as if nothing, no matter how strong or fearsome, could stand in his way. There was no way Johnny could stop him now, was there? Of course not! So why did he still feel that nagging worry that somehow Johnny would still find a way to win?

He couldn't wait, simply couldn't wait, to stand over Johnny's dead body. Then, finally, he could relax. Even then, he imagined Johnny would find a way to come back from the dead and get revenge. What was wrong with him, was he going crazy? He began to wonder if his obsession with Johnny was affecting his mind.

He decided he needed a distraction. He looked around from his perch on General Stupid's shoulders and saw an old, metal bus on the side of the road.

"Hey Stupid, blow that up!" Ripper pointed. General Stupid stopped, making all the other robots stop as well. He turned his head to aim and then shot a missile from his arm. It hit the bus and exploded, making the bus fly into the air in pieces.

"Yes!" Ripper said, shaking his fist. "That was awesome."

"Two missiles remaining."

"What?" Ripper said, irritated. "Why didn't you tell me you only had so many missiles?"

"You did not ask."

"So, do you have any more?"

"There is a supply-"

"Let me guess. Back at that dump you came from."

"Correct."

"Do the rest of your stupid metal junkheaps have missiles too?"

"Five are equipped with surface missiles. Six have surface to air missiles. Two are equipped with phosphorous grenades. Two have sleeping gas cannisters. The last five have lasers."

Ripper felt a headache coming on. These robots were more trouble than he expected. "From now on, keep track of what you got. And before you shoot something, let me know who's doing it, and what…" Ripper thought about what he was saying. Even talking about it was making his head hurt. "Forget it. Just don't shoot anything unless I tell you to."

"As you wish, Mr. President. For your information, I am at 52 percent energy."

"No!" Ripper said. It would just be Ripper's luck to get to Johnny and have all the robots die from lack of juice. *That was how Johnny could win,* he thought. It was almost as if there had to be something, and now he'd found it.

"So how do you recharge?" Ripper asked.

"There are recharging stations back at the Pentagon in the Executive Underground Shelter," General Stupid said.

Great, all the way back where they'd come from, Ripper thought. And what if the robots died half way there?

"What happens if you die on the way to that place?" Ripper asked.

"There are portable recharge units, but they have not

been used in over a century. They are currently out of charge."

"Great. Okay. Just don't do anything you don't have to. Save your energy for the fight. And that goes for your robot army, too. From now on nobody do nothing but march!"

Ripper settled back, not happy at all. But then he saw something that made him very happy. Ahead, the dark outline of the wall of cars the Tribe had made came into view. The battle was about to start. He gripped General Stupid's head with his hands, so excited he could barely sit still. It wouldn't be long before he enjoyed his revenge.

CHAPTER 22

Johnny, Starbucks, Misterwizard and Foodcourt stood alone on the wall, watching and waiting. The rest of the Tribe returned to New Sanctuary where they busied themselves gathering weapons and hiding, hoping Johnny and Misterwizard found a way so the robots never reached them.

It was daylight now and they could see the robots well, even though they seemed far away. They were golden in color and tall, their bodies shaped like tin cans stuck together. They looked terrifying and menacing. Behind them, Ripper's army stood, waiting for the call to advance.

"There's so many of them!" Foodcourt said, sounding somber. "Even without the robots, Ripper has a huge army now."

"Yes, he has amassed a considerable force,"

Misterwizard said. "Hello, what's this?"

Misterwizard put a pair of binoculars that he'd brought from New Sanctuary up to his eyes and peered through them. "Johnny, do you know where your young maidens are at this moment?"

Johnny frowned, wondering what Misterwizard was talking about.

"Look through these binoculars," Misterwizard said, handing them to Johnny. "I'm afraid you may not be pleased at what you see."

Johnny peered through the binoculars. Not sure how to use them, it took him a moment to realize they made everything look bigger. Then he saw the robots, just as if they were right in front of him. And then he saw the girls.

"Oh no! It can't be!" Johnny's face showed the horror he suddenly felt. Inside, despair began to grip him. Things just seemed to be getting worse and worse.

"What is it, Johnny?" Starbucks said.

The girls sat on two robots, one on either side of Ripper and General Stupid. On the ground next to them, two Gangers walked along, keeping an eye on them.

Johnny handed the binoculars to Starbucks, so he could look. When Starbucks saw the girls, his face filled with grief and sadness as well.

"How did he get them?" Johnny said, horrified.

"This changes everything," Starbucks said with dismay. "We can't risk hurting the girls, and if we fight back, Ripper will kill them."

"We have no choice now but to run," Johnny said, disappointment filling his voice. Fear filled his heart for Deb and Super. If Ripper killed them, Johnny knew he'd just as soon die too. Without Deb, life would not be worth living.

"We can't just keep running," Foodcourt said. "Sooner or later, he'll catch up with us."

Johnny turned to Misterwizard, feeling sad. "Maybe there's just too many bad people now, Misterwizard. Maybe we can't build a new country after all."

Misterwizard smiled sadly and patted Johnny's shoulder. "You're not the first good man to have doubts, Johnny. It's not easy fighting for justice and freedom. But evil only triumphs when good people do nothing! We shall win, though it may not come without suffering, loss and heartbreak. History is replete with men suffering and dying for freedom. It's an unfortunate reality that good men often must sacrifice themselves, so others they love can live free. Anything worth fighting for is worth the sacrifice. We may suffer. We may die. We may experience death and dismemberment. But fight on we must, for the sake of our country and our progeny!"

"What's a progeny?" Cinnabon asked.

"Not now" Starbucks said. "The robots are moving again!"

Johnny and the rest looked. The steady tramping sound of the robots' feet came again. They marched towards Johnny and his friends, getting closer every second.

"Well, this is it," Johnny said. "We need to leave before they see us."

Suddenly Johnny heard a familiar sound, one that made his heart jump with joy, but also filled his mind with worry. It was Deecee's bark! Where was he? Was he in the path of the robots?

Johnny and the others looked around. Then they saw Deecee! Johnny smiled, happy to see his dog-beastie friend back. Deecee saw Johnny up on the wall and barked happily at him. Then Johnny looked at the robots. They were almost to the other side of the old Capitol building. Deecee saw them too and ran towards them.

"No!" Johnny said desperately. "Deecee, come back!"

But Deecee was too far away to hear. He ran until he was twenty feet in front of the robots and crouched. He snarled and barked at the robots.

"Deecee!" Johnny yelled, cupping his hands to his mouth to try and be heard over the din of the robots. "Deecee, get back here!"

The robots saw Deecee. Johnny watched helplessly as every robot stopped, including General Stupid. Their heads all turned to look at Deecee. Ripper, who had been looking at the wall of cars ahead anticipating its destruction with glee, noticed the sudden lack of movement. He looked down at General Stupid.

"Hey!" He yelled.

He heard Deecee's bark and looked over at him. Then he turned around as best as he could and looked at the other robots. He looked back at General Stupid.

"Hey! It's just a dumb dog-beastie. Keep moving, Stupid!"

"Hi Deecee!" Deb yelled, waving from her perch on the robot.

Deecee barked happily in reply.

"Deecee, can you bite this thing?" Super yelled.

General Stupid's voice emanated from its voice-box in a flat, menacing tone. "A Wild Animal Infestation. Executive Order 411 E Eliminate all wild animal infestations to restore order."

As Johnny yelled, General Stupid fired a rocket. The area where Deecee stood exploded and the air filled with smoke and flying debris.

"No! Deecee!" Johnny yelled. Johnny, Misterwizard and the others stared at the flame and smoke, trying to see if Deecee was dead.

There was a moment of silence, as they all held their breath. Then somewhere in the smoke and flame, they heard a familiar bark.

Johnny was relieved but still terrified for his dog-beastie. "Deecee, get out of there!"

The smoke cleared, and they saw Deecee. He had moved behind a broken stone pillar when General Stupid fired. Now he came out again and barked at the robot again and wagging his tail, as if it was all a game.

General Stupid and all the other robots turned and marched towards Deecee. Deeceee, barked again and took off running. The robots stomped after him.

"Stop!" Ripper yelled. "Why aren't you stopping! Stupid!" Ripper beat on General Stupid's head, but the robot didn't seem to even notice, it just kept marching after the dog-beastie.

"Johnny, look!" Foodcourt said. "Deecee is leading the robots away!"

"He's giving us a chance to escape!" Starbucks said happily.

Johnny was afraid for Deecee, but even more for Deb and Super. "But what about Deb and Super?"

Starbucks frowned, remembering. "Maybe this is our chance to save them."

"At least the people will be safe in New Sanctuary,"

Starbucks said.

"No, they won't," Johnny said, frowning. "Ripper knows we live there. Like Misterwizard said, the robots look like they're able to destroy buildings with the rockets they shoot. We have to find another place where Ripper won't find us until we can find a way to destroy them."

"Where can we take them?" Starbucks asked.

Johnny had been thinking about that already. "To the Undergrounders."

"Yes!" Foodcourt said, nodding his head. "It is a place that Ripper knows nothing about."

"But it will only work if he doesn't see the Tribe going there," Johnny said.

Misterwizard nodded, stroking his short beard.   "A very novel and ingenious solution. And I have come up with a possible way to counteract our enemy's new metal allies. It may not succeed, but I believe it is worth expending the effort in the attempt. It involves a device that, while I have never actually fabricated, I believe I have the parts to create. The largest detriment is the time it will take to bring it to fruition."

"Where's fruition?" Johnny asked.

Misterwizard chuckled. "It is not a place, Johnny, but a goal. The object I will create is called an EMP. It stands for Electro-magnetic Pulse."

"Electro..." Johnny tried to repeat what Misterwizard said.

"It is a device which can render mechanisms that run on electricity inert, for a brief time. It dampens the electrical field, making the movement of electrons impossible for a short duration."

Johnny shook his head, not even trying to

understand. "How long will it take you to make it, Misterwizard?"

Misterwizard scratched his head and scrunched up his eyes, deep in thought. "There lies the conundrum, Johnny. If I were back at Castle in our old city of Philadelphia, I could make it in a matter of a few hours. Here in Washington D.C. it will take me that long just to find the components necessary to fabricate it."

"All the way back to Philadelphia?" Johnny said, dismayed. "Can you get there and back in time?"

"If I go fast, it could only take me a few hours. I'll need a very fast mode of transportation."

Johnny knew what Misterwizard was thinking. He wanted to use Johnny's Harley. He wondered if Misterwizard could ride it, and then he remembered Misterwizard had taught him.

"My Harley is on the street on the other side of the Mall."

"Splendid!" Misterwizard said with a smile. "I've always desired an opportunity to experience the adrenaline rush that is created by the speed and innate sense of danger riding a motorcycle creates! I will go at once!"

"And me and Johnny will go see if we can save the girls."

Johnny looked at Foodcourt. "Dad, can you help sneak the Tribe out of New Sanctuary? I'd help, but-"

"I understand, Johnny. You must save your lovely ladies. I will do my best. I will have to do it quickly, before Ripper and his robots return!" Foodcourt took off down the ramp as fast as he could run.

"Oh, oh," Johnny said, looking on the other side of the Capitol building. "We talked too long. The robots are coming back!"

Johnny was right. Ripper had finally gotten the robots to stop pursuing Deecee. They marched back towards the Capitol. When they reached it, the turned towards the wall again.

"I'm off for Philadelphia!" Misterwizard said, and he ran down the ramp on his short stubby legs.

"And we need to find a place to hide so we can rescue Deb and Super," Starbucks said.

Johnny and Starbucks ran down the ramp too. The top of the wall was empty as the robots approached.

Ripper finally managed to get the robots to stop pursuing the stupid dog-beastie. It ran around a building and disappeared, but it still took Ripper a long time to convince General Stupid to stop chasing it.

What finally worked was when Ripper pounded on General Stupid's head and yelled, "I am President! Obey me!" The robot stopped climbing over piles of rubble and seemed to listen to his commands again. Ripper wondered if the years sitting in that old building had broken something inside General Stupid's head. What would he do if the robot suddenly went mad and attacked him? Ripper decided not to think about that possibility too hard.

He led the robots back to the old Capitol building and finally they faced the wall of cars the Tribe had constructed.

Meanwhile, Misterwizard hurried over to Johnny's Harley, which was parked on the street behind a building on the right side of the Mall on the street where Johnny and his friends went exploring. Misterwizard beamed with pleasure as he looked it over, excited at getting to ride it. He climbed on with a happy chortle and bounced up and down on the leather seat, grabbing the handlebars.

Misterwizard looked silly in his green army shorts and green army coat on, a round little bald man with a white beard sitting on a big, shiny Harley. He made himself look even sillier when he pulled a pair of goggles from the handlebars and fit them over his eyes. He turned the Harley on and turned the throttle on the handle. The bike roared to life. Soon the engine puttered loudly.

"Ha ha!" Misterwizard said, "This is living! I must see to the procurement of one of these for my own use, when things finally reach a peaceful plateau. My little Moped does not create the same sense of elation."

Misterwizard took a cigar out of his pocket and shoved it between in his teeth. He turned the throttle on the bike and the Harley began to move. He turned the Harley around, so it was pointed towards the broken stick building, the direction of Philadelphia.

Looking towards Johnny, who was somewhere trying to save Deb and Super. "We will meet again, Johnny, one more meeting of the type we have so often. From the frying pan into the fire, and out again!"

Misterwizard took off in a roar, creating a cloud of dust. In a few seconds he was gone.

CHAPTER 23

Foodcourt ran into New Sanctuary, puffing and out of breath. Everyone ran to the entrance to greet him, many holding rocket launchers, rifles and explosives.

"Where's Johnny?" Carny asked. "What are we going to do?"

Foodcourt looked at them, his hands up in front of him. "Listen, everyone. We aren't safe here. Ripper will simply destroy this place with us in it."

Everyone started talking at once in scared voices. Foodcourt yelled to quiet them down and be heard. "But! But we have a place we can go. As long as Ripper doesn't see us leave, we can hide there until Johnny comes up with a plan."

"Where?" Cinnabon asked, putting the question they all wondered to words.

Foodcourt looked at them, trying to be ready for their

reaction. "The Undergrounders' place."

His words created a new panic, just as he thought it would.

"We barely know them!" One woman wailed.

"They're cannibals, aren't they?" A man said, his voice full of fear.

"Weren't there some other monsters down there that they were afraid of?" Another woman said.

"Listen to me!" Foodcourt said, and finally everyone stopped talking. "Johnny suggested it. And if it wasn't safe, he wouldn't have. We have no choice. Now get ready to move, fast! We have to leave before Ripper gets here. Everybody out the back door!"

There was a rush for the back door. Carny, Teavana, Thegap and Bathandbody works stayed behind and gathered around Foodcourt.

Foodcourt looked at them. "Somebody should stay to make it look like the Tribe is here."

Teavana grabbed her husband's arm. "No, Foodcourt! You'll be killed!"

"Don't worry, Teavana," Foodcourt said, gazing at her with an affectionate smile. "I'll be careful. And I'll leave before they can do anything."

"You realize that they're likely to destroy the Museum," Bathandbodyworks said.

Abercrombie and Microsoft joined them. "Oh, what a shame!" Abercrombie said. "This beautiful place destroyed!"

"Ripper doesn't care much for beauty," Lady Stabs said. "All he cares about is killing."

They didn't realize Lady Stabs had stayed too. They all nodded in agreement.

"You can't do it alone." They all looked to see who

spoke, and they were surprised to see it was round, short Thegap, Deb's father. He wore a look of determination. Bathandbodyworks walked up and hugged him, looking worried.

"Whatever we do, we have to do it fast!" Foodcourt said. "Teavana, you, Abercombie and Bathandbodyworks are going to have to lead the Tribe to the Undergrounders' home. Do you know where it is?"

"I think I remember where they came out of," Teavana said. "It's on the street on the other side, behind the buildings."

"Good. Get going, ladies."

"I'm staying here with you too," Lady Stabs said.

Teavana took Foodcourt's hands. "Be careful. And leave as soon as there's danger."

Foodcourt kissed her. "I'll see you soon. Now get going!"

"Fire on that wall!" Ripper yelled, pointing.

Three of the robots raised their arms. Their hands popped up and three rockets sped towards the car wall. Three explosions erupted in three different places.

Ripper watched with pure enjoyment as the wall of cars collapsed backwards with a loud crash. Some of the cars burned from the rocket fire, smoke pouring from their interiors out their broken windows. The cars still stacked up as part of the wall burned too, and soon the whole wall became a sheet of flame. Ripper's men cheered and raised their weapons high. Ripper looked at them and grinned in victory, enjoying the moment. The robots just stood, waiting for more orders.

Ripper pointed a finger forward. "March! Through those holes!"

General Stupid and the robots marched again, with Ripper's army following.

Out a window of New Sanctuary, Foodcourt watched through Misterwizard's binoculars. He saw the robots march through the ragged opening, past the burning cars. They stomped on the cars on the ground and right over them.

Foodcourt looked at Thegap, who stood peering out a window on the other side of the door. "Here they come!"

"Yep!" Thegap said in a high, squeaky voice. His small body shook with fear.

"As soon as they see us, we'll run!" Foodcourt said. "And not a minute later!"

"Yep!" Thegap said again, just as squeaky.

Foodcourt looked through the binoculars. "Any minute now!"

The robots had reachd the middle of the Mall now, marching right for New Sanctuary. The smashed through the old, rotten shacks of the Wildies as if they were tissue paper. The Wildies and Gangers poured through the car wall more slowly, avoiding the burning cars. To Foodcourt there seemed to be hundreds of them, like a hill of ant-beasties.

"I'm going to shoot at them, let them know we're here," Foodcourt said, as he raised his gun. "Maybe with luck I can hit that rotten leader of theirs."

"Okay," Thegap said in a wavery voice. He looked miserable and scared, his round little eyes watching Foodcourt.

Foodcourt used the tip of the gun to smash the glass of the window. The sound of the breaking glass made Thegap jump. He peered out the window again and watched the steady approach of the robots.

Foodcourt stuck the tip of the gun out the window. He put the butt of the gun against his shoulder and squinted through the rifle's scope. He moved the gun until he had Ripper in his sights. Then with a steady and careful aim, he fired.

Teavana, Abercrombie and Bathandbodyworks ran out the back door. They saw the Tribe standing around with wide eyes, waiting. The women passed by the old yellow buses, still sitting where they were when the Tribe arrived.

Teavana and Abercrombie looked at the buses and them at each other, both thinking the same thing.

"Do you think we should take them?" Abercrombie said.

"Yes!" Teavana said. "That'll get us there way faster."

"If they still run," Bathandbodyworks said.

The three of them looked at the buses as the rest of the Tribe waiting behind them, watching. "If they don't work, we'll waste a lot of time trying," Abercrombie said.

Bathandbodyworks looked puzzled and spoke in her raspy voice. "Does anyone know how to drive them besides Foodcourt and Thegap?"

"I guess we'll figure it out," Teavana said, a humorous smile on her long, thin face. "Or die trying. Let's get everybody on board!"

Quickly they spread the word, and the people filed back onto the old yellow buses one more time, again doing it because they were running from Ripper and his Gangers.

"Yay, another bus ride!" Sephie said, as she hopped on the first bus.

After the last person except the girls were aboard, the three gathered by the door of the first bus. The three ladies looked at each other. Inside the buses, the tribe members all talked at once, already creating a din.

Abercrombie looked at Teavana and Bathandbodyworks and said, "So what do you do to make them go?"

Teavana said, "I watched Foodcourt. I think I know. You turn the key to start it. Then you press the pedal on the right of the floor to go, and if you want to stop, you press the pedal on the left."

The ladies smiled at each other. "Sounds easy!" Bathandbodyworks said. They all nodded agreement and headed for a bus.

Abercrombie took the first bus, Teavana the second and Bathandbodyworks the third. Sephie sat in the first row of her mother's bus. She had trouble getting her large, round body up into the driver's seat, but finally managed it. The noise inside from the tribe members' talking was so loud she could barely think.

"Quiet down, everybody!" Abercrombie yelled, and they did, a little. She smiled and looked down and saw the key sticking out of a hole on the panel next to the steering wheel. She reached down with a long, slim hand and turned it, and the engine roared to life. Encouraged by this success, she smiled and looked at the controls. What to do next?

She looked in the mirror on the side of the bus and saw Teavana in the driver's seat behind her. Teavana grabbed a lever and shifted it, and her bus lurched forward, heading right for Abercrombie's!

In a panic Abercrombie grabbed the same lever and pulled it down. The bus lurched and started going backwards! Quickly she shifted it again, and it stopped, but didn't move forward either. She pulled it down one more notch, and this time the bus leapt forward into motion, throwing everybody out of their seats.

"Are you trying to kill us?" Cinnabon, who happened to be in her bus with her son Wheaties said.

"Sorry," Abercrombie said waving her hand. Looking back at Teavana again, she saw her holding onto the big wheel and turning it. The bus seemed to go in the direction Teavana turned. Abercrombie grabbed the wheel and turned it, and just in time for the bus almost hit a concrete pillar. The bus ran over a pile of rock and everyone inside bounced up and down. Soon they were all complaining except Sephie who jumped up and down, having fun.

Abercrombie looked down and saw the two petals on the floor. She stepped on one and the bus sped forward. Everybody yelled. She took her foot off that petal and put it on the other one. The bus came to a screeching halt, and once again everyone was thrown from their seats.

"Sorry," Abercrombie said with a weak smile, as they all yelled at her. "I'm getting the hang of it now."

This was driving? she thought. *It's easy!* She sat back with a grin. *This was going to be fun!*

CHAPTER 24

Ripper sat on General Stupid's shoulders facing New Sanctuary. This was the moment he'd been waiting for. He looked around, enjoying the moment for as long as he could. He gazed at the tall, golden robots lined up in two rows in the grass. He looked at Deb and Super. Johnny's girl, ready to watch his destruction! He looked beyond the robots at his army, loaded with the weapons from the fallout shelter, ready to kill and maim. It was the greatest moment of his life.

He turned and opened his mouth to give the command to fire. And then he heard a gunshot and felt a stinging pain in his arm. He grabbed it and felt himself slipping off General Stupid. His arm exploded in pain as he fell, the world slipping by him.

In an instant he saw a man's face looking out the window of New Sanctuary. He instantly recognized it as Johnny's father Foodcourt. Then he hit the ground with a thud and everything went black.

Johnny and Starbucks watched the robots cross the grass from a building on the far side of the grass. They saw the girls still riding the two robots, looking frightened.

"When are we going to move, Johnny?"

"I don't know. There are a lot of Wildies and Gangers out there. I don't know how we can get them away from the robots and all the way back here without being caught."

"We have to do something soon. When Ripper realizes the Tribe is not inside New Sanctuary, he may decide to take it out on the girls."

"I know. Look at all those weapons Ripper's men have. Where did they get them all?"

"I don't know, but things have never looked so bad before. Why couldn't that jerk just get eaten by the tiger-beastie and save us all a lot of misery?"

"I agree. We'll just have to make sure he's good and dead next time."

Meanwhile, Deb and Super were making plans of their own. Deb looked over at Super and spoke in a quiet voice so only Deb could hear.

"We have to make a run for it, Deb. When the fighting starts, these robots are going to be right in the line of fire."

Deb looked back and shook her head no. "There won't be any fight, as long as we're on these robots. Johnny won't dare letting us get hurt."

Super nodded sadly. "We're just going to have to jump for it and run before that happens."

Deb looked down at the ground. The robot was ten feet tall, and the ground below looked far away. If they jumped, they would risk getting hurt, but there seemed to be no other way.

"When Ripper starts attacking New Sanctuary, that's our chance," Super said. "We jump for it."

Deb nodded. "What about the guards?"

Super looked down at the two Gangers walking along next the robots. They seemed to have forgotten the girls. Instead they looked at New Sanctuary, anticipating the fight, like all the others around them. "We'll just have to take 'em out. We killed the wolf-beastie, we can take them."

The girls looked at each other and nodded.

Johnny and Starbucks could see Ripper and his army were close to New Sanctuary now. It wouldn't be long before they attacked.

"I'm going to stand up," Johnny said.

Starbucks looked at him, wide-eyed. "What for?"

"It's me he wants. Maybe we can end this thing, right here and now."

"He'll kill you!" Starbucks said.

"As long as he lets Deb go, I don't care."

Suddenly a shot rang out. Ripper fell from on top of General Stupid. The robots stopped. Facegash and the rest of Ripper's army ran up to see if he was still alive.

As the shot rang out, the guards watching Deb and Super

ran away. Super saw it first and turned quickly to Deb.

"Now's our chance!"

Without another second, Super lifted her leg over the robot's head, turned around and jumped. Deb saw her and did the same. They both landed on the ground and fell on their faces. Luckily, they were in the grass and it cushioned their fall.

Without even looking back, the girls took off running across the grass towards the other side of the Mall and the broken white buildings there. Halfway across the grass, Deb glanced back. She smiled when she saw no one had even noticed them leaving! She giggled, thinking how much trouble the guards were going to be in when their escape was discovered. Then another thought came to her, one of dark hope. Maybe Ripper was dead! She didn't like wishing harm on someone, but Ripper was an exception.

The girls made it to the nearest building on the other side and disappeared through the open door into the dark, cool interior. They stopped just inside the doorway and peeked out from either side.

"We made it!" Super said, happiness filling her heart. Deb nodded, a big smile on her face.

"And where do you two think you're going?"

Deb and Super looked at each other with dread. They turned around and looked to see who had caught them.

It was Johnny and Starbucks.

Misterwizard sped down the lonely, empty highway littered with cars. The roar of the Harley made the only sound, melancholy in the still morning air. Weaving between the rusted hulks turned this way and that as if thrown on the ground by an angry child, Misterwizard squinted through the goggles, his eyes intense. His short, round body hugged the bike tightly and he gripped the handgrips tight. Being short and the handlebars being long and silver, his arms were almost vertical as he gripped the throttle. The bike was not made for a short person like him, but he made the best of it he could.

A skinny dog-beastie, its ribs showing and with a long snout, trotted out from behind an old car to stare at the strange shiny object roaring down the road. It watched him with sad eyes as he sped past. Then it went back to foraging for scraps.

A deer-beastie leapt onto the road and Misterwizard looked at it with a smile. The animal stood still and watched until he was gone. Then it leapt across the road and disappeared behind the trees.

Misterwizard sped past three Wildies fighting over a blanket. He passed so fast by the time they looked up he was already down the road beyond them. All three stopped and stared at the strange loud thing with a man on it, for a moment forgetting their argument. Then when he was just a dot in the distance they forgot all about him and fought over the blanket again.

Misterwizard grew close to Philadelphia. He smiled, happy to see it again. He looked forward to once again sitting in his own home with all his favorite objects there to comfort him. He knew he wouldn't have much time to enjoy them, for he had to work fast. Still, a cup of tea wouldn't be out of order, and maybe a couple tomatoes from his garden on the roof.

"Open Sesame!" Once more the door to his yard

swung open. He sped in and yelled over his shoulder, "Close Sesame!" The door closed again.

Misterwizard quickly hopped off the Harley and ran inside. The Gangers had trashed his home, knocking things over, smashing other items and using markers to destroy his priceless paintings. He looked on the mess with dismay. "Ruffians!" He thundered. "Hooligans!" He added. "No goodnicks!" He wanted to say more, but he had no time.

He took off the goggles and his hat and set them on a round antique table by a window.

"Tea first!" He said out loud. He ran through the doorway into the room he made into his kitchen. Finding a silver teapot, he filled it from a plastic bottle of water he kept in the corner. The electricity was off, so he started a fire in the old cast iron stove he had as a backup on the corner, its black round chimney pipe leading out the window.

The room filled with smoke, and he coughed. He chided himself. "Flue!" He ran over and flipped a lever and the smoke started to clear.

Putting the tea pot on the top of the stove, he ran back into his main room. "Now. EMP."

Having no "computers," Misterwizard had been forced to go back to old traditional books for his source of learning. On one side of the room bookshelves filled the wall. On the middle shelf an old brown set of encyclopedias sat, fifty volumes.

"E... E..." Misterwizard moved his finger down the spines of the books. 'Electron Gun to Fish Ladder. That's it!"

Misterwizard pulled the large, dark brown book off the shelf. It was heavy, so he had to grab it with both hands. He carried it over to the round table in the middle of the room. The table was covered with maps and drawings. Holding the book awkwardly under one arm, he used the other to sweep all the papers onto the floor. Then he plopped the book down, creating a cloud of dust. He opened it and found the passage on EMPs. Then he began to read, his lips moving as he moved his finger down the text.

Teavana sat in the driver's seat, her thin, frail body looking tiny in the huge chair. Abercrombie sat down to drive the other bus. Her large, round body seemed just the right size.

The buses rolled down the empty street, weaving from side to side. Every few feet one swing so far in one direction it would smash into the side of an old car or even ride up on the sidewalk and hit the side of a building, but then the bus would go back the other way, back on the road, and keep going.

Inside the buses the members of the Tribe hung on for dear life, looking out the windows nervously. In her bus, Abercrombie gripped the big black steering wheel s with both hands and stared out the window, eyes wide and a look of fright on her face.

"This thing just won't go straight!" She yelled over the roar of the engine. "I think it's because of all the junk on the road!"

Sephie, wore a big smile sitting in the front row holding onto Kermit. She yelled, "This is fun!"

Sephie looked like she was having the most fun she'd

ever had.

The buses finally reached the door down into the subway and the Undergrounders home, but at first it looked like they weren't going to stop. As the people in Abercrombies bus saw the entrance getting close, they all yelled at her at once to stop, even Sephie. Panicked, Abercrombie looked at the floor. She pressed the left pedal with all her might, but the bus wasn't stopping! The people yelled so loud Sephie covered her ears. A big wall came rushing up at the front of the bus. Abercrombie yelled, "Hang on!" and once more slammed on the pedal. Finally, the bus slowed down, but too late. With a sickening lurch it struck a wall, and everybody pitched forward, ending up on the floor.

Abercrombie turned around and looked at them all, hands to her face. "I'm so sorry! Is everyone all right? The pedal stopped working!"

Everyone got up groaning. With relief it looked as if no one was too badly hurt. But then Abercrobmie looked out the window. The second bus with Teavana was heading for them, looking as if it wasn't going to stop either. As realization dawned on the rest of the people in the bus, the yelling rose again to a din. They all watched, eyes wide in fear at the other bus.

As they all yelled and watched, the second bus barely missed them and drove on past. They all looked through the side windows to see the people on the second bus peering at them, looking just as terrified as they'd been. As they watched, the second bus finally stopped on a pile of rock and rubble, looking as if it was going to tip over at any second.

Abercrombie opened the door, and everyone rushed to get out, as if their lives depended on it. "Slow!"

Abercrombie yelled. "Don't trample each other!"

Finally, everyone was off the bus except Abercrombie in the driver's seat and Sephie, who was smart enough to stay put in her seat. Abercrombie slumped down and closed her eyes, exhausted from the ordeal. She felt a small, soft hand in hers. She looked up to see Sephie standing next to her, a big grin on her face.

"You did good, Mommy!"

Abercrombie smiled at her and put a hand on her cheek. "Thank you, Darling. But I'm not sure everyone in who rode with us might agree."

They laughed and then Abercrombie led Sephie lead her off the bus, holding her hand.

Ripper woke up to see Facegash and a group of Wildies staring down at him. His arm felt wet and it throbbed. After his mind ceared, he looked at his arm. He saw a small round hole in the middle of his forearm. Blood poured from it. Someone shot him!

He jumped up, enraged. He gritted his teeth and stared with absolute hatred at New Sanctuary. He pointed at it. "General Stupid, fire at that building. Every robot fire everything you have! Knock it to the ground!"

"As you wish, Mr. President."

The robots raised their arms to fire.

CHAPTER 25

Foodcourt watched Ripper fall off General Stupid with glee. "I got him!"

Thegap and Lady Stabs smiled from their positions at the other windows. "You sure did," Thegap said.

"I hope he's dead," Lady Stabs said.

They all waited, watching Ripper as he lay on the ground, holding their breath, hoping he didn't get back up. But then he did.

"Blast him!" Foodcourt said, as he saw Ripper cradle his bleeding arm. "I only winged him."

"Oh, oh," Lady Stabs said, as she saw Ripper say something to the robot in the green coat next to him. "I think it's time for us to leave."

All three jumped down and took off running, just in time. The front of the building exploded, sending debris flying inwards in a shower of dangerous rock and metal.

Foodcourt, Thegap and Lady Stabs hurried to the back door. Behind them they heard explosions that made their ears ring. They felt the ground shake from the impact of the missiles.

"Such a shame!" Foodcourt, said, looking at the building sadly as they ran out the back door. They ran across the street and hid in the doorway of a building and watched the beautiful museum be destroyed. It shuddered and shook, and finally, as if surrendering, the roof collapsed inward. All three watched sadly, their faces glum.

"I really loved that place," Foodcourt said.

"I did too," Lady Stabs said. "That jerk."

"Let's get out of here before he sees us," Thegap said.

Slowly and reluctantly the trio walked away, not looking back.

General Stupid fired his missiles. Soon all the robots fired their missiles, lasers and bombs. The first missile hit New Sanctuary and the wall exploded. Another hit and another. The wall crumbled and the pillars out front fell.

As Ripper watched with joy, the roof collapsed, falling inward. Dust rose in a giant cloud, billowing out until it enveloped Ripper, the robots and his army. Ripper closed his eyes and his mouth as the dust covered him. He coughed, not expecting such a large dust cloud.

Suddenly it was hard to breathe, and he bent over. The wound on his arm filled with dust, making it hurt more.

Finally, Ripper looked up as the dust cleared. He smiled. The whole building was destroyed, lying in a pile of rubble. The Wildies and Gangers cheered, and Ripper laughed. Take that, Johnny!

Ripper looked and saw something strange. Some of his men lay on the ground. "What's wrong with them?" Ripper asked General Stupid, pointing.

"They must have been close enough to be exposed to the sleeping gas some of the robots deployed."

"Sleeping what?" Ripper said, frowning. Then he shrugged. "Whatever." It was only a few men, and he really didn't care about them. Then he noticed something else he did care about! Johnny's girl and the other girl were gone!

Ripper cursed in frustration. Why did something always go wrong whenever he was trying to enjoy his victory? Now they'd spoiled his great moment. Rather than enjoying seeing Johnny and the Tribe destroyed, now he had to instead waste time punishing the guards who were supposed to watch the girls.

He stomped over, frustration and anger making him so mad he could barely walk. He found the guards who were supposed to be watching the girls.

Shaking so bad he could barely talk he pointed at the robots who had been carrying the girls. "Where are they?" he said to the guards.

They looked terrified and contrite. They fell to their knees in front of him. "We're sorry, Your Majesty. We were worried about you. We left to see you were all right. Please forgive us."

Still so mad his words came out in choppy bits Ripper turned to General Stupid. "Shoot them! Shoot them both!"

Everyone turned to General Stupid, expecting to watch the guards die. But General Stupid just stood there.

"I cannot, master."

This wasn't happening!

"Why not?" Ripper stammered out.

"You told us to fire everything at the building. We have no more ammunition."

"Gaah!" Ripper stomped around in a circle, frustrated beyond tolerance. He fumed and stamped his feet on the ground. What to do now? He looked at the guards, his face dark with evil. "Then pick them up and throw them, as far as you can."

"No, please have mercy!" One of the guards said. The other was smarter. He stood up and took off running.

"Don't let him get away!" Ripper said, feeling as if no one was doing what he wanted them to.

General Stupid stomped after the fleeing guard, but he was so slow, the guard was halfway across the grassy Mall before the robot had gone ten feet.

"Come back!" Ripper called out, waving his hand, so mad now his head hurt. His stomach ached, and his arm throbbed in pain. Nothing was going the way he wanted it to!

General Stupid turned and stomped back. The other guard, seeing what the first guard did, jumped up and took off running too. Ripper jumped up and down. "You stupid robots! You're worthless!"

The second guard disappeared behind the rubble of New Sanctuary.

Ripper sighed. Facegash, the Wildies and the Gangers stood around looking at him. Ripper realized he began to look foolish. He had to get control of himself. Standing up tall, he scowled. Then he looked at New Sanctuary and smiled. He'd all but forgotten. He'd just killed Johnny and the whole Tribe.

All thoughts of the girls or the guards disappeared, as he thought of how he was going to get to see Johnny's lifeless body.

He walked towards the rubble pile, a big grin on his face, like a child about to open a present. Facegash and the army walked forward too. It was an impressive sight. Half of the roof remained intact, lying on the pile of rock that had been the walls. The whole pile smoldered, smoke rising into the bright sunlight.

Ripper laughed, an insane sound. He leapt up and down, forcing himself to enjoy his victory. He'd really won!

Then he heard a bark. A very annoying bark! It was that stupid dog-beastie again!

He looked to see Deecee standing across the Mall, looking at them. The robots started to turn.

"No!" Ripper yelled quickly. "Do not go after the animal infestation!"

The robots stopped. "Ignore it, you stupid, annoying piles of junk!"

Ripper pointed to the pile of rubble. He looked up at General Stupid. "What I want you to do is pick this pile up, rock by rock, until you find the bodies. Then show each one to me until I find the body of Johnny Apocalypse."

"As you wish, Master."

The robots advanced on the rock pile to obey.

Deb ran and jumped into Johnny's arms. Johnny pulled her close. She put her head on his shoulders as he hugged her tight, eyes closed, joy filling his heart.

Super sauntered over to Starbucks and grinned at him. "Miss me?"

"Like a bad tooth," Starbucks said. Then they smiled at each other, took hands and kissed.

"I missed you, that's for sure," Johnny said. Deb lifted her head up and kissed Johnny. He kissed her back, deliriously happy after being afraid he'd lost her.

Starbucks grinned at Johnny and Deb, his arm around Super's waist. "Uh, maybe we should get out of here."

They all laughed and walked towards the back door of the building, away from the grassy Mall and New Sanctuary where Ripper and his army stood.

Deb frowned and looked at Johnny. "He's going to destroy New Sanctuary, Johnny! Everyone will be killed!"

"They're not there," Johnny said.

Deb frowned with confusion.

Starbucks said, "They're going to the Undergrounder's place to hide, until Misterwizard comes back with a thing he's making that will stop the robots."

"Is that what those things are?" Super said, as they reached the back door of the building. The metal door hung crooked on one hinge. Johnny swung it open cautiously. It creaked loudly, and he winced.

"That's what Misterwizard called them," Johnny said.

"The Undergrounders?" Deb asked. "What about the Rat People? They're still down there."

Johnny shrugged. "We don't have much choice. Those robots are powerful. We can't fight them."

When it seemed clear, the four snuck out the door

onto the back porch of the building. A small stairway of three stone steps led to the sidewalk and beyond it was the street. Most of the old cars that had been on the street were gone, used for the car wall. What was left was an empty ribbon of gray, stretching in both directions.

"Well, I guess we join them, for now," Starbucks said.

"There's not much cover," Johnny said. He pointed across the street. "Let's go over there to that building and try to stay in the shadows."

An explosion rocked the air from somewhere behind them. They turned towards the sound. They knew it was Ripper destroying New Sanctuary.

"That rotten creep," Deb said, a sad look of regret on her face.

"I sure hope you get to give him what he deserves, Johnny," Super said.

"Let's just get out of here before he realizes you girls are gone."

With that, the heroes took one more look to make sure the coast was clear then darted across the street, on their way to the Undergrounder's.

Ripper waited impatiently, pacing back and forth for the robots to finish sifting through the rubble of New Sanctuary. He looked up to see how far they had gotten, saw they were still working, and then looked down again and went back to pacing. His army stood around, looking bored.

Ripper had a new bandage around his arm where

he'd been shot, and the wound ached so much it made his teeth hurt. This wasn't the way it was supposed to go! Why did his victory seem so unexciting, so anti-climactic? He just killed Johnny and his whole Tribe. Why didn't he feel happy?

Then he realized why the victory seemed so hollow. He never got to see Johnny's face before he died. He didn't get to see him sad and full of fear. And he didn't get to see the annoying old man die either. It was a clumsy way to kill them, and he wished he could do it over, make it more dramatic.

The robots were so slow! They would pick up one rock, slowly turn around, walk away from the building and drop it. Then ponderously turn around and go back. Ripper worried the work would use up all their power. This victory was turning out to be a bust!

General Stupid stomped over to him.

"What is it?" Ripper asked irritably.

"We have finished removing enough debris to determine there are no human remains."

Ripper couldn't believe it. His mouth fell open and a blank look came over his face.

He stomped up to stand right in front of General Stupid and craned his neck, so he could look up at his face. With fists on his hips he said, "What? You, stupid piece of junk! Don't you know a dead body when you see it?"

"Affirmative. There are no dead bodies present."

Ripper screamed. He was so angry he walked around in circles yelling. Why did everything have to be so hard? No bodies meant the Tribe escaped! Johnny escaped. His girlfriend escaped! It was just like Ripper feared, somehow Johnny was winning! His head started to hurt.

He put a fist on it and tried to think.

Wait, he thought. That means I have another chance to kill him, in a better way. But what if he wins, a small weak voice in his head said? He won't, he told himself, though with less conviction than before.

As if to annoy Ripper even more, Facegash walked up. "What do we do now, Ripper?"

Ripper turned on him and snarled, "Be quiet and let me think!"

Facegash shrugged and walked away. Ripper stared daggers at him. He hated Facegash. He hated everybody! Where was Johnny and his tribe?

As he tried to think, he heard a strange sound off in the distance. It was rumbling sound, like a motor running. It was barely audible, as if it came from far away. He looked up and realized it came from behind the buildings on the other side of the grassy Mall.

"What's that?" Ripper asked.

Facegash shrugged.

"Go find out, Stupid."

The robot started moving towards the sound.

"Not you, Stupid, I meant this stupid." Ripper pointed at Facegash.

Facegash ran across the Mall and down the side of the building until he could see the street beyond. Then he ran back, close enough to yell at Ripper.

"It's the old man! On a bike!"

"Well, follow him!" Ripper said, excited. "Find out where he's going!"

Ripper turned to the robots and his army. He pointed towards Facegash. "Everybody, go that way!"

Then he took off running.

CHAPTER 26

Misterwizard sped along, a big smile on his face, enjoying the feel of the wind on his face and the heat from the Red Eye on his back. He thought what a pleasant day it was. If not for the ongoing conflict and threat of imminent death, it would be a good day to simply ride around and explore.

On the way to his old castle, he had enjoyed driving recklessly, doing circles and running up onto sidewalks. Now, with the fragile device strapped to the seat behind him, he was very careful to drive straight and avoid any bumps. A square box two feet tall and wide, it had wires on top and sides of metal. It was the second one Misterwizard made. The first one he used as a test, and it worked well, shutting down all the electronic equipment in his castle that he had just fixed and got working again This second one was set and ready to go. He just hoped it would be powerful enough to shut down twenty-one large robots.

He drove down the empty streets of Washington D.C. feeling the pleasant rumble of the powerful Harley beneath him. The streets were mostly empty, all paper trash from the world before long disintegrated. All that was left were the old rusted hulks of car, old rusted mailboxes and the occasional empty frames of old streetcars. He reflected how everything around him, the cars, buildings, even the street, seemed white and washed of all color, like old bones bleached in the sun. Here and there the concrete beneath the bike was cracked and grass sprouted up. Other places the street was broken entirely, and one half of the street sunk lower than the other half. It made riding down the road a tricky endeavor, for if he wasn't watchful, he could run over a small tree in the road or a dip and crash, a very unpleasant prospect.

To Misterwizard the road's roughness was a challenge, and he made a game out of weaving around, finding a safe route. He'd grown so good at it he could move fast over small dips in the road or around junk cars. If he hadn't been on such an important mission, he would have liked to simply ride around all day, seeing what tricky roads he could discover.

He was feeling so good, in fact, he totally forgot to be cautious as he drew close to New Sanctuary. He motored along the street next to the buildings opposite the grassy field, thinking about making sure he didn't drive into the hole Deb and Super fell into. He watched the ground, trying to make sure to see it before it came on him suddenly. He was so intent on watching the road, he didn't see Facegash standing next to the building watching him as he sped by. Nor did he see Facegash run back towards New Sanctuary. He simply kept on going, weaving around rocks and broken pieces of buildings, speeding up and slowing down to keep from falling.

He saw the hole and smiled, glad to have seen it before he fell in. It was not easy to spot, for the road curved and hid the hole from view of the side he was on. The road here had collapsed in many places. He could see how the girls could have been caught unawares when it broke away under their feet. *It was fortunate they hadn't been hurt worse than they were,* he thought. He slowed down to be sure his weight didn't cause more of the road to fall away, and carefully wove his way along a sidewalk on one side until he was well past the jagged opening.

As they all piled out of the buses, the people of the Tribe were greeted by bright sunshine and heat from the Red Eye. It was a beautiful, sunny day and as they realized no one was seriously hurt, they all cheered up and began laughing and talking.

Teavana, Bathandbodyworks and Abercrombie met and smiled at each other. Abercrombie nodded at the buses. "That was easy."

Teavana grinned. "No, it wasn't."

All three laughed. Then they turned and looked at the foreboding entrance into the subway where the Undergrounders lived. A rounded tunnel of glass and steel led to a black hole with no door, for Johnny had blown the door off when he led the Undergrounders out. The black hole looked dark and foreboding. Now that the ordeal of the bus ride was over, and everyone had recovered, their thoughts turned to what they had to do next. The cheerful talk changed to whispered tones full of worry and fright.

Teavana looked at Abercrombie and Bathandbodyworks. "Well, I guess we're the leaders now." Abercrombie and Bathandbodyworks each nodded with smiles of determination. Teavana walked down the glass tunnel, waving her hand for everyone to follow.

Talking excitedly in quiet voices the people of the Tribe all followed her. Sephie walked along holding her mother Abercrombie's hand. When they reached the entrance into the subway Teavana stopped. Everyone looked at her with worried expressions.

"Do we really have to go down there?" Cinnabon asked, holding Wheatie's hand.

"It's going to be all right," Teavana said. "The Undergrounders live there all the time. It's either join them, or… " she didn't finish her sentence, knowing they all knew what she meant.

"But we don't have any way to see," Carny said, holding Miracle. "How are we supposed to walk in the dark?"

"We will just have to see what's inside we can use," Abercrombie said, interrupting. "It's better than being blown up by robots."

The people all started talking again, mostly in agreement.

"We'll go in two rows. I'll lead the way," Teavana said. "If I see a problem, I'll yell, 'stop!' Then everybody stop moving, until I figure out what it is."

"I don't like this," Wheaties said. "It's dark and scary

in there."

"Don't be afraid," Sephie said to him, smiling. "Johnny and Deb went down there. We'll just pretend we're as brave as them."

Wheatie scowled at her, not liking taking advice from a girl. "You think you're so brave. Let's see you go first then."

Sephie stood up tall. "Okay." She went over and took Teavana's hand. She looked up at her and said, "Let's go."

Everyone laughed and pointed. Teavana smiled at Sephie, and together they started down the entrance. Carny followed next with Miracle. Abercrombie waited to the end to make sure everyone made it. Then she too descended into the darkness.

The Tribe followed Teavana, Sephie Abercrombie and Bathandbodyworks as they led the way into the dark tunnel, each holding a flickering torch. The walls of the passageway were covered with square yellow tiles about a foot in size. Age and dust had faded them until they were almost white. Ragged paper posters adorned the walls as well, faded and rotted so that they seemed sinister, even though they showed smiling people on them or happy scenes.

It was cold in the tunnel, and the air was stale. The flickering torches made dancing shadows on the walls, causing the people in the old posters to seem to come alive. The people of the Tribe gazed around, half crouching, eyes open wide with fear, as if the people in the poster were going to come alive and grab them.

"How far do we have to go?" One old man with white hair, a long face and big eyes asked in a high-pitched voice.

"Are you sure there aren't monsters waiting for us inside?" A woman, short and round in an old dress and shawl asked.

Miracle lay in Carny's arms. She coughed. Carny looked at her with a worried look. Then she looked at Teavana and said, "I don't think this air is good for Miracle, mother."

Teavana looked at her granddaughter in Carny's arms, concern on her face as well. "Poor baby. We'll have to be sure to bundle her up warm and keep him away from any water."

Cinnabon held Wheaties' hand so tight, he hit her arm to make her loosen her grip. "How long does this stupid tunnel go?" Cinnabon said.

They passed by the half- buried statue of Lincone and all stared at it in amazement. The hole leading up to the museum was now filled with dirt and rock, caused by the explosions from the robots.

"Who's that?" Abercrombie said out loud, looking at the statue of a man sitting in a chair with a beard.

"I don't know," Teavana said. "But he looks like he was someone important."

They reached the edge of the platform. The torches shone only a little way into the darkness, revealing what looked like a dark abyss in front of them. Suddenly a white face appeared out of the darkness and everyone in the tribe shrieked in fear, except Teavana. Even Abercrombie and Bathandbodyworks made a scared sound and backed up a few feet. Teavana just smiled. It was Slon, the leader of the Undergroudners.

He smiled when he saw them and turned his head to yell back at his people in an excited and happy voice. "The People of Johnny are here!"

Out of the darkness, more white faces appeared, like ghosts floating on the air. All wore smiles of pleasure, and their friendly faces made the people of the tribe relax and smile back. Slowly their fear dissipated, and they seemed to relax.

Loki ran up and Teavana turned to him and spoke, rather than to Slon.

"Hello, Loki!"

A young, slim girl walked up next to Loki. It was Harp. She took Loki's hand, and Teavana saw Loki had found a girlfriend.

Loki smiled back. "Guess what? We have found a way to join you in the Bright World." Loki held up his black piece of cloth to show her. He put it over his eyes to demonstrated.

Teavana frowned, and was about to answer, when Sephie did it for her.

"We're here to join you! Some bad robots are after us!"

The smiles on the faces of the Undergrounders turned to frowns of concern. Slon scowled with anger. "What does the little one mean?"

Teavana looked at him. "Do you remember the battle we fought with the evil men above?"

Slon nodded, still frowning, as if knowing he wasn't going to like what she said next.

"An even more evil man, one who caused us to come to this land, has joined them. And he has found some giant machines to help him try and destroy us."

Sephie cut in. "So, we're coming down here to hide."

The Undergrounders whispered to each other in fright. Loki and Harp looked at each other and then back at Teavana. Slon shook with anger and pointed a finger at the Tribe.

"You brought this on us. We were safe, until your kind came and opened the door to the World. Now we will all die, because of you!"

Teavana's eyes narrowed as she grew angry herself. "As I recall from Deb and Super, you were not safe at all, but about to be eaten by the Rat People. And you were dying down here in this festering dark hole, without light or hope. If you'd like to stay down here, that is fine with us. But for now, we need to stay here with you, just long enough for my son to come up with a plan to save us."

Slon's lip curled as he prepared to give her a sharp answer, but Loki stepped forward and extended a hand. "Welcome to our home. We are happy to see you again."

Teavana smiled at Loki as Slon sputtered, feeling as if his authority had been taken from him once again.

Bathandbodyworks stepped forward and pointed a finger at the Undergrounders, her big nose seeming even larger in the torchlight. "Listen to this. What happens to us, happens to you. We're all in this together. So, straighten up!"

Teavana turned to her and said in a diplomatic fashion, "I'm sure they understand that, Bathandbodyworks. We are stronger together, not apart. Slon, being a great and wise leader, understands that, I'm sure."

Slon stood up taller and smiled, glad someone recognized his authority. "Yes, I suppose it's true. Though there isn't much room down here, or food. And it won't be long until the Rat People attack again. And the water continues to rise. Soon, the whole village will be covered with water."

"We'll just have to come up with a plan before that happens," Teavana said. "Won't we, Slon?"

Slon didn't answer, wondering what she was up to.

Teavana looked at Loki. "Loki, we can't see down here as well as you and your people."

"Don't worry," Harp said, "we'll light the torches."

Slon narrowed his eyes. "Those are only for-"

"Special occasions," Harp finished for him. "What's more special than a visit from our friends?"

Slon looked angry again but didn't argue.

Harp stepped forward and took Teavana's hand. "Let us show you our village. It isn't much, but it's where we live."

Teavana nodded graciously and let Harp lead her to the stairs leading down onto the track area. The rest of the Tribe followed, talking and pointing at the walls and ground. Slon stood back and let them pass, his eyes dark and angry. Then he spoke.

"Wait! Where are the angels? And where is Johnny?"

Teavana stopped and turned. Everyone grew quiet and looked at her, waiting for her response.

"Johnny is out looking for the 'angels,' Deb and Super. Starbucks is with them."

Slon's eyes narrowed. "What are you not telling us?"

The Undergrounders all waited for her answer.

"The robots captured Deb and Super."

The tunnel exploded with frightened voices as the Undergrounders reacted to this news. Slon nodded, as if he was somehow proved right.

"And where is the short old man with the beard who

was so smart, your Misterwizard?"

"He has gone to find a way to fight the robots. When he returns, we will have a way to destroy them, hopefully."

Slon looked unconvinced. "A lot of hopefullys and maybes."

"Johnny will win," Loki said. "He's a hero."

Slon snorted. "We'll see."

Johnny, Starbucks, Deb and Super reached a spot where they could see the long awning that led to the door into the Undergrounders' home. Deb smiled. "I'll be glad to see Loki again. I missed him."

Super grinned with dark humor. "I am not looking forward to being in that dark pit again."

Somewhere in the down the street came a sound. They all turned and listened. It was the sound of a Harley!

"Is it-" Deb said.

"It sure is!" Johnny finished. "It's Misterwizard!"

They all smiled with joy, excited.

"Yay! Misterwizard!" Super yelled.

Johnny nodded. "I just hope he was able to make the EMP he talked about."

As he drew close, they saw him hunched down, goggles on, speeding down the road on the bike. When he saw them, he sat up and smiled with joy. He raised a hand and waved. They all waved back, big smiles on their faces. Then they looked up and their smiles disappeared like a small cloud in the sunshine.

Two blocks down the street behind Misterwizard, the

robots marched towards them. Misterwizard had brought the enemy right to their doorstep.

Misterwizard stopped the Harley in front of the tunnel and climbed off, a big smile on his face as seeing his friends. He was especially happy to see Deb and Super safe and sound. He walked over and gave Johnny a big hug, then hugged Starbucks and the girls as well. Then he stood back and smiled at them.

"Well done, Johnny! I see you saved the fair maidens once again!"

Misterwizard noticed neither Johnny or his friends smiled back at him. Sensing something was wrong, he saw they were looking beyond him at something.

He turned and saw the robots.

"Oh my," he said with distress. "I seem to have made a minor error in judgment."

"Did you make the EMP you were talking about, Misterwizard?" Johnny asked.

In answer, Misterwizard walked to the back of the Harley and picked up the box. "Affirmative. It should work very satisfactorily."

"Then it's good they found us," Johnny said.

"How so, Johnny?" Deb asked.

"Because we're going to lead them down into the tunnels and trap them there."

"A capitol battle plan!" Misterwizard said, nodding in appreciation. "Once they are in the tunnels, I will set off my EMP. Then we shall be able to seal them in and have them at our mercy for a change."

"Well, we better do something soon because here they come!" Starbucks said.

Down the middle of the road the robots marched. General Stupid led them with Ripper on his shoulders. Ripper saw them. He grinned, his face dark with evil.

"Let's get inside, fast!" Super said.

They ran down the covered path to the metal door into the subway as the constant thudding of the robots' metal feet grew closer and closer.

"I see them! Now we've got them!" Ripper was so excited he bounced up and down on General Stupid's shoulders. "That must have been where those white weirdos came from! We'll shoot missiles at them and bring the whole place down on them!"

"We have no more missiles, Mr. President."

Ripper frowned, remembering. "Oh yeah. Well, then we'll just have to go in there and you guys can rip them apart." Ripper laughed insanely. "I can't wait!"

From somewhere behind him came a loud whirring sound. Ripper turned to see what it was. One of the robots had stopped moving! "What's wrong with him?" Ripper asked, looking concerned.

"He is out of energy," General Stupid replied.

"No!" Ripper yelled. "Not now!"

"We are all down to less than twenty-five percent."

"Not now! Not now!" Ripper pounded on General Stupid's head.

"We still have an average of two hours operating time."

"Then move it!" Ripper said. "Into that tunnel. And once you get inside, kill everything that moves!"

Inside, Johnny, Misterwizard and their friends were met with a very happy reunion. Both the Tribe and the Undergrounders cheered as soon as they saw the heroes appear, big smiles on their faces. Sephie, as usual ran up and gave Johnny a hug. Teavana also hugged Johnny. Bathandbodyworks was so happy to see her daughter Deb that big tears fell down her cheeks and her big nose ran.

Teavana and Abercrombie held torches made of rags and old sticks. The flames flickered on the faces of everyone there and danced on the walls of the tunnel. Loki and Harp walked up, but rather than greeting Johnny they said hello to Deb and Super first. When Slon saw them, he looked relieved as if a big weight had been removed from his shoulders.

After the welcomes were over, Teavana talked to Johnny. "Johnny, did you see your father Foodcourt anywhere? He and Thegap stayed behind in New Sanctuary to give us a chance to escape."

Johnny shook his head. "No, I'm sorry, Mother."

Sephie said, "Johnny, where are the robots?"

Johnny looked at all the people gathered in front of him with a serious frown. "They're heading this way."

This set off a new panic, and everyone started talking at once. Johnny raised a hand to quiet them.

"But we have a plan to end Ripper's evil once and for all."

"Misterwizard has a machine," Deb said. Misterwizard held it up for all of them to see.

"What does it do, Misterwizard?" Sephie asked as she gazed at it, holding Kermit tight in her arms.

"It will render the mechanical monsters inert," Misterwizard said.

Everyone smiled with joy and started talking again.

"Listen!" Johnny held up a hand. "We want to trap Ripper's army down here, in the underground. If we seal off all the entrances, they'll be trapped here, and they won't be able to harm anyone anymore."

Slon walked up. "Tell us what to do, Johnny."

Johnny turned to Misterwizard. Misterwizard smiled mischievously. "I have a plan of action that should render us the victors, if executed with precision, and if Fate lends us its assistance."

Quickly they listened as Misterwizard told the plan to them. The Undergrounders would hide at the far end of the tunnel to the right, where they hid from the Rat People with Deb and Super. Here the water was still rising, and in some places, it was already waist deep, but they would only have to be there for a short time, if everything went according to plan. The Tribe would lead Ripper's army and the robots through the village. When the robots and all of Ripper's army were inside, the Undergrounders would run out the door into the subway and seal it with a rocket launcher Johnny gave them. Then Misterwizard would set off his EMP, disabling the robots. Johnny and the Tribe would escape out the hole Deb and Super fell in and then seal it off too, trapping Ripper and his army inside.

It seemed like a workable plan. Just then Foodcourt, Thegap and Lady Stabs appeared from down the tunnel.

"We came in the back way," Foodcourt said, smiling, meaning the hole where Deb and Super fell.

Everyone cheered and welcomed them. Then they all began to take their positions. The Undergrounders ran down the tunnel and hid. Johnny and the Tribe gathered in the lower track area to await the coming of Ripper and the robots.

They were ready just in time, for just then they heard tramp-tramp of the robots' heavy feet. Ripper and the robots had arrived.

CHAPTER 27

Johnny, Misterwizard and the Tribe heard the excited voices of Ripper's army and the frightening tramp of the robots' feet in the side tunnel. The people of the Tribe turned to Johnny.

"Everybody down the passageway except Misterwizard, Starbucks and the girls. Meet at the hole to the street."

The people of the Tribe didn't need to be told twice. They took off running down the tracks, their faces white with fear. They ran around the subway cars and through the village, anywhere they could, no longer afraid of the darkness as much as they were of the robots and Ripper's men.

Teavana turned to Johnny. "Will you need the torch?"

Johnny shook his head. "No, mother. You and the Tribe need it more. We'll be okay."

Teavana smiled and nodded, and her and

Abercrombie followed the others down the tracks.

"Foodcourt!" Johnny yelled to his father. Foodcourt, who was just about to join the others, turned and looked at Johnny, his face anxious and pale. "Catch up to the Tribe and make sure they find the hole out. Most have no clue where they're going."

Foodcourt grinned with excitement, nodded and without a word ran after the tribe members. The only ones left were Johnny, Misterwizard, Starbucks and the girls.

Johnny turned to Misterwizard. "How long should we wait until you set off your EMP, Misterwizard?"

"Let me guess," Starbucks said. "Until we see the whites of their eyes."

Misterwizard grinned and nodded, amused. "Absolutely."

Ripper watched with glee as General Stupid smashed the wall of the subway with his arm, making an entrance big enough for the robots to enter. Ripper stayed on the ground and walked behind the robot. The low ceiling of the door and tunnel meant there was no room for him to ride. He didn't mind, though. The ground was just as good a place to see Johnny and the Tribe die.

General Stupid stomped into the tunnel. The ceiling inside was higher than the awning outside, but still General Stupid's head was only a foot from the ceiling. The robot tramped down the yellow tiled tunnel as Ripper hopped along in excitement following him. This was so much fun! Ripper thought. Killing and smashing things with robots! He'd never had so much fun in his life. He loved the world now, with no rules or laws, just murder and mayhem and destruction! Why didn't they have a Great War a long time ago?

Ripper followed right behind General Stupid. Behind him, the other robots who were still operational followed in single file. Ripper had lost two to running out of power and one that stupidly walked into a wall and it fell on him. Robots could be so dumb! But Ripper still had enough to do the job.

Behind the robots followed Ripper's army, carrying the weapons. Ripper didn't even know if he needed them, the robots were going to kill everyone. Still, he had to have some people to rule afterwards.

General Stupid passed the half-buried statue of Lincone. Ripper looked over at it curiously. "Who's that old codger?"

"Abraham Lincoln, sixteenth president of the United States and the president during the Civil War," General Stupid intoned. "He was elected and held office from March 1861 until his assassination in April 1856. He was assassinated in Ford's Theater by John Wilkes Booth on April 14, 1865."

"Did I ask for all that detail?" Ripper said, annoyed. "You just keep your eyes peeled for Johnny."

General Stupid reached the edge of the platform and the lower track area.

"I detect life forms to the right, approximately one hundred yards away."

Ripper didn't even hear what General Stupid said, he was too excited, standing in the middle of the tracks by an old subway train was none other than Johnny and his friends!

Ripper pointed, so excited he could barely talk. "There he is! Kill him! Kill him!"

General Stupid turned towards Johnny. "I have no missiles."

"Then chase him down and rip him apart you stupid pile of junk! He's your main mission! KILL HIM!" Ripper jumped up and down in anger.

"As you wish." General Stupid marched after Johnny and his friends, who melted into the darkness next to the old subway train.

Loki, Harp and the Undergrounders saw the strange, tall golden man of metal with the funny green coat and Ripper standing next to him. Other metal men of gold stood behind the first one in a line, stretching off up the tunnel.

Behind Loki and the Undergrounders the tunnel was blocked, choked with rock and debris. They sat on chunks of rock and clung to the walls as much as they could, but some had no choice but to stand in the slowly rising water. They were very careful not to make a sound, none moving, almost not daring to breathe. If Ripper and the robots heard them, they would be helpless with nowhere to go.

Loki watched Ripper point at Johnny and heard him yell. Johnny and his friends disappeared down the tunnel. He heard Ripper talk to the metal man again in a loud voice. Then the metal man walked to the edge of the platform and stepped off. He landed on the lower track with a thud, and Ripper yelled at him angrily. Then the metal man tramped down the track after Johnny and his friends, with Ripper following close behind.

Loki had never seen Ripper before, he'd only heard people say his name. Now that he saw him, he could tell for himself the man was evil.

He heard the metal man speak! "Twenty percent power remaining." Its voice was flat and lifeless, as if it was dead.

"Stop telling me about that!" Ripper yelled, hitting the robot on the back with his fist. Just use your energy to do what I say!"

Loki thought Ripper didn't treat the robot very nice. One by one the other metal men walked up and jumped off the edge of the platform onto the tracks below. One fell on his side and lay there not moving, making Loki laugh. Then came Ripper's men. To Loki they looked mean and scary, with wild hair and dirty faces. Their clothing was ragged and filthy, and they grinned evilly. They held strange weapons, long sticks or small metal things with a barrel at the end. Some held swords or clubs. They all looked as if they couldn't wait to hurt someone.

Slon looked at the rest of the Undergrounders and in a very soft voice, whispered, "Remember. As soon as the last one is gone, we run for the tunnel to freedom, then outside into the World Above. Then we seal it up!"

They all nodded in the dark. Loki's heart pounded so hard, he was sure it was going to go flying right out of his chest. He felt a soft hand in his and turned to see Harp smiling at him. He suddenly felt not afraid at all, but happy. He smiled back at her and squeezed her hand. They were going to win he just knew it.

Ripper felt giddy, almost as if he was flying. His forehead was wet, for he was sweating. His vision kept blurring and refocusing. He wondered if he was getting sick, or if it was just the long drawn out battle.

"I'm going to win now. I'm going to win." His mind kept repeating it over and over. "Johnny's going to die. He's already dead!" He laughed insanely, feeling reality slip away and then come back, as if he was drifting in and out of a dream. He had to win this time. He had to!

He just saw Johnny. It wouldn't be long now! He cheered himself up with the memory of killing Lord Algon again, and even more entertaining was the death of Leader Nordstrom. He thought back to how he'd killed the boyfriend of that annoying sister of Johnny's Carny. What was his name, Buildabear? He'd done a lot of fun killing. Now he just had to kill the one he wanted dead most in the whole world, Johnny.

The robots' heavy feet hit the ground with loud thuds. Ripper looked down to see the ground was mushy and soft. He worried the robots might get stuck.

"General Stupid."

"Yes, Mr. President."

"Is this ground hard to walk on?"

"The composition of the floor of the subway is soft shale and composite. It is soaked with water that has seeped from the nearby river through cracks in the subway walls and is the consistency of mud. The ground is unstable for a depth of thirty feet to bedrock."

"Just answer my question! Man, I'm beginning to

hate you!" Ripper glared up at General Stupid's face.

"It is difficult to maneuver. The weight of each robot is eight hundred pounds. If we were to stop moving forward, we would sink into the ground at a rate of one inch every thirty seconds."

"Why can't you just give me a straight answer?" Ripper gave up not understand half of what General Stupid aid, and just hoped that the robots would make it to the Tribe before sinking in the muck.

The robots disappeared down the tunnel, walking on either side of the old subway car. The Wildies and Gangers followed behind them, and soon they too were swallowed up by the darkness. Loki waited for Slon to give the all clear, but Slon just sat there, eyes wide, a nervous frown on his face. Finally, Loki couldn't wait any longer.

"Let's go!" Pulling Harp along with him, Loki ran through the waist deep water as fast as he could, heading for the side passage.

"Wait!" Slon yelled, but it was too late. Others took off too, and soon Slon had no choice but to follow them.

Soon the whole tribe of Undergrounders slogged through the water towards the side tunnel. Loki and Harp reached the ledge first. Loki helped Harp up then jumped up himself. They turned and waited for the others to join them.

In twos and threes, the rest of the Undergrounders made it to the landing and climbed up. On their backs or in their arms they carried what belongings they could gather from their homes, the most precious things to them, knowing they would probably never see their village again.

Slon was the last to arrive. He stood at the edge of the platform on the track, wearing an unhappy scowl.

"You should have waited! What if they see us?"

Loki's father Bott, who held the missile launcher Johnny gave them, answered for Loki. "We can't wait for you to get a backbone."

Slon's lip curled in anger. Loki saw a big argument coming, so he tried to head it off.

"Slon, what should we do now?"

Slon turned and glared at Loki, not willing to be mollified so quickly this time. "Why don't you ask your father? He seems to be so much braver than me."

Bott looked regretful. "I'm sorry Slon. We're just all afraid. I shouldn't have said that. It was mean. You are a brave man, and a good leader."

Slon snorted and climbed up the ledge. He continued to frown but looked less angry.

Everyone looked at him, waiting for him to tell them what they already knew they were supposed to do.

"Well?" he said, pointing the way. "You know what to do. Don't forget to put the cloths over your eyes."

Everyone headed down the side passage towards the silver metal turnstiles that came before the tunnel up to the surface. They pulled their black cloths out of their pockets as they walked.

Loki and Harp waited for Slon and walked beside him. Loki felt ashamed at the way Slon was treated. He was the leader of the Undergrounders, and deserved respect, even if he had faults.

"My father was right, Slon. You are a good leader."

Slon smiled at Loki sadly, this time seeming to really let go of his anger. "Thank you, Loki. I know I'm not as good a leader as Johnny."

"You try your best!" Harp said. "I bet it's not easy to be leader."

Slon smile genuinely at her. "You are right," he answered. "But with good helpers like you and Loki, it becomes easier."

They smiled at each other, and Loki felt like maybe they had finally become friends.

The Undergrounders reached the metal gates and started passing through turnstiles, making the metal bars rotae. As each Undergrounder passed through, a clicking sound happened and a little counter on the top of the turnstile added one number, for a count that no one would ever care about again.

When they had all passed through they walked up the yellow tunnel with its old posters up to the door to the surface world.

When they reached to door out, the Undergrounders all turned and waited for Slon. When he arrived, he turned to them and spoke in an official tone.

"This is it. When we walk out here, we leave our home for good."

Some started weeping, and everyone looked sad.

Slon was different. He smiled with hope. "But we leave for a new world with new friends."

This brought smiles to some faces, though others remained sad.

"A whole new land awaits us. But first we must help destroy the evil, eradicate it like a bad growth that threatens to make us all infected. We must do our part in the battle for good, as our friends do their part, a much more dangerous one, at the other end of the tunnel. And we will do our part!"

Loki rolled his eyes. Like all leaders, Slon couldn't pass up a chance to make a speech. But time was going fast. The bad men might catch them at any moment. Loki decided he had to hurry things along.

"Okay!" He interrupted. "I'm going outside!"

Slon looked at him with a frown as Loki grabbed Harps hand and headed to the door. Slon looked at the people. They looked at Loki and Harp and then back at him. Slon sighed. "All right. Single file, everybody out!"

They all moved to the door and one by one, left their village for good, walking out into the bright sunshine.

Once outside and wearing the black cloths over their eyes, they placed their arms over their eyes to better shield them, for even with the cloths the Red Eye hurt them. When they were all outside Slon led them across the street to a sidewalk where an awning gave them some shade.

"Who has the weapon?" Slon asked, looking around.

Bott walked up holding the missile launcher Misterwizard gave them. Slon looked at the missile launcher warily, as if it was a snake that might bite any second.

"Do you know how to use it?" Slon asked Pak.

Bott smiled and leveled the missile launcher at the door into the subway. "Watch."

As everyone in the tribe watched with mixed feelings of hope and sadness, Bott pressed the trigger. A missile flew out of the launcher and sped through the air. They all oohed and aahed at it as it flew in a straight line, right into the hole of the doorway.

They waited for a second, and nothing seemed to

happen. Then they heard a dull explosion and a cloud of dust filtered out of the opening. Loud rumblings sounded far down below, and as they watched, rock and stone filled the opening. The street buckled above the entrance and sank, cracking and folding inward. The two buildings above the entrance sank down and leaned towards each other as the ground below them crumbled. More dust and debris filled the air, and everyone cheered.

Slon smiled. Loki too.

"That'll fix 'em!" Loki said.

The Undergrounders stood around, a strange looking people, slim, tall and white, but with black cloths over their eyes. Most held bags full of possessions, and a few held little white Scrabblers in their arms. They looked at the ground, not up at the Red Eye, for the light still hurt their eyes. Now that their victory was over, they waited for someone to tell them what was next.

"Now," Slon said, forgetting he was talking out loud and trying to see as best as he could through the black cloth on his eyes. "where do we go?"

"To the hole where the Newcomer will come out," Bott said, smiling, his eyes covered. "There to wait for Johnny and the Angels. All the bad men are inside now and can't hurt us."

"Just so," Slon said, nodding, as if he was the one who thought of it. He turned to look at where he thought Loki was. "Does anyone know the way?"

"I do," Loki said. They all turned and looked at him, not able to see very well. "Remember, I found the angels."

"Good!" Slon said, can you lead us there with this annoying cloth on your eyes?"

"I think so," Loki said. "I will risk the brightness if I

have to, even if it hurts me."

Slon looked in every direction, to where he thought the people were. "Everybody take someone's hand. We will walk slowly, single file."

They all did as Slon said, and made a very odd-looking procession, like a group of blind people trying to find their way.

Then Loki led them, but as he did he came up with a very wicked idea that made him smile. Loki found Harp and walked over to her. He touched her arm and she peeked out from under her cloth at him, squinting from the light.

Loki whispered, "I've got a plan to make sure the bad men are gone for good."

"I'm going with you!" Harp said.

Loki shook his head. "No, Harp, don't. I have to do it alone."

Harp looked at him, her face full of worry.

"Don't worry," Loki said. "I'll be careful."

Harp nodded, though she didn't like the idea of Loki leaving. "I don't want you to leave."

"I'll be back, I promise. Look up for a moment. You see that big building ahead, with the glass wall?" Loki pointed.

Harp lifted the cloth off her eyes enough to see what Loki pointed at. "Yes."

"Just below that is the hole where the angels came from. I have to get there before our people and do something. Can you lead them there?"

Harp nodded. "Are you sure you should do this?"

Loki nodded and squeezed her hand one more time. "Don't worry, I'll be all right."

Loki smiled. He reached over and kissed Harp. She

smiled, but the worry remained on her face.

"I'll be back, I promise."

Loki ran fast down the street. Harp turned around and walked backwards. "Loki had to do something. He put me in charge of leading you."

Slon lifted his cloth enough to expose one eye and glared at her. "Who decided that?"

"He did," Harp said. "Don't worry. He told me just what to do."

Slon lowered the cloth over his eyes again, but he didn't look happy. "I wish everyone would stop making decisions without asking me first."

Loki ran ahead to where the hole into the underground was from the top. He peered down the hole, wondering if what he was planning was really very smart. He was going to jump back down in the subway, with the entrance now sealed. What if Johnny and his friends didn't know he was there and left him inside?

It was a chance he had to take, to make sure Ripper and his men were finished for good. Stealing his courage, Loki climbed into the hole. Gritting his teeth and yelling, he leapt to the ground, hoping he didn't hurt something on the way down.

When he hit the ground he rolled, and was happy to find his light, thin body helped keep the fall from hurting him. He stood up to see the Johnny and the Tribe hadn't arrived yet. He looked down the tracks towards the entrance.

He heard voices! Johnny and his friends were almost there. Loki decided he'd wait to make sure Johnny and his friends got out safely, and then put his plan into action. He ran down the dark tunnel, to where the Rat People lived.

Johnny and the tribe ran through the deepening water. Misterwizard led the way, his flashlight making a round spot of light wherever he shone it. Carny ran next to her mother Teavana, holding Miracle tight. Foodcourt ran next to them, a big grin on his face. "Those Gangers are in for a surprise."

Teavana looked at him, amused at his excitement. He was like a little boy on an adventure sometimes, just like his son Johnny. "Let's just hope it isn't us who get the surprise."

"How much longer until we get to this hole, you guys?" Cinnabon said, peering back nervously in the dark behind them.

"Not very far," Deb said. "I know exactly where it is. I'll never forget it."

"We're not going to have much time to get everyone out," Starbucks said. "Ripper's army have guns and explosives. If they catch us before we're ready... "

"Positivity is needed, Starbucks," Misterwizard said, and he slogged through the muddy water. "And a little Serendipity."

"What's that?" Super said.

Johnny laughed. "Don't ask."

They all laughed. Then Misterwizard stopped and turned with a happy smile. "Behold, the doorway to freedom."

Ahead they all saw it. The ragged hole where Deb and Super fell, before seeming like a dangerous and scary hole, now it seemed like the entrance to a magical land.

Everyone in the tribe cheered as they all gathered around the opening and looked up.

"Wow," Starbucks said, pointing up at it "You fell down that?"

Deb and Super both grinned. "We sure did," Super said. "And it wasn't fun, let me tell you."

"And we must ascend," Misterwizard said, "without delay." He turned to the men of the Tribe with a ladder they'd fashioned for the purpose. "Quickly, our mode of escape."

Gum sat in the dark behind the big slap of square rock, scared to move. The rock he hid behind fell from the sky long ago, making a cave out of three pieces that leaned on each other. The cave was far back down one side tunnel where there were no openings, so the rat-beasties never came down it. Since there were no rat-beasties here, his people never came down the tunnel either, so it made a perfect hiding place.

He knew his tribe wanted to eat him. He dared not peek his head out of his hiding place, for he knew they were looking for him. They might even come down the side tunnel, for they were all very hungry. Someone would spot him for sure. Then they would point and yell, letting the whole tribe know. Soon they'd come with sticks and rocks. That would be it for him, he'd be nothing but meat in somebody's belly.

He was so hungry his stomach growled. He thought longingly of the delicious meal from the pot. How he wished he had some now! The thought of that juicy meat only made his hunger worse. He didn't know if he would last much longer. He was growing weak.

Then he heard something he never expected to hear again. It was the voice of Loki the meat boy!

"Gum, where are you?"

Did he dare look? Gum sat still for a moment, wondering if it was just a trap, one of his own people faking the meat boy's voice. Then slowly, he peeked his head out of the cave just far enough to see. It was Loki! Loki stood at the entrance to the main passage, looking around for Gum. For some reason he didn't understand, seeing Loki again made him feel happy.

Loki turned and saw him. He smiled at him.

"Gum! Are you still hungry?"

The thought of food made Gum forget to be cautious. He moved out a little farther and nodded.

Loki motioned to Gum with his hand. "Then follow me. Tell all your people too. Lots of yummy food!"

The mention of his people made Gum scared again. They wanted to eat him! He shook his head fearfully.

Loki didn't understand why Gum was so scared. "Lots of food! Yummy, yummy!"

Gum shook his head again.

Loki grew frustrated. "What's wrong with you? You were ready to eat me!"

Gum just stared.

"Okay. If you want yummy meat, follow me, you ornery monster. If not stay here and starve."

Loki started to walk away. Gum watched him, not sure what to do. He was very, very hungry. Finally, his hunger overcame his fear, and he crept out after Loki.

Loki walked down the passage, with Gum following far behind in the dark.

Suddenly a pair of eyes stared at Loki from the main passage. It was a Rat People! Loki ran fast, before the Rat People saw him.

Gum was not so lucky. The Rat People saw him. It turned and yelled back at the other Rat People. "Here Gum!"

Gum yelped and ran after Loki as fast as he could. In front of him, thousands of rat-beasties ran too, thinking Gum and his people were after them again to eat them.

Gum saw Loki far ahead, running even faster. Loki disappeared in the dark, and Gum wished he'd never left his hiding place. He dared to look behind him. The whole tribe of Rat People followed right behind him!

The men holding the sections of subway car that had been fashioned into a ladder ran up. Quickly it was hoisted up and set against the tunnel wall.

"Women and children first," Misterwizard said. "And that means you, Carny and Miracle."

Suddenly they heard a thousand little squeaks from the tunnel ahead of them. Thousands of rat-beasties appeared, covering the ground like a disgusting living carpet of gray.

Everyone screamed and panicked. They ran to the old subway car and tried to climb up its sides or jumped up on rocks, trying to get their feet away from the moving floor of vermin.

"Don't worry!" Johnny yelled. "They won't hurt you!" But no one listened. Some even ran down the passage, back towards Ripper's oncoming army.

Sephie looked terrified and screamed. Teavana picked her up and together they stared down at the moving river of disgusting rat-beasties that ran around Teavana's legs.

"Don't run off!" Foodcourt said, as she saw some people do just that. Some came back reluctantly. Others didn't listen and disappeared in the darkness.

"Hurry!" Cinnabon said, pressed against the tunnel wall as tightly as she could with Wheaties in her arms. "Please, get us out of here!"

"Johnny!" Deb said. "This means the Rat People are coming! We've got to hurry!"

Johnny turned to Carny. "Carny go!"

Carny, holding Miracle in her arms, started to climb the makeshift ladder. It was difficult and tricky.

"Let me up there!" A large, fat man from the tribe rushed forward in a panic. He tried to climb up and almost knocked Carny off. Johnny grabbed him and dragged him back down.

"Wait your turn, or you're staying down here permanently!"

The man looked at Johnny with wild eyes. Then he relaxed and nodded, ashamed. He backed away and stared down at the rat-beasties running by.

Then they heard something even more frightening than the thought of the Rat People. A voice came out of the darkness in the direction of Ripper and his army. It was the tramp of the robots and the voices of Ripper's men. They were almost upon them!

Johnny turned to Misterwizard. "Misterwizard, wouldn't this be a good time to use your machine?"

"Capital idea, Johnny."

"Everyone, line up and get ready to leave!" Starbucks

yelled. The people of the Tribe obeyed, lining up in a ragged makeshift line that trailed off towards the subway car.

As those waiting to climb watched anxiously, Misterwizard set his machine down on a rock. Some gathered around to watch him, including Teavana and Sephie. Misterwizard smiled at her interest, and Sephie grinned back, showing a missing tooth.

Misterwizard opened the box, revealing a black panel with buttons. He flipped a switch, and lights came on behind gages and under buttons. Some oohed and aahed, fascinated, despite the danger. Foodcourt stood right over Misterwizard's shoulder, peering down with avid interest.

Misterwizard looked up at everyone. "As they say, here goes the absolute absence of any verifiable substance!"

He flipped a switch. They all waited. Nothing seemed to happen. They all looked at each other.

"Keep climbing!" Foodcrout yelled, and the mad scramble for the ladder continued.

Ripper slogged through the deepening muck. Around him, the robots tramped on, but very slowly. The only light came from the robots' red eyes, but the combination of all of them lit up the tunnel enough to see, though everything around had a red tint to it, as if it was bathed in blood.

Each time the robots set a foot down, it looked as if the soft gooey ground grabbed it and held onto it. Then when they lifted the foot up again, a sickening sucking sound happened. Ripper worried the effort of just walking through the muck must have been using up a lot of the robots' energy.

Ripper looked ahead. In the middle of the tracks sat an old, rusted subway car lying on its side like a giant dead dinosaur. They would have to split up and walk on either side.

Then he saw something else far ahead beyond the subway car. Dark, evil joy filled his heart. It was the flickering light of torches! The Tribe was just in front of them! There was no way the Tribe could escape now.

Ripper jumped up and down and looked to see if Facegash or his men saw. They slogged along, heads down behind the robots, all looking bored. Well, he had something to cheer them up.

"Look!" Ripper yelled. All the mens' heads came up and they looked at him with curiosity. Ripper pointed ahead. "There they are!"

The men cheered, instantly excited again, and they began trotting faster through the muck.

Ripper walked faster goo. He could hear faint voices! He grinned, getting so excited he could barely contain it. Then he saw a faint light above the heads of the Tribe. They'd found a way out! No, it couldn't be!

He turned to the robots. "Hurry! Kill them!"

He looked up at General Stupid's face and was alarmed to see the red lights of his eyes flickering.

Ripper stopped. "General Stupid. General Stupid!"

The robot didn't answer. Suddenly the third robot in the first row fell over! It almost landed on a Wildie but he jumped out of the way at the last second. The robot lay in the soft dirt, half buried already from the impact.

Another robot on the other side fell. And another! The last one did hit a Ganger. He lay with his leg pinned under the massive robot screaming in pain, but no one took any notice.

"What's going on?" Ripper yelled in a panicked voice. "General Stupid!"

General Stupid still didn't answer. Ripper looked at him. His eyes were dark! He looked at the rest of the robots. All their eyes were dark! They were dead! As Ripper watched, the heavy robots started slowly sink into the thick soft dirt, as if they were standing in quicksand. This couldn't be happening!

Ripper's men ran up and looked up at the metal men, now just huge metal statues. Facegash looked at Ripper with fear. "What happened?"

Ripper scowled and shot back, "How do I know? They're asleep."

"Well, wake them up!" Facegash said, his voice rising in panic. "Wake 'em up!"

"Really, Stupid?" Ripper said, giving Facegash the same name he gave the robot. "I didn't think of that."

The thing Ripper feared had happened. The robots had run out of juice, just when he needed them most! Ripper screamed and beat his fists in the air, so frustrated he could barely think. In his mind a crazy, terrified old man with wild eyes and a look of utter despair that looked like a much older version of himself ran up and stared at him. The old man wailed in a scared, high-pitched voice, "the only one who's trapped is you! He's going to escape, and you're going to be trapped!"

He realized the man in his mind was a version of him, trying to take over. He shook his head, making the man go away, for the moment. He found he was breathing hard, almost as if he was panicking, and forced himself to relax. It would be okay. He smiled, remembering he still had a whole army. His enemy was trapped in a dark, wet tunnel with nowhere to go. All he had to do was hunt them down and kill them like rat-beasties in a barrel. Take that, crazy cowardly man!

Ripper, Facegash and his men gathered in front of the now silent robots. They looked ahead into the blackness. Without the light of the robots' eyes the tunnel was black. They could see the dark round hulk of the subway train in the middle of the track, but little else. Even the light of the Tribe's torches far ahead seemed to have disappeared.

"We should have brought a torch," Facegash said.

"Ya think?" Ripper said with a sneer. "Get ready. We don't need the robots and we don't need no torch. We're going to kill them all the old-fashioned way, and the light we see will be their bodies burning."

Ripper walked again. Facegash looked at the men next to him, motioned with his head and followed. The rest of the Wildies and Gangers fell in behind them.

Gum ran faster. Ahead he a strange light from above. He wondered what it could be from. He saw a familiar sight. It was the old hulk of the subway car. Then he saw something that made him forget about everything else. It was meat! It was not white, but he could tell it definitely looked tasty. He licked his lips and his stomach grumbled in response to the sight. He forgot all about the other Rat People chasing him as he stared at all the yummy meat!

The Rat People behind him saw the meat too. One pointed at another. "Gum not eat now. Meat look!"

With big grins of hunger, the Rat People ran for the Wildies and Gangers.

Gum was in the lead. He couldn't wait to eat again, he was so, so hungry.

Ripper and the Gangers slogged on through the black tunnel.

"It's dark," an old Wildie said in a scared voice, peering down the tunnel.

"That's right," Ripper said, grinning evilly, his face terrible in the flickering light. "That means it's dark for them too. And they're going to be scared."

The Wildies and Gangers grinned, and their eyes lit up with cruel fire.

Ripper walked past the old subway car. "Get your weapons ready. It's going to be a slaughter."

The Wildies and Gangers laughed, hoisted their missile launchers and rifles on their shoulders, and followed him into the darkness. Behind them, the robots, frozen in immobility, stood silent and still.

Without the light from the robots, it was dark now, so dark that Ripper couldn't see two feet in front of himself. A voice in his head cautioned him that he should turn around before it was too late, but he ignored it, wondering if he was being really stupid. His heart pounded in his chest, and he could hear himself breathe. It was stuffy and hot in the tunnel, and the ground was wet. Did Johnny and the Tribe really go down here, he wondered? How was it they weren't afraid of the dark? How did they know where they were going?

And then it occurred to Ripper. The weird white people. This is where they came from. Ripper grinned. He could get rid of all of them at the same time. All he had to do was-

Suddenly he saw the men ahead of him running back towards him with eyes open wide in terror. What was going on now?

Ripper stopped and watched them. They ran out of the darkness, hands in the air. And they looked as if they'd seen a monster.

Then Ripper saw the monsters come pouring out of the dark too. Strange, gray creatures with big heads, bulging, gray arms, no ears or noses and sharp teeth. As he watched in shocked horror, the creatures leapt on Widies and Gangers and bit them as they fell to the ground screaming.

It wasn't real, Ripper thought. Somehow, he'd fallen asleep and into a nightmare. *You see?* said the frail, crazy old man in his head. *I told you. Johnny always wins.* Ripper finally let go and let himself go mad. What did it matter now? It was all over. Ripper ran back down the dark tunnel, his mind slowly slipping in and out of reality like a machine starting and stopping because it is slipping gears. His heart pounded in his ears, and he wondered how long it would be until he died.

He turned to see the creatures swarming all over the men, hundreds of them. They were all huge and strong, and his men had no chance against them. He watched as Facegash fought one, his face a mask of terror. The huge creature bit Facegash's shoulder and he screamed.

A Ganger saw one of the creatures bounding towards him. In his hands the Ganger held a missile launcher. He pointed it at the creature and fired. The creature leapt out of the way and the missile hit the side of the tunnel. It exploded, throwing creatures, Wildies and Ganger in

the air. It also sent chunks of rock and tunnel wall out in a spray of dangerous projectiles. Then from the hole where the missile hit, water gushed out. The tunnel would flood!

Ripper ran desperately away as men screamed. The monsters saw the water and turned and ran back the way they had come, leaving the dead and maimed men lying on the ground. A few men and women had survived, and they joined Ripper in running down the tunnel as the water level began to rise.

CHAPTER 28

Loki watched with grim satisfaction as the Rat People attacked the bad man's army. Though he felt bad that the men were being killed, he knew they had it coming. They were evil, and only wanted to hurt his people and Johnny's. He heard the screams of the men as the Rat People attacked them, and it sent a chill down his spine. *If it wasn't for Johnny and his Tribe,* Loki thought, *that would have been his people. It all ended the way it was supposed to, with the good people winning.*

A bright arrow of flaming light streaked across the tunnel, followed by a loud hiss. Loki recognized it as another missile! He saw it was aimed at one of the Rat People, but the monster moved at the last moment and the rocket missed. It hit the wall! Loki watched with dread as the wall exploded and water poured out of the hole. It was definitely time to leave!

He ran as fast as he could down the tracks, back to the opening where Deb and Super had first appeared. He hoped Johnny had kept his promise and waited until he returned to seal up the hole, or he was just as doomed as Ripper's men.

He reached the hole and with relief saw the makeshift ladder still there. He looked up with pleasure to see Johnny looking down through the hole, grinning at him.

"Are you finally done goofing around?" Johnny asked.

Loki laughed. Then he frowned, thinking about Ripper's men. "They're all going to die down here, Johnny."

Johnny nodded sadly, understanding how Loki felt. "I'm sorry, Loki, but we didn't really have any choice. Now, get up here!"

Loki grinned and started to climb.

"Not so fast, freak."

Loki turned. It was Ripper. He looked insane, his eyes wild and his scarred face covered with blood and mud. "You're not going anywhere."

The last two to climb out were Misterwizard, who needed a little help, and Johnny. Everyone cheered and laughed, so happy to have escaped Ripper and his men. They all wore smiles of joy, wondering if their long, scary ordeal was finally over.

Greeted by the warmth and brightness of the Red Eye high in the sky, the people of the Tribe sat on the rocks and old cars, simply enjoying the peace and quiet.

As they all looked, the Undergrounders walked up, all

holding hands and with black cloths over their eyes. The people of the Tribe ran to them and greeted them, and soon more smiles abounded as the two different peoples, now one, got to know each other.

Cinnabon walked up to Johnny holding Wheaties' hand, a big smile on her face. Johnny smiled back at her.

"Thank you, Johnny, for saving us. You're a good man, and a good leader." Then she kissed him on the cheek.

Johnny grinned, grateful, but a little embarrassed. He looked to see if Deb saw him get kissed, but she was busy talking to Super. "Thank you, Cinnabon. I just hope we're truly, finally free and can start to finally build a home here."

"We will be able to, thanks to you," Cinnabon replied. She looked over at Deb. "It's a good thing she grabbed you first, or I'd be doing it."

Johnny laughed, not knowing what to say, as Cinnabon grinned one more time and then left.

Then Johnny heard something that made his heart leap for joy. It was Deecee's bark!

As Johnny watched, Deecee came running up to him. Johnny knelt and Deecee jumped on him, knocking him down and licking his face.

Everyone gathered around, cheered and laughed as Johnny struggled to get his face away from Deecee's tongue, filled with happiness.

Finally, Johnny sat up and hugged Deecee as the dog-beastie wagged its tail and still tried to lick him.

"Where have you been, boy?" Johnny said, petting Deecee's head. "Having an adventure of your own?"

Deb came over and petted Deecee too. "Hi Deecee! We missed you so much!"

Deecee looked at her and licked her cheek too. Soon everyone surrounded them, all trying to pet Deecee at once.

Misterwizard strolled over on his short little legs, rubbing his hands with glee, a big smile on his round, cherubic face. It made him look more than ever like the yellow minion picture on the wall of his castle. "Well, the total quantity proceeds agreeably that culminates agreeably, as they say."

Johnny shrugged, once again having no clue what Misterwizard meant. Starbucks stopped petting Deecee and said, "We should seal the hole now, Johnny so Ripper and his men can't get out. "

Johnny nodded. He looked at Sephie. "Watch Deecee for me, will you Sephie?"

She grinned and nodded and put an arm around Deecee, happy to be given the task of watching him.

Johnny and Starbucks walked towards the opening when a girl from the Undergrounders ran up. It was Harp. They turned to see what she wanted.

"Johnny, please wait! Loki went inside the hole. He said he had to do something."

Johnny and Starbucks looked at each other, curious. Johnny looked at her.

"Do you know what he was going to do?"

Harp smiled mischievously. "He didn't tell me, but I think I know."

"What?" Starbucks asked, eager to hear the answer.

"I think he was going to lead the Rat People to the bad men."

Johnny and Starbucks grinned at each other. "I don't say it's nice, but it is fitting," Starbucks said.

Johnny looked worried. "That's why we saw the rat-beasties. I hope he didn't get caught by them himself."

Harp frowned, starting to worry too.

Johnny touched her arm and smiled at her, though his face was serious. "I promise, we won't seal it up until he gets out."

Harp smiled, but still looked worried. Johnny looked at Starbucks.

"Don't say it!" Starbucks warned, thinking he knew what Johnny was thinking.

"I have to," Johnny said. "If Loki is in there alone, I may have to go in and help him."

Starbucks shook his head. "Don't you ever take a hero break?" He looked at Johnny and laughed.

Johnny laughed too. "Nope."

Johnny walked over to the hole, laid down, put his head in the hole as far as he could, and peered around. At first all he saw was darkness. Then he heard screams of terror, far away in the darkness. He saw a hulking gray shape flit by the opening. A Rat People!

He heard an explosion, and then the rushing of water. Just what was going on down there?

Then he saw Loki! He was at the bottom of the ladder! Johnny grinned, relieved. Loki looked up and saw him.

"Are you finally done goofing around?" Johnny asked.

Loki laughed. Then he frowned, thinking about Ripper's men. "They're all going to die down here, Johnny. I'm kind of sorry."

Johnny nodded sadly, understanding how Loki felt. "I'm sorry too, Loki, but we didn't really have any choice. Now, get up here!"

Loki grinned and started to climb.

"Not so fast, freak."

Suddenly a dark, wild face appeared at the bottom of the ladder. It was Ripper!

As Johnny watched helplessly, Ripper grabbed Loki's leg. As Loki yelled, Ripper dragged him off the ladder. Loki fell to the ground. As Johnny watched, Ripper stood him up and put a knife to his throat. Ripper stared up at Johnny.

"All right, Johnny. You think you won. You saved the day again, didn't you? Well come down here and fight me like a man. It's time we finished it, you and me. Or this white freak dies."

Johnny scowled. "All right, Ripper. You'll get your fight. I've been wanting to give you what you deserved as much as you've wanted to kill me. Let him go, and let's do it."

Johnny grabbed a short sword and climbed on the ladder. He started down.

Starbucks, who was standing nearby, saw Johnny start down the ladder. "Johnny, what are you doing?" He turned to the Tribe. "Johnny's going back inside!"

They all rushed over to the hole and peered inside. Loki climbed out and they all looked at him as he put his black cloth over his eyes.

"Where's Johnny, Loki?" Deb asked.

Turned, trying to see who was speaking with his blindfold on. "He's down there, fighting Ripper."

They gathered around the hole, trying to catch a glimpse of Johnny and Ripper, who were down in the subway, fighting to the death.

CHAPTER 29

Johnny reached the bottom of the ladder. He turned around and looked at what was happening. He saw a scene straight out of a nightmare. The subway was dark. Dead bodies and abandoned weapons lay everywhere. Some men and women, still barely alive but torn and bloody, some with missing arms or legs struggled weakly.

A huge gusher of water poured out one wall, and the ground below was covered. In some spots, small lakes had already formed, and papers and dead bodies floated in them. It wouldn't be long before the whole underground would be flooded.

Johnny looked for Ripper. He found him standing ten feet away, sword in his hand held ready, a crazy smile on his face and a strange, wild gleam in his eyes.

"This is how it was meant to be, Johnny. All the way from the beginning."

Johnny scowled with hatred and walked towards Ripper. He held his sword in front of himself and stopped when he was five feet away. The two men faced each other, staring.

"Maybe it was. But is still doesn't have to. This place is going to be flooded any minute. Surrender, and you can leave with me," Johnny said, this, knowing perfectly well Ripper would never say yes. But he felt as if he had to try.

"Neither of us are ever leaving here," Ripper said. His voice sounded strange. Johnny realized Ripper was now insane. "We were both meant to die here, to rot here, until there's nothing left but our bones."

They circled each other, the light from the opening above the only illumination. It shined on Ripper's face, then as he moved, it shined on Johnny's instead.

"Maybe you," Johnny said. "I have a life to live."

Ripper shook his head. "Why should you get a life, when you stole mine?"

Ripper lunged, his knife stuck out straight in front of him. Johnny yelled and jumped back. The knife missed Johnny's stomach by an inch. Ripper turned and slashed the knife in a deadly arc, and Johnny backed up. Then Johnny jabbed with his sword, but only caught the ragged sleeve of Ripper's torn and dirty shirt. The sword got stuck! Ripper, seeing his chance, tried to grab the hilt of Johnny's sword and stab him with his knife. He missed as Johnny pulled his stomach back.

Finally, Johnny got his sword free. He swung it at Ripper and managed a glancing blow on Ripper's arm. Ripper yelled, a small gash appearing. He stabbed again, and this time connected. The knife stuck into Johnny's left arm and he yelled. Ripper grinned, his eyes lit up with an unholy fire. Johnny swung his sword at Ripper's arm, but Ripper pulled the knife out and pulled his arm back before Johnny could hit him.

Because Ripper had to pull back, the cut in Johnny's arm wasn't as deep as it could have been, but it still hurt, and it was bad enough to start bleeding. Luckily, Johnny was right-handed, but the pain made him weaker.

Ripper, like all wild animals, sensed the weakness in his opponent. He grinned and moved around, looking for an opportunity to strike.

"You're big, Johnny, and strong. But I'm older, and a dirtier fighter. You ain't got a chance. Give up now, and I'll make it quick."

Johnny smiled grimly and moved too, trying to keep Ripper from getting an advantage. "You may be older, but you're also stupid. You just don't know when to realize you've lost and give up."

Ripper leapt at Johnny, but the ground was soft under his feet, and instead he fell on his face. He realized what happened fast and rolled away, just before Johnny's sword came down where his head would have been.

Johnny chased Ripper, who rolled away until he was in a muddy pool. Then he stood up and ran away laughing as Johnny pursued him.

The water had filled the tunnel up to a foot everywhere now, and they had to slog through it. They ran past the subway car, Ripper laughing insanely. They reached the place where the robots stood, now ankle deep in mud, their golden bodies now rusty and brown from the effect of the water. Ripper taunted Johnny as he ran. "I'm going to get that girl of yours Johnny. When you're dead, I'm going up there and bringing her down here. I'm going to drown her."

"You're insane!" Johnny yelled. "We're both going to drown, if you don't give up."

Johnny finally realized he didn't know why he was chasing Ripper. Loki had gotten away, and Ripper was running away from the opening. Johnny knew the real reason he came down was to get revenge, but Ripper drowning in the filthy subway tunnel, wasn't that enough?

Johnny turned to go back. Ripper saw he was leaving and stopped.

"COME BACK HERE!" Ripper yelled, a sad, miserable frown on his face. "You promised me we'd fight!"

Johnny stopped and looked at Ripper. "I'm done fighting. It's time for peace. We're going to build a new world, one where everyone has freedom and liberty."

Ripper sneered. "You're a fool, Johnny Apocalypse. You'll never tame this world. There will always be more people like me to fight you."

"Maybe," Johnny said. "But there will always be good men like Misterwizard to help fight back."

Johnny started to walk again. Ripper yelled, "We're not done!"

Suddenly behind Ripper, General Stupid's eyes lit up. A soft whirring sound began deep inside his chest. Ripper didn't notice, but Johnny did. He looked up at General Stupid, mouth open in surprise and dismay. If Ripper got the robots back, could he still win?

The eyes of three of the other robots lit up too. Their arms began to move, like puppets brought to life. General Stupid's head turned. He looked at Ripper. Ripper finally realized something was happening behind him. He turned and looked up. He saw General Stupid's eyes and he grinned drunkenly.

"Welcome back to the party, General Stupid. Great time you pick to wake up!"

Ripper looked at Johnny. "See what I mean, Johnny? Bad always wins, because they're so much of it. Good can never win!"

Ripper turned to General Stupid and pointed at Johnny. "That's Johnny, the one you were supposed to kill. Tear him apart!"

Johnny backed up a step and watched the robot. His heart sank. Could he really be killed, now and his Tribe lose, after all they'd been through? It was too terrible to think about.

Ripper seemed to get some of his old self back. He turned and grinned at Johnny.

"Time to die, Johnny Boy."

General Stupid lifted his right leg out of the muck and took a step forward. Then he spoke.

"Dangerous Infestation. I love a good party." His voice sounded sketchy, like a bad record that skipped or had static. General Stupid took another step.

"Two times two is forty-eight." He took another step. Ripper stood back, frowning at him.

"What's wrong with you, you stupid pile of junk. Kill him!"

"When in the course of human events, mix in two eggs lightly salted."

General Stupid turned and walked, toward Ripper!

"What are you doing, you stupid?" Ripper began to look afraid.

"The dog is in the meadow, the cow is in the barn."

General Stupid reached down and grabbed Ripper by the arm. He lifted him up in the air. Ripper screamed and flailed around, as the grip of the robot crushed his arm.

"I sing the body electric," General Stupid said. Then as Johnny watched in horror, he ripped Ripper apart, throwing his body parts in different directions.

Johnny backed up and started running. General Stupid finished with Ripper. He turned around and wandered into the dark subway.

"Hello. May I take your coat?"

Johnny ran to the ladder. He took one more look at the scene of mayhem. The water was up to three feet and rising. Some of the robots fought the mud to get free, but they moved like broken toys, jerky and slow. It wouldn't be long before they all were destroyed by the rising waters.

Johnny climbed the ladder to freedom and a new life.

CHAPTER 30

Two weeks had passed since the victory over Ripper and his army. The car wall had been torn down, and a stronger wall of rock and stone had was under construction with a much larger area enclosed. The Museum of American History that Ripper's robots destroyed was being cleared of rock and debris. Meanwhile the Museum of Natural History next door became New Sanctuary, though in reality all the buildings around the grass square were turned into part of the Tribe's new home, and there was enough room for everyone to choose where they wanted to live.

The Undergrounders adapted well to their new world, though they still preferred the indoors. They moved into the President's old Bunker underneath the Museum of American History. The Tribe had learned to accept them, even care for them.

Johnny sat in the old Capitol in the old President's chair. Misterwizard had insisted he take off his leather pants and vest and put on a totally uncomfortable and ugly blue suit. Across from him sat Misterwizard, in green shorts and a shirt with a picture of a strange looking man Misterwizard said was Herman Munster. He held what huge brown book in his hand. It was open, and he leafed through the pages, a serious look on his face.

Johnny had never been so bored in his whole life.

"We have so much to accomplish, Johnny, I really don't know where to start. You have so much to learn, years and years of schooling must be condensed into as short a time as possible if you are to be President.

"Starting today, you must learn the Constitution and the Bill of Rights. Then you will need to understand the structure of a democratic government and the inner workings of the judicial system. When that is done, you must learn finances and basic accounting. So much to do, so much to learn!"

Johnny groaned, not sure why everything Misterwizard said lately made him feel so unhappy. They had won, hadn't they? It was what he always wanted for the Tribe, a new start in the new world.

And yet, every day Johnny felt more and more depressed, as if the world had taken on a dark and hazy gloom. Johnny gazed out the window. The light from the Red Eye had just begun to illuminate the old, broken buildings surrounding the grassy Mall.

Johnny's mind wandered. He thought about the subway filled with water, old, broken robots and the skeletons of the dead. He thought about Lord Algon's castle and its land, filled with strange, stone tablets. In his mind, all their adventures played back. He saw

Sanctuary, the old mall where they lived. He remembered how dark and gloomy it was, and how it always smelled like mold.

He remembered how magical and amazing Misterwizard's castle seemed, with all its gadgets and wonderful things from before the Great War. The memory of being chased in the museum by the dog-beasties with Deb, Starbucks and Super came back to him, and how close they'd come to being eaten that day.

Then in his mind, he saw him and Deb on his Harley, her holding him tight, and the feeling of joy he felt as the wind whipped through their hair. And then he knew why he was so sad.

Misterwizard droned on, until Johnny interrupted him.

"Misterwizard, can we take a break for a moment? There's something I have to do."

Misterwizard stopped talking and looked up, a frown of displeasure on his face. "Must we, Johnny? We've only just started, and we such a long road to travel ahead of us."

"Please, Misterwizard."

Misterwizard shrugged. "As you wish. But only a short one. Time waits for no man!"

Johnny stood up and moved about uncomfortably. He'd never worn anything that felt so miserable as the suit he was wearing now. It was like torture. Johnny hurried out of the room.

As soon as he was out of Misterwizard's view, he ripped the jacket off and threw it down, like it was some kind of monster trying to smother him. He pulled the shirt open, buttons flying everywhere. Finally, he felt like he could breathe.

He walked outside into the bright sunshine from the Red Eye. He had to find Starbucks.

Johnny found Starbucks lying on the grass in the middle of the square, simply staring up at the sky. Johnny instantly envied him. He sat down next to Starbucks, who grinned at him. From somewhere, Deecee came running. He lay down next to Johnny and Johnny smiled at him and petted him.

"How goes the training to be president?" Starbucks said, still looking up at the sky. "I bet it's a load of fun."

Johnny laughed and laid down next to Starbucks. He looked up at the sky too. Deecee laid down next to hm, his head on his paws.

"Misterwizard says he's going to start classes for everybody soon," Starbucks said, closing is eyes. "Classes in Reading, Riting and Rithmatec, whatever they are."

Johnny smiled and stared at the sky. Then he frowned and said, "Starbucks, can I tell you a secret?"

Starbucks opened his eyes, suddenly fully awake and interested. "Sure, Johnny. What?"

"This is just between you and me."

Starbucks turned his head to look at Johnny, who still stared up at the sky. "If you say so, Buddy."

"I don't want to be leader anymore."

Starbuck sat up, losing all interest in the sky or anything else except what Johnny was saying. "What do you mean, Johnny?"

Johnny turned his head and looked at Starbucks.

"Way back before any of our adventures happened, when I used to go see Misterwizard at his castle all by myslef, he told me about a land called Cally-forna. He said it was full of things called Pam Trees. He told me about a place called Taxes, where the bug-beasties fly and there are thousands of horse-beasties roaming around free."

Starbucks grinned. "Cool."

Johnny lay back again and looked at the clouds rolling by in the sky.

"He told me about a place called New Ork, where buildings go up so high you can barely see the tops. And a place called Forida, where weird beasties called allygators roam about, with big teeth and long tails. And then there's Australia."

Starbucks sat up and looked at Johnny, wondering where this was going.

Johnny sat up too and looked at Starbucks. "He also told me about being leader, something called Congress, and Voting, and Elections and Terms. It's all very confusing but it looks like you have to argue with people and always make decisions and have people mad at you all the time."

Johnny looked miserable. "And read books. Lots and lots and lots of books. I used to like books, but now they give me a headache."

"Just what are you saying, Johnny?" Starbucks said. "Misterwizard will help you with the books. He can explain anything."

"But I don't want him to. I'm only fifteen seasons, well sixteen in a few days. I don't want to be the Leader Nordstrom anymore. I thought I did, and maybe I do some time, but not yet. The thought of being leader gives me a headache, and an ache in here." Johnny pointed to his chest.

"So, what do you want to do, Johnny?"

Johnny looked at the buildings around them, and then at the distant mountains on the horizon.

"I want to get on my Harley and ride. I want to explore the world. Misterwizard showed me a paper with a picture of America. It's goes on forever, Starbucks. We just left Sanctuary, where we were stuck in the dark, like rat-beasties. Now we're free, and there's a whole big country to see. I want to leave the Tribe behind, just for a while, and just go. Alone, just me and Deecee."

Starbucks frowned. "I can go too can't I?"

Johnny smiled and slugged Starbucks' arm. "Of course. How could I go without you?"

Starbucks smiled. "And I'll take Super. Will you take Deb?"

Johnny and Starbucks looked at each other. "Do you think she'd go with me?"

"Of course, she will, Dummy. But what are you going to tell Misterwizard?"

"I don't know. I don't know if I can even go. He'd be so disappointed in me. I can't let him down, after all he's done for me."

Starbucks stood up, and so did Johnny. Deecee stood up and wagged his tail, sensing they were going to do something fun.

"You should tell him how you feel, Johnny. He wouldn't want you to be unhappy. And I bet he'll understand."

"I want to tell Deb first."

"Can I tell Super?"

"Sure." They boys walked towards the Museum of Natural History, New Sanctuary.

Johnny, Starbucks and Deecee walked into the Museum of Natural History. They found Teavana and Foodcourt sitting in the lobby near the big hole where Johnny fought Ripper and the tiger-beastie at a table. Foodcourt was eating something Johnny didn't recognize and seemed to be enjoying it a lot. Teavana sat across from him with a book in front of her.

"See... Dick." Teavana said, squinting hard and concentrating. "See... Dick run."

Foodcourt took a bite of what he was eating and said with a mouthful, "See Dick run."

Johnny walked over and looked at them. Deecee eyed the food Foodcourt had with hungry eyes.

"What is that?" Johnny asked, pointing at Foodcourt's food.

Foodcourt lifted it up and grinned with excitement. "It's called a 'hambooger.' Misterwizard showed us how to make it on the big flat oven thing in the room over there with the pictures of food on the walls. It's delish. You have to try one, Johnny!"

Johnny grinned. "You don't have one to give Deecee, do you?"

"Forget Deecee," Starbucks said. "I want one."

Teavana smiled and patted Deecee's head. "I'll make him one. And one for you too, Starbucks."

Starbucks looked at Johnny and then said, "Maybe later."

"Thanks, Mom," Johnny said. "Have you seen Deb around?"

Foodcourt took another bite and then mumbled, "She's in the room with the weird bird-beasties, you know the ones with the long necks and black and white feathers. Her and Super."

Johnny and Starbucks grinned at each other. "Of course, they're together," Starbucks said. Inseparable, just like you and me."

Johnny laughed, nodded and left Deecee with Teavana, so she could make him his hambooger. Then he and Starbucks went to find the girls.

They found them on a bench talking. They looked up when the boys approached.

"Hi Johnny!" Deb said. "Are you done with your studies with Misterwizard already?"

Johnny shook his head, looking serious. Super looked at Starbucks.

"Are you distracting him, Starbucks? I'll take him off your hands if you like Johnny and keep him out of your way."

They all laughed. "No thanks, Johnny said. He looked at Deb. "We need to talk."

Deb saw Johnny looked serious, and she frowned, curious.

"And you and me, talk too," Starbucks said. He grabbed Super's hand and dragged her to her feet. "Come with me."

"Oh, oh," Super said, laughing, "he's going to pop the question."

Deb laughed. "It's about time!"

Starbucks and Super walked into a separate room as Johnny sat down next to Deb.

"Deb," he asked looking into her eyes, "Do you like it here?"

Deb, wondering, said, "Yes, Johnny, don't you?"

Johnny looked miserable. "I do, but I feel...it's hard to explain."

Deb slid over and took Johnny's hands. "It's okay, Johnny. I'm listening."

Johnny looked at her, his face set and determined. "I'm leaving, Deb. I want to get on my Harley and ride. I want to explore the world."

Deb looked worried. "Are you taking me with you?"

"If you want to go."

Deb put her arms around Johnny's neck. "Just try and get away from me."

They kissed, long and hard. Johnny put his arms around her and they held each other, eyes closed, just happy to be together.

Starbucks and Super returned. Super jumped up and down with excitement. "Road Trip!"

Johnny walked back into the President's Office at the Capitol, to find Misterwizard lounging in a chair, smoking a cigar and holding an enormous glass with a brown liquid in it. He looked as if he was two seconds from falling asleep, his eyes closing.

Johnny sighed, trying to prepare himself for what he had to say.

"Misterwizard?"

Misterwizard woke with a snort and opened his eyes. His cigar fell out of his mouth and on his lap. He yelped and quickly picked it up, almost dropping his glass.

"Were you sleeping, Misterwizard?" Johnny asked.

"Nonsense, my boy, just resting my eyes. I began to wonder if one of your fine companions waylaid you, Johnny. They are notorious time wasters."

Johnny sat down on the edge of the desk. Misterwizard stood up and grinned. "Ready to resume your studies?"

Misterwizard noticed how grim Johnny looked, and he frowned, growing concerned.

"Johnny is everything all right?"

Johnny looked miserable and torn, and Misterwizard walked over and sat next to him.

"Johnny whatever it is, you know you can tell me. I have only your best interests at heart."

Johnny looked at Misterwizard. "I know you do, Misterwizard. And that's why it's so hard to tell you this."

Misterwizard waited for Johnny to continue, his face grim as well.

"Do you remember all the stories you told me about the world? Other places in America, the strange beasties and people that used to live there?"

Misterwizard smiled. "Of course. We had some marvelous episodes in the castle, didn't we?"

Johnny decided there was nothing to do but say it. "Misterwizard, I don't want to be President. I want to get on my Harley and explore."

Johnny waited for Misterwizard's reaction, but rather than being angry Misterwizard grinned. Then he laughed!

Misterwizard patted Johnny on his arm, still chuckling. "Of course, you do, Johnny!"

Misterwizard put his glass down, put an arm around Johnny and led him out the door into the hallway of the Capitol.

"You've been such a stalwart and responsible

individual Johnny, I forget you're only fifteen seasons. Naturally you want to experience the fullness of life, its colorful tapestry and ever-changing hues."

"You're not mad, Misterwizard?"

"Not at all, Johnny. After all you've done for this Tribe, myself included, you deserve to do something for yourself."

Johnny grinned, relieved. They walked outside the Capitol. It was a beautiful sunny day, and they gaze out at the grassy field where children from the Tribe and the Undergrounders both ran and played.

"Just what is your plan, Johnny, if I may ask?"

Johnny shrugged. "Just ride and see what we find, I guess."

Misterwizard looked at Johnny seriously. "You realize the world is likely to be wild and untamed, with many more Rippers and Leader Nordstroms."

Johnny nodded. "I know. But I don't care. I just want to see it."

Misterwizard chuckled. "And see it you will. And have many more adventures."

Misterwizard looked at him questioningly. "You will return, won't you?"

"Sure," Johnny said. "I'd miss everyone too much not to."

"Good," Misterwizard said. "Then that's just fine. When you return, you must tell me all about your new adventures."

"Who will be President?" Johnny asked.

"Don't worry about that," Misterwizard said. "Your father Foodcourt will do quite nicely, at least until we become organized enough to have free elections. He is more the age of most presidents in any case, and I have a suspicion he would enjoy the position."

Johnny grinned. "I bet he'll love it. He always likes to help people. And he likes to have people look to him for advice."

One week later, Johnny, Starbucks, Deb and Super walked out of the Museum of Natural History to see everyone waiting for them. In front of the crowd sat Johnny and Starbuck's Harleys.

They walked up to see Misterwizard standing next to the bikes. Everyone looked at Johnny and the others, sad looks on their faces. Johnny, Starbucks and the girls looked sad too. Deb seemed to be trying to keep from crying.

"Johnny," Misterwizard said, "we will all miss you, but we understand why you are going."

Foodcourt stepped forward and shook Johnny's hand. "Take care, my son. Come back safe."

Teavana was crying. She sniffed and ran up and gave Johnny a hug. "Be careful," she said, and then walked back to stand by Foodcourt.

The parent of the other three came up and hugged them as well, saying their goodbyes. The rest of the Tribe waved and said sad goodbyes.

Sephie ran up and Johnny picked her up. She was crying too.

"Hey," Johnny said. "I'll be back."

"I know, Sephie said, sniffing. "I'm just going to miss you."

"I'm going to miss you too."

Misterwizard motioned for Johnny to come over. "I want to show you a modification I made to your Harley, Johnny."

Johnny walked over, still holding Sephie, curious. When he saw what Misterwizard had done, he laughed. When Starbucks and the girls saw they laughed too.

There in a side seat on Johnny's bike sat Deecee, wearing a pair of custom made goggles.

"This way, you can take Deecee wherever you go!"

The rest of the Tribe laughed too.

"Thanks, Misterwizard."

A few minutes later the adventurers finished their goodbyes. Johnny, Starbucks and the girls climbed on the bikes and started them up. As everyone watched, they drove away, past the broken stick building onto the street beyond and towards the setting Red Eye.

Johnny's real adventures had only just begun.

www.ingramcontent.com/pod-product-compliance
Lightning Source LLC
Chambersburg PA
CBHW060319100726
47907CB00002B/459